Gale Borger

Totally Buzzed

Echelon Press
Publishing

TOTALLY BUZZED
An Echelon Press Book

First Echelon Press paperback printing / 2010

All rights Reserved.
Copyright © 2010 by Gale Borger

Cover Art © Nathalie Moore

Echelon Press
9055 G Thamesmeade Road
Laurel, MD 20723
www.echelonpress.com

All rights reserved. No part of this book may be used or reproduced in any manner whatsoever without written permission, except in the case of brief quotations embodied in critical articles and reviews. For information address Echelon Press LLC.

ISBN: 978-1-59080-790-3
1-59080-790-1
eBook 1-59080-957-2

Printed in the United States of America

10 9 8 7 6 5 4 3 2 1

*To the loves of my life, Bob and Shannon.
I couldn't have done it without you.*

Without the love and support from the real Bill-n-Gerry Show, I would not have had the background material to mold my characters. I love you both. I only wish you could have shared this with us, Dad.

Big thanks go to Sadie Sullivan Greiner–the finest witch in the west. Thank you for your expertise and your friendship– you too, Froggie!

Finally, huge thanks to Karen, Kat, and all the folks at Echelon Press for your hard work, and for holding my hand through the process.

1

"Okay Buzz, let's do it; rock, scissors, paper," my younger sister Fred said.

I stood, hands on hips, staring at the open door to the crawlspace under our parents' farm house. "Rock, scissors, paper my butt, who do you think you are talking to? It stinks to high Heaven down there! You are not getting me under that house."

"C'mon, rock, scissors, paper!" Fred shook her fist in the air–like that was going to convince me to do something as stupid as to play her little game.

"C'mon now Buzz, we've always made major decisions this way. We can decide fairly and impartially who has to go under the house, get the lamp, and drag out whatever died down there. I promised Mom." She wore that condescending look that never failed to piss me off, as if she were conversing with a foreign, slow child.

I felt my blood pressure rising. "Impartiality my ass, you cheat. I never did know how, but I know you cheat. If you think Mom's ugly old floor lamp is under there, you go. No *way* are you getting me under that house!"

I sniffed, confirming that it reeked under there. "I can smell something rotten in Denmark."

I bent to look in the black hole. "*Oooo*, looks like some big hairy spiders are waiting for you Fred."

Her face crumpled and her voice took on the nasty grating whine that told me she was getting desperate. "Aw geez Buzz, you know I have arachnophobia! I won't be able to breathe, I'll die down there! If I wasn't sure the lamp was there I would never suggest you going.

"I remember we stuffed the lamp under there about five years ago, hoping she'd forget she owned it. Just go under there, get Mom's cowboy lamp." She sniffed. "And uh, while you're there you can drag that dead coon, or whatever the heck is rotting down there, out. I'll even pay you, I swear!"

I sighed. "Damn right you'll pay me!" Fred opened her mouth and I held up a hand. "Okay, okay, rock, scissors, paper. I don't know how you Bogart me into this stuff, I never win anyway." I went for rock, and lost like I knew I would.

"Crap, I really hate it when that happens," I mumbled as I crouched down and prepared to enter the crawlspace from Hell. "A few spiders and you'd think Godzilla was down there! I can't believe I have such a wienie for a sister."

"Oh Buzz, you're the best."

"Spare me, Spider Girl, and shine that flashlight under here."

The reality of it was the crawlspace under our folks' house really *was* a damp, spider-infested, creepy place all four of us avoided at all costs–even when we were kids. Not that we were girlie-girls, well, except for Al, but we don't usually claim her as a sib anyway.

Staring through the door, I saw a string tied to one of the rafters and smiled. I remembered one time when I was really pissed at my youngest sister, Al. I'd put a noose around her Beach Girl Barbie's neck and hung it about four feet inside the crawlspace. No one would rescue her and Al cried and tattled to Dad. He cut down the little Prima Dona's stupid Barbie doll and I got my butt kicked. That would have been about 40 years ago. The tell-tale string still hung, mostly rotted, to the rafter. I sighed. *Ahhh, those were the days.*

Coming back to the present, and resigned to my dismal

fate, I took a deep breath, cracked my knuckles, and squeezed my not-so-petite butt through the opening under the farmhouse.

Inching through that damp, smelly crawlspace, I continued to cast aspersions on Fred's integrity, our ancestors, and any future-born children she might have. I huffed, I puffed, and I clawed my way through five thousand spider webs and 54 years of old junk.

I heaved myself along what must have been the length of two football fields. Straining to look behind me for the opening, I realized I had gone about eight feet. *Damn*, feet *s*chmeet; I was getting the hell out of Dracula's Den as soon as I laid a hand on Mom's stupid floor lamp.

I crept further along, the smell of dead animal making me nauseated. The feeling of being trapped in this moldy, dark place brought every horror flick I ever saw to life. The tickling of panic settled in the back of my throat. In the ever-narrowing, coffin-like confines of the foul-smelling crawlspace, all I could think about was the many ways I could murder Fred.

The rub was how to convince my parents she had run away to Alaska to count whales. It crossed my mind that it had been much easier to wind my way around broken pram wheels, rotten dog bones, and old window screens when we were younger... *much* younger.

"Are you there yet? Are you there yet?" floated the sing-song mantra of my lovely–and soon to be dead–whale-counting sister. She sounded so smug and triumphant. I gritted my teeth and thought about bringing back a couple giant tarantulas and slipping them into her underwear drawer.

"To Hell with this mess; I'm out of here."

Scrambling around on my belly so I once again faced the door, my elbow smacked into what I thought was another empty box. When pain shot up my arm, I thought whoever thought up the words 'funny bone' should be shot. I nudged the box and figured this had to be where Mom must have stashed that butt-ugly cowboy lamp. Eureka! Now to get the Hell out of Hell.

In the dim light, through an open corner, I could make out the cowboy boot which made up the base of the floor lamp. That was all the incentive I needed.

I would have made Jesse Owens proud as I high-tailed it down Black Widow Boulevard and exploded out of the door, dragged in great gulps of fresh air.

Looking much like Medusa must have on a bad hair day, I heaved the heavy box with the cowboy lamp to the door. I swept the spider webs out of my hair and choked on the foul smell emanating from the crawlspace. A brief moment of great joy rushed through me as I flicked six of those eight-legged little buggers off my sleeve in Fred's direction. Watching her screech and dance out of the way was the highlight of my entire morning.

"Man, for a woman who owns a pet store, you sure are freaky about spiders, Fred."

She gave me a 'You're number one' with the wrong finger, and I chuckled as we lugged the box around the corner of the house. We agreed we would clean up and de-bug the lamp before hauling it into Mom's kitchen, so we headed toward where Mom's garden hose lay in the back yard.

Struggling with her end of the box, Fred waddled around the corner of the house. "I wonder if this thing s as ugly as I remember it."

"I remember it as being butt-ugly, but not this heavy. Boot, rattle snake–distinctly Mom's taste. I wonder what made her decide to go for the southwestern décor again."

"Don't know, maybe she was watching a John Wayne

marathon and the mood struck. So how about if we accidentally drop this ugly sucker on the way in?"

While I agreed the idea held merit, I figured nothing short of a sledge hammer would destroy it. We also thought about accidentally leaving it behind the pickup truck and letting Dad run over it, but we figured Mom might make him fix it. I didn't think Pat carried that much duct tape at the hardware store, so we just dropped it in the back yard.

The box was slit up the side, so we decided to just flip it open. As the flap came loose, the putrid odor of rotting flesh lambasted our unsuspecting nostrils and sent us both stumbling backward.

"Oh, my God! Something must have crawled in there and died," Fred yelled, falling over my feet, and gagging to beat the band.

"No shit, Sherlock, and it don't smell like any dead raccoon, either." I poked the box with a long stick, but nothing moved. As Fred continued to choke in the background, I lifted the flap on the box, again exposing the cowboy boot.

Much to my dismay, I noticed I had overlooked one minor detail about the lamp down in the crawlspace. The cowboy boot base, which normally would have been attached to a rattlesnake on a pole, was instead connected to a blue-jean covered leg. By Fred's shriek and the gagging noises coming from behind me, I guessed she saw it too.

"Damn, I hate dead bodies," I said lifting the rest of the flap. I pinched my nose and stared at the bloated and decomposing body of a woman.

2

Dead bodies really piss me off. Twenty-three years of wading through blood, guts, and bad guys, too much booze and a bleeding ulcer later, retirement never felt so good. I have had about enough of staring at dead bodies in my lifetime, and I wished this one would have found its way somewhere else. What made my stomach churn about this particularly odoriferous cadaver however, (aside from being really, *really* smelly) was the fact that something struck me as familiar about it.

I let the flap fall back in place and stepped back. I turned and sucked in a lung-full of clean air, then pulled my tee shirt over my nose–like that was going to help. "Well, at least we know one thing, Fred. We don't have to go back under the house to look for a dead raccoon."

Fred stared at me with those saucer-like eyes of hers, then turned and puked in Mom's Knockout Roses–what a pansy.

Swallowing the bile rising in my throat, I saw my chance for revenge.

"*Hmmm*, was it something I said, Fred?" I slapped her on the butt. "Come on, Spider Girl, buck up."

Fred wiped her mouth and took in great gulps of air. Her hands flapped wildly and she began by hyperventilating. "Who is he, Buzz? Where'd he come from? Is it a man or a woman? What's he doing under Mom's house? Oh man! What are we telling Mom? We gotta call Mag! We gotta tell Dad; we gotta call the cops!"

I could see she was about to lose it, so I reached over and rapped her on the back of the head.

"Good Lord, Fred. Take a 'lude and slow down for a minute. Let me call J.J. and let's keep this quiet. We don't want those little old ladies hearing this over their police scanners, and we definitely don't want to give Mom a heart attack."

I took her by the shoulders and squeezed until her glazed stare focused on me. "So here is what we're going to do...."

Under my arm, I could feel the hysteria bubble to the surface though I tried to calm Fred down by rambling on about my plan of action. She tore herself out of my hands and flew to her car, hands still flapping. She grabbed her phone and dialed 911 at lightning speed.

I rolled my eyes. What did I expect from a woman whose highlight of the day was cleaning the poopy papers out of a puppy cage? I grumbled as I resigned myself to setting up a crime scene. I halted in mid-stride when the thought hit me I still had to tell my mother.

"Crap. This ain't going to be pretty. Drag the dead woman out of the crawlspace, puke all over, and leave Buzz to break the bad news to Mom. Good job, Fred, you're smarter than you look"

I scuffed my way toward the back door, rehearsing how I was going to break the news to Mom, and break the neck of my younger sister.

I had my hand on the screen door when I realized I probably got the better end of the deal. Mom would be more concerned with having enough coffee and snacks for the Sheriff's deputies than how a dead woman came to be in her crawlspace. Fred, on the other hand, had to deal with a lazy, incompetent town constable until the real cops arrived on scene. I probably didn't even have to tell Mom now; the bad news might send her into a tizzy. Or, I could tell Dad and make *him* tell Mom! Hah! Sometimes my own genius surprised even me. I took a seat on the swing and waited for the chaos to begin.

Sure enough, in less than five minutes a dust cloud formed at the end of the long gravel driveway. The engine roar of the township's new squad announced that the little weasel wearing a badge was on his way in. If the noise wasn't enough to raise the dead, he laid on the equally new siren. At the same time, the squad skid sideways and almost went through Dad's new fence.

Animals scattered and the local pigeons had heart attacks as our bungling, inept excuse for an elected official with a gun raced up the long drive. Dad poked his head out of the barn when he heard the commotion, shook his head when he realized it was Ted.

Telling Constable Ted Puetz (correctly pronounced 'Pets', but most folks just call him Putz) that the victim was already dead and there was no hurry to mow over the local flower and fauna obviously had fallen on deaf ears.

"We'll be lucky if that little piece of shit zipped his pants and dropped off his latest bimbo before making ruts in my driveway," Dad shouted as he stomped toward me.

"Dad!"

"What the hell would Dead Butts be wanting way out here, I wonder? There ain't a donut shop for miles."

Dead Butts, as Dad called him, was not about to be left out of any headline if he could help it, I thought.

Topping the final rise, Ted hit the brakes of the speeding squad, slid sideways and sprayed gravel in a tidal wave over the front quarter panel of Dad's new truck. In that second, I almost felt sorry for Ted. Almost.

My father despised Ted to begin with and that new truck cost him more than what he originally paid for the farm. A smart person would not even breathe hard in the direction of Dad's new truck, but no one would ever accuse

Ted of having a brain.

By the time he made it over to his new truck, Dad had called Ted every name in the book. In a loud voice, my father told Ted he hadn't voted for him last election, and he would run himself if it meant Ted wouldn't win in the next one.

Ted, blissfully ignorant of the insults hurled his way, turned off the squad. He smiled and waved as Dad passed the squad. Dad flipped him the bird.

Ted wrestled his considerable bulk from behind the wheel of the squad chuckling at Dad's ravings. While Dad checked out the damage to his truck, Ted brushed the white donut powder from his potbelly. That belly of his is quite a wonder in itself. It always made it around a corner a split second before the rest of Ted's five-foot-three frame did. He continued to flick the residual doughnut crumbles from his tie as he lumbered toward my dad. Ted was mostly deaf in one ear, and he made an art form out of 'turn a deaf ear' when he wanted to.

Speaking of deaf, I yelled, "Hey Ted! Turn off the siren!"

Ted looked at me, and looked at the squad. I took a deep breath. *"Turn off the siren!"*

He raised his hands and used sign language to tell me he couldn't hear me. I stomped over to the squad, leaned through the window, and turned off the siren. I walked up to Ted and yelled in his good ear. "I said, TURN OFF THE SIREN!"

Ted rubbed his ear. "Oh, uh, okay." He hitched his pants in true Barney Fife form. "Well now Bill, what do we have here?"

Not bothering to turn around, Dad ran his fingers over the dings the flying gravel had made in the door of his new truck. "You mean, of course, besides an auto body shop estimate for the damages you caused to my new truck? Nothing is going on, Putz. Nothing that would interest you, like say, work. Why don't you waddle back to the taxpayer's new squad and go wreck someone else's $40,000.00 vehicle?"

"Uh, well now take it easy there, Bill. I'm an officer of the law, you know…"

Dad spun around and gave Ted an evil scowl. Ted had the sense to back away a couple steps.

I jumped right in. "Hey Dead–uh, Ted, I think Mom has some of those fudge brownies you like and a new pot of coffee going in the kitchen. Why don't you go on in and check it out? I'll be sure to call you if anyone wants you."

The sarcasm took wing over Ted's head, and he scuttled off toward the kitchen door. "I guess you'd be right, Buzz, I could use a good cup of joe right about now. Can I get you anything while I'm there, Bill?"

Dad's temper boiled over. Through gritted teeth, he seethed, "You mean like maybe some rubbing compound and a new Town Constable, you damn maniac?" Dad fumed as he watched Ted hitch his pants again and stroll through the kitchen door.

"*Humph*!" Dad looked at me and grinned. "That idiot is deaf as a doornail and twice as dumb. Ha-ha, wait until he gets a belly full of Ger's coffee. That stuff has been known to melt the enamel off your teeth, but at least it keeps me regular." He patted his belly. "Ger will keep Dead Butts eating and talking local gossip so he won't mess up anything. Now what the hell is that smell, Buzz?"

Sharp as a tack, my dad. "Well, Dad, to make a long story short, I was looking for Mom's nasty cowboy lamp under the house, and I found a dead body instead." At his raised brows, I gestured. "There it is, over in that box. Fred panicked and called 911 and Edie over at Dispatch must have called Ted."

"At least now I know why that idiot came screaming up the drive like a bat out of Hell, wrecking my new truck. Speaking of old bats, don't tell your mother about this yet, okay?" He looked beyond me to his truck. "Say, do you think I can buff this scratch out?" He bent over again, running his fingers lovingly over the truck door.

"Uh, Dad, did you just tell me to not to tell Mom about the dead body?"

"No, go ahead and tell her about that, just don't tell her that the new truck is all scratched up–she'll have a fit!"

My head spun trying to keep up and to focus my father on the more important situation at hand. "Dad, listen to me, you have a dead person in your back yard. The cops are going to want to know how it came to be under your house! What are you going to tell them?"

"Hell, I don't know. Isn't it the cop's job to find out who he is? I didn't put him there and your mother sure as hell didn't, so what am I going to do about it now? Besides, that's more up your alley anyway, Buzz. I figure you'll look into it–that *is* what you do, isn't it?"

"No, that is what I *did*. I'm retired, Dad. I don't do that anymore."

"You won't be able to stay away Buzzi, and it will make your mother feel better about having a corpse under the house."

"I suppose it would be kind of traumatic if she was the one to find it. Good thing Fred cheezed me into looking for that snake lamp, I guess."

"I think I'd rather have a dead guy I don't know under the house than that damn snake lamp next to my chair. You didn't find the lamp, did you?" He pinched the bridge of his nose. "Geeez, every time I turned the lamp on that damn snake stared me right in the eye." He shook his head, thinking back. "That damn lamp always did give me the willies. Do you think we could accidentally drag it behind the manure spreader or bury it in the garden? I hate that damn thing." He rolled his shoulders and resumed his search for dings across the rear fender of his truck.

Just when I was about to scream, my third sister Mag strolled around the side of the house. "Yo, what-up Buzz? Mom called and said I'd better come over. Sounded like a royal summons–" She stopped dead in her tracks and fanned the air with her hand. "Man-o-man, what is that smell? You eat some bad burritos, girl, or were you letting that Bulldog of yours eat sauerkraut again?"

She turned to Fred and laughed at her own joke.

Fred burped. She still looked rather green. "Shut up, Maggot, Buzz and I found a dead body under the house." She fish-eyed me and amended, "I mean, *Buzz* found the body; she thought it was that cowboy lamp of Mom's."

Mag looked at me. "Hah! Great detective work from the Sherlock Holmes of our generation–Buzz Miller. What kind of a moron mistakes a dead guy for a snake? Whew! The smell alone would knock a buzzard off a manure wagon! Let me give you a hint big sis. With very few exceptions, most people do not look like snakes." She bent to get a closer look at the box. "You know, I think you might be losing it old girl, you might as well call old Dead Butts to investigate or someone equally stupid…wait, ha, ha, there isn't anyone more stupid!"

Fred looked at the ground, still hyperventilating. "I already called him–he's in the kitchen eating brownies."

"You didn't! And I thought Buzz was losing it. What were you thinking?"

I smiled. "Fred already lost it. It's in the rose bushes behind you."

Mag sighed and rolled her eyes. "Why, did she see a

little spider?"

Circling the smelly box, Mag kept her nose pinched and her nasal commentary going. "And I had such high hopes for you, Freddie." She sighed. "So, dead person in Mom's back yard and Dead Butts is in the kitchen? Good place for him. He can't find his ass in the dark, but he never misses his mouth."

"I heard that," Ted yelled from inside the house.

"*Shhh*–don't piss him off Maggie," Dad said shuffling past us on his way toward the house. "That might have spoiled my chance to get my truck fixed by the Township."

He sighed and muttered to himself as he walked toward the house. "Guess I'll go in before Butts gobbles up all the brownies. Maybe I can still get my truck fixed."

He paused, looked back toward us, then scratching his head, continued on to the back door. "I sure hope she frosted those brownies this time. Maybe Andy, in town, can pull those dings out for me. I wonder who put a dead guy under the house. Chocolate frosting would be nice...." Mumbling to himself, Bill bustled through the kitchen door.

We all watched him walk away with varying degrees of awe, incredulousness, and resignation. I slowly shook my head, "You know, he gets more like Mom every day. Maybe dementia flows from both ends of the gene pool. Should we be afraid?"

"Afraid for whom, them, us, or our offspring?" Mag quipped.

"You don't think it's like, hereditary or anything, do you?" Fred looked worried.

I shook my head at Fred and looked at Mag. "Yep, you'd better be especially afraid, Fred."

Mag whooped. Fred gave us both an injured look. "Was that a joke? I don't get it. What did you mean? Are you guys laughing at me?"

By this time Mag and I were rolling. Gasping for breath, I said, "Yes!"

I looked at a teary-eyed Mag and signaled toward Fred with my head. "I can see Mom in the making...be very, very afraid!"

The roar of another car engine shifted our attention back toward the driveway. I groaned, watching a cloud of dust billow out from behind Al's car as she raced up the drive.

"Awe crap, did Mom call the Queen Bitch too?" Fred ducked her head and hid behind Mag. I saw red. "Fred, have you ever thought about counting whales in Alaska?"

Both Fred and Mag looked confused. "What?"

"Never mind." Following more sedately behind her was every county squad on day shift patrol–all three–plus the Sheriff and the Coroner.

Mag took in the scene and mused, "I wonder who is taking care of the county since everyone is at the Miller farm?"

"I don't know," I mumbled, "But maybe the coroner will do a three-for-one deal after I kill Al and Fred."

"A dead body in White Bass Lake is a big deal. Maybe Al called the newspaper."

"Al being here is a big deal," I said. "Don't let her near me, okay?"

A sheepish looking Fred saluted me with one finger "Aye-Aye, Captain!"

Al minced her way across the driveway in her very inappropriate high heels and power suit. Mag began humming 'Hail to the Chief'. Fred tried to sneak off before I murdered her for calling Al.

Fred is a featherbrain, but means well and can be tolerated for short periods of time. She's a little wacky, but in a nice way–like Mom. Mag is mostly a bitch and proud of it, but great to have around in a crisis. We get along great. Al is just a plain pain in the ass. From the time we were kids she was a snot-nosed-Prima-Dona-tattling little shit. Baby of the family, she got away with murder and never failed to rub our noses in it. She had boyfriends do her homework when she was twice as smart as they were. She said it made them feel needed. She acts like a helpless wimp while she rules with an iron fist. She is well suited to her career choice as a Librarian. Not just any librarian, but the Librarian from Hell. That is, an anal-retentive bookworm with a Dewey Decimal obsession and a Wicked Witch of the West attitude. Both Mag and I mess with her any chance we get.

Being the diplomat I am, I hide my animosity well. I squared my shoulders and pasted a phony smile on my face. "Yo Big Al, does it take a dead body to bring you down to visit with us lesser beings, or did you hear about the opportunity for a photo op?"

Well, I guess I have to work on the 'hide it well' part.

She looked down her nose. "As usual, Buzz, your unprepossessing personality shines through in a moment of crisis."

She almost minced past, but stopped and spun and shook her finger at Mag and me. "And don't think I don't know it was you and Mag who filed all of my Presidential Debate videos under Fantasy and Fairy tales! It took me hours to straighten that mess out!"

I shook my finger right back at her, but not my index finger.

She sniffed. "Mature as always. I thought you might get past childhood since I've been out of your life for so long."

Mag and I both smiled. Mag spoke out of the corner of her mouth, "Not long enough, evidently."

Al flipped her long blonde hair over her shoulder, raised her nose in the air, and sashayed closer to the body in the box. When the smell of the corpse hit her full in the face, she reeled, gagging. She teetered on those stupid stiletto heels of hers and started to windmill her arms, trying to keep her balance. The heels sank into the ground but Al continued her forward momentum. She suddenly pitched forward and rammed into Mag, who toppled like a domino into Fred. I jumped out of the way and Al grabbed empty air.

I twiddled my fingers in Al's direction. "See you later, Queenie."

She screamed and lost it, sending all three of them collapsing on top of the dead body box–a whoosh of fetid air exploded in all directions. I didn't know whether to vomit or laugh, but it struck me as being funnier than it was sick. I grabbed my sides and roared with laughter. Mag scrambled off the box and we looked back at the floundering Al and Fred.

I looked at Mag and she looked back at me. We fell on the ground howling. While Al and Fred gagged, screamed, and clawed at each other, no less than four deputies careened around the side of the house to the rescue. Looking like a NASCAR photo finish, the deputies bumped and shoved each other. Each elbowed the other aside trying to be the first to assist Al.

Did I mention that although Al is a royal pain in the ass, she's an absolutely gorgeous pain in the ass?

The unlucky deputy who got to Al first yanked her up and tried to steady her on her one remaining heel not quite sinking into the grass. She was still screeching and flailing her arms, knocked the glasses off the hapless deputy. She skewered another deputy's foot with her stiletto. She backhanded the third and he lost his balance, tripped on the box and ended up beside poor Fred.

Fred was finally hauled off the box by the County Coroner, Mee-Me (Malcolm) Evans, a great guy and friend of the family. Mee-Me reached down, grabbed Fred's wrist, and yanked. Fred flew through the air and landed with a whoomp against his stocky body. He held Fred about the waist and she threw her arms around his neck. She sobbed into his neck. He awkwardly patted her on the back. She incoherently blubbered out her story. Mee-me didn't care. He just closed his eyes and smiled serenely while he continued to pat her on the back. When they realized where they were and what they were doing, they sprang apart and stared at each other. They both began to babble.

"Oh, Malcolm, I am so sorry."

"Fred, are you okay?"

"Thank you so much for saving..."

"I didn't mean to grab..."

An awkward silence prevailed. Mee-Me stubbed his toe in the ground. He rubbed the back of his neck. "Uh, gee, Fred I h-hope you're uh, are you okay?"

Fred took a deep breath and looked down at the box. She gulped in some air and looked at Mee-Me. "Yes, Malcolm, thank you. I'm okaaa-akkk!" and threw up on his shoes.

Malcolm looked at his shoes, then up at a horrified Fred. "Good, Fred, I'm glad you're feeling better. Would you excuse me for a moment, please?" He walked stiff-legged over to Mom's garden hose and calmly rinsed the puke off his shoes.

Mag elbowed me. "Poor Malcolm. It's never easy being the Coroner."

"Frankly, I was wondering where Fred came up with the stomach contents. She already unloaded once."

Fred watched Mee-me. I thought about Malcolm for a

minute. Mee-Me got his name the day we read a report about a body Mag had found down by the lake. He initialed, rather than signed, the report. Because his name is Malcolm Edward Evans, Medical Examiner, the initials were MEE, ME. Of course being the tasteful friends and consummate professionals we are, we never let him live it down, much to his despair.

Mee-Me has always been sweet on Fred, but being painfully shy, he has never pursued it. Fred knows about it too. However, she tries not to encourage him. She would never intentionally hurt his feelings, but I really don't think she could take the heat if she was going out with the County Coroner.

With the trauma the box suffered under the onslaught of my sisters' respective flying bodies, it was laid open and the entire length of the body inside was now exposed. I vaguely registered the fact Mag had ceased laughing, and now she, too, was throwing up behind me.

I stared numbly at the body, realizing that not only was the body female, but it was our neighbor and friend, Carole Graff.

As I said, dead bodies piss me off, but dead bodies of good people I know send me into a rage. At this point I'd had about enough of the theatrics of my lunatic sisters, and the bumbling of the Three Stooges, so I took off in search of the only sane person on the premises–Sheriff James J. Green.

I saw him coming out of the back door of my mom's house, sporting brownie crumbs on his graying mustache. Dragging him over to the box, I said, "Yo, J.J., get rid of the brownie crumbs and look at this–we got trouble."

"Hey, Buzz, what's up? I gathered we had some trouble when I got the frantic 911 from your sister, and I understand that your Mom made brownies."

I grabbed his shirt. "No, you don't understand, J.J. It's Carol Graff from down the road. She's dead in the box."

Hands on his hips, he stared at me. "As in Graff's Garden Center Carol Graff?" He pushed his ball cap back and scratched at his forehead. "If that doesn't beat all." He rubbed the back of his neck looked down on the body. "Damn. Nice lady, too. Sometimes I hate my job. I'm going to have to be the one to go break the news to Glen and Rob."

I felt that old sick feeling in the pit of my stomach. "I agree, my friend. I hated that part of your job too. That's one of the reasons why I don't do it anymore. If there's anything I can do to help..."

"As a matter of fact, Buzz, you know, you can help me out here. I know you still look into things now and again. Moe is my only detective now since Brian got hit with the shrapnel when Paul Stewart's still blew up last week."

"Moe? Oh, you mean Phil."

"Is that his name? I can only keep them straight as the Three Stooges."

"But Phil isn't a detective, even on a good day. Where's Brian Adamson? Can't he do the initial?"

"He's off on Workman's Comp and I'm left with the Three Stooges and Shemp over there for line staff. I'd almost be better off using that sawed-off excuse of a constable to investigate. Hell, I hope I'm never that desperate. Come on, Buzz, help me out here. Hey, I'll even put you on the payroll–at Captain's pay."

"Captain's pay! Forget it, J.J. I have my pride."

Grinning, J.J. threw an arm over my shoulder. "No you don't, Buzz–who are you trying to kid? How about it? I'll also squeeze your expenses out of the training budget. Will that do it for you?"

I felt myself wavering, but I held my ground. "Plus an

Unmarked for the duration?"

J.J. gave me an incredulous look. "You want an unmarked squad too? Why don't you bleed me some more? How about a new grill and a year's supply of beer to go with all that?"

Confident now, I crossed my arms over my chest. "No, my grill is just fine, thank you very much, but I could use a year's supply of dog food. Just the squad and a free hand in the lab should do."

Being an intelligent man, Sheriff Green knew when he'd been beaten. "I'll go for the dog food, Buzz, but the only squad I have is mine, so forget it. Now let's go and see what Malcolm has to say." He grabbed me by the belt loops and yanked me against his side. I yelped and he noogied the heck out of the top of my head.

"Cut it out you moron, I said I'd help!" I jabbed him in the ribs with my fist.

He let out a whoosh of air and let me go. He shot me an injured look. I smiled, savoring my victory. It would have been cheaper for them to buy me a squad rather than to feed Wesley and Hilary for a year! We strolled back into the melee, where Mee-Me was gloved up and doing an initial examination of the body, ignoring the chaos still reigning around him. Moe, Larry, and Shemp strung police tape around the box, while Curly attempted to make time with Al.

Mee-Me looked up from his clipboard, reminding me somewhat of an adorable, near-sighted Bulldog. "Hey, Buzz, hey J.J. Too bad about Miz Carole, eh?" We both nodded.

J.J. rubbed the back of his neck. "I just can't imagine who would want to kill her."

Malcolm pointed to the body with his pen and said, "I don't know who, but I have a hunch about how she died.

Want to hear it?"

We both nodded and looked solemnly on while Mee-Me extrapolated in great medical detail about his initial examination. Our eyes began to cross and I elbowed J.J. When Mee-Me finally took a breath, J.J. interrupted him. "So in your professional opinion, Malcolm, what does all that mean?"

Mee-me shrugged and considered his notes for a few minutes. He sighed heavily and scratched his brow. "All that means, ladies and gentlemen, is that she is dead. Murdered, actually, and with great prejudice."

3

J.J. expelled an exasperated breath. "Come on, Malcolm, a blind man could see she's dead. Hell, he'd only have to take a whiff around here to know someone was dead! I'm thinking she didn't crawl under there by herself and die of natural causes, so cut the crap. I meant what is your unofficial opinion? What's your initial, unconfirmed best guess at what happened here?"

Malcolm became serious. He consulted his notes, checking off points. "Well, I see numerous contusions and lacerations on her arms and face. Doesn't look like anything is broken–except maybe her nose. Her hands are in tough shape, however. She has been beaten, dragged, and if the bullet hole between her eyes is any indication, I'd say she was either shot by a very good marksman or executed. I can't tell that until I do powder testing. Until I get her down to the cool room (Mee-me hated the word 'morgue'), I cannot be any more specific than that."

J.J. whistled. "That was specific enough. Thanks, Malcolm. Any thoughts on how long she's been dead? Ballpark?"

"I can't give you that with any amount of accuracy until we run tests, J.J. Normally I could look at the body and hypothesize according to our weather and the extent of decay, but the Miller girls kind-of wrecked that theory when they fell into the evidence."

J.J. continued speaking quietly with Malcolm. I walked back over toward the body. I crossed my arms and said, "Damn, I was afraid of that. Don't let that worry you Carole, we'll get him."

The longer I studied her body the more I felt that old, eerie calm settled over me. Thoughts were trying to surface and I fought them back. I examined and mentally noted the obvious and the relevant. I began to feel a little queasy and must have called J.J., because he suddenly appeared beside me and handed me Malcolm's clipboard.

"You going to be okay, Buzz?"

I took a deep breath and pulled a pen out of my back pocket.

"Yeah, sure. I felt Carole for a second, but I think I'm okay. Can you stick close just in case though?"

"You bet. But if you go too deep, I'm going to pull you back, so don't get mad."

I smiled and he pulled me close for a second. I smelled a hint of man and Veveter by Axe and almost swooned. *Whoa Buzz, what are you doing? This is J.J. your best friend, your partner before you wimped out and quit the department.*

J.J. has seen me at my best, and at my very worst. He picked me up when I was beaten and bloody, said nothing when I slipped into a vision, and sat with me and Jack Daniels through the aftermath.

He always did know what I was thinking before I did. Kind-of creepy, but I bet I've creeped him out more than once over the years, too. Kidnappings, rapes, lost pets and people; sometimes pictures would flash in my mind, but on really bad days, I would witness an entire scene in a flickering, 8mm kind of way. J.J. knew all this. He pulled out his mini-recorder and stayed with me as I began the inspection of the body. I expected J.J. to go the opposite direction and draw his own conclusions, but he must have thought I was going to whack out, because he was never more than a step away from me. J.J. almost ran me over when I stopped near Carole's waistband. I zeroed in on the tiny change pocket of her jeans. The short hairs on the back of my neck prickled as I leaned in and flicked a tiny piece of plastic protruding from that pocket with my pen.

Pulling out my cell phone, I snapped a couple of pictures.

I touched J.J.'s arm and halted him, pointing silently to Carole's jeans pocket. With a nod from him I slowly removed a piece of plastic wrap, which was taped closed. Inside the plastic was what appeared to be a paper towel wrapped around something lumpy.

I snapped another few pictures. Drugs, was my first thought.

"Drugs?" J.J. eyed the tiny bag and looked back at me.

I shrugged and looked around for Malcolm. "That would be my first guess, but Carole didn't seem the type. Maybe her kid. Hey Malcolm!"

Mee-Me hurried over to us, holding out an evidence bag. I dropped the plastic inside, confident he would properly seal and label it.

Turning to speak to J.J., I suddenly felt that creepy feeling slither up my spine. A wave of vertigo swept over me. I wavered and grabbed J.J.'s belt.

He took an arm and as if in a tunnel I heard, "Buzz? Are you alright? Are you with me here?"

I opened my mouth to answer but nothing came out. I held out my hand and reached toward the bag Malcolm still held in the air. J.J. saw my fingers wiggle and he grabbed the bag out of Malcolm's fingers.

I touched the plastic. "Seeds."

J.J. looked confused. "Seeds? What seeds, are there seeds in here?"

J.J. shoved the bag into my hand. There was remove buzzing in my ears and the world waved and shimmered in front of me. J.J.'s mouth moved but I could not hear his voice as he faded into a thick grey mist.

The noon sun fell away, giving rise to a full moon and a large farmhouse on a hill. I smelled damp earth felt the crisp bite of an autumn evening. I recognized the scene but could not place it.

I knew what was happening and tried to fight back, to tamp it down. My great grandmother called it 'The Sheeny', or the 'Irish Magic'. I called it the bane of my existence. The Sheeny was what made me an exceptional detective, but it also ate holes in my stomach and gave me nightmares. It made me drink too much and had failed me at the moment I needed it most. I dreaded it and I feared it, because I believed in it and knew enough not to fight it when it came. I gave myself over to the feeling of vertigo and it engulfed me like a tidal wave.

I felt a chill and materialized as a part of the scene, an objective observer of what was about to happen. I stood at the bottom of the porch now, and realized I was at Graff's Garden Center–the greenhouse and nursery next door to my mom's and dad's farm. I braced myself for what was to come.

* * *

Lightning exploded as horrific screams tore through the night. Non-stop and agonizing, the screams were wrenched from a soul so tortured death would have been a blessing. The front door flew open. Carole Graff stood in the opening, listening. Giving no thought to her personal safety, Carole tore out of the house. She followed the screams to the old horse barn at the back of her property and slid to a halt at the open door. I ceased being the objective observer and was one with Carole. I could feel the blood pounding in her ears as we drew a ragged breath. We stood paralyzed as we stared at the gruesome scene before us. Blood was sprayed everywhere; it coated the floor and spattered across the walls. Carole's face was a frozen mask and I could taste the metallic sting of blood on my tongue. A screaming horse was tied in the cross ties, bleeding from its nose and mouth. The creature fought for its life, sweat pouring off its sleek coat. Veins popping, it reared high, clawing at the sky. It screamed in agony, tossing its head and spraying everything with blood. As the poor beast fought for its life, several men stood off to the side and looked on.

Carole stood paralyzed as the dying horse made one final attempt to free itself from whatever torture it was forced to endure. It reared again, lost its footing on the blood-slicked floor and flipped over sideways.

The resounding crack of the mare's broken neck echoed in the dense silence. We watched the dead horse dangle in the cross ties, streams of blood pouring from its mouth and nose. Carole stood rooted in the sudden silence. A tiny sob escaped her lips.

All heads turned in our direction. Crap, I thought, as Carole realized she had stumbled into a situation she was never to have witnessed.

"Go," I yelled, "Carole, run!" Of course, no one heard me.

Two men pulled guns from their waistbands. One man rolled a cigar in his mouth, pointed at Carole, quietly said, "Get her."

In that split second of comprehension, instinct took over. Carole whipped around and ran blindly into the night. Footsteps clattered behind her. Shouts of, "Stop that bitch! Now!" rang in my ears.

"They'll catch you at the house, don't run to the house," Carole chanted to herself as she ran.

We tripped over field stubble as we ran blindly across the hay field behind the barn. Years of physical labor paid off for her as she hit the back fence at a full run. She half climbed/half fell over the top. I could feel the bite of the jagged claws of the barbed wire tearing at her clothes and ripping her skin.

She stayed on all fours for a minute, breathing hard. She turned and saw the bouncing beams of flashlights, and heard the curses and yells of the men chasing her. They were gaining ground. "Go, Carole, run," I screamed silently. She stumbled forward, heedless of the brambles shredding her clothing and gouging her arms. Her chest felt tight and her lungs ready to explode by the time she got to Mom and Dad's property line. Barely hesitating, she hurdled the fence and stumbled toward the farmhouse.

"Get to Millers, Call 911, Get to Millers, Call 911," she chanted to the pounding of her feet. She saw Miller's house up ahead. Blood pounding and chest heaving, I felt a surge of relief run through her as she thought, for the first time, she would make it. We neared the farmhouse and I became the observer once again.

Suddenly Carole was lifted off her feet as she was tackled from behind. She landed face first in the dirt. The air exploded out of her as a body landed on top of her. "Air," she gasped. "I need air." She was roughly hauled to her feet. Head down, hands on her knees, she sucked in gulps of air. Turning to run, she was again knocked down and dragged by the collar of her tee shirt over a low rise. She fought her attacker, kicking and screaming. "Please, someone hear me!"

I winced as the man dropped her on the ground and flipped her over. Primal instinct for survival gave her energy and she fought like a wildcat, kicking and clawing at anything she could reach. Someone stomped on her stomach and the fight went out of her. Lying in a fetal position, gagging and sucking in air, she fought to remain conscious.

To pass out now out surely meant death. "Where are the Millers? Don't they hear me?" she cried.

I felt helpless as I stood aside, forced to watch– knowing what was coming and dreading the inevitable.

The men argued. One told another to shut up–there might be people in the house. Carole was more frightened than she ever thought she could be. She was not only afraid for herself, but she realized she had just put the Millers in jeopardy. She looked at the old farmhouse. A single tear cut tracks through the dirt on her face as she thought about her elderly neighbors. She sobbed, "Please be gone."

Tears coursed down my face as I realized that even facing death, Carole would have rather gone it alone than see my parents hurt.

She began to pray in earnest when she heard she 'saw too much', and with shocking clarity realized her life was about to end. She thought of her husband and son, pulled herself together, and got ready to run. Her legs trembled so hard they wouldn't support her, so she propped herself up on her elbows and waited for an opportunity to escape. When the men turned away to argue, she dragged herself a couple of feet away. The conversation stopped. She stopped...and waited.

When they started arguing again, she clawed the ground and slowly made it to the woodpile near the house. She crawled over the top, breaking off fingernails and bloodying her hands. Her blood-slick hands slipped off a log making a soft clunk. She froze and listened for her attackers. Hearing no break in the conversation, she continued on to the top.

Gathering the last of her strength, she curled her legs underneath her body. Taking in a huge breath, she thought one more time of her son and sprang off the woodpile. She was airborne about two seconds before a bullet hit her between the eyes. The force of the bullet whipped her head back and hurled her body against the woodpile. The sound of her head splitting on contact was like a sopping wet sponge hitting the woodpile. I gagged and tried to rush forward, but my feet were rooted to the ground. Her head flopped to face me. I watched in horror as the light in her eyes faded, dimmed, and went out.

Hatred and rage welled up so deep and so fast, it erupted like lava and poured from my soul. I memorized their faces so when I hunted them down, I knew the faces and names of the men I put a bullet through–for Carole.

One of the men looked at the other and spit at his feet. "Good shot, cowboy. You probably woke the whole damn county with that. Now you can get rid of her. Clean up your mess, amigo. Now." He turned and walked away.

The short, thin man, standing with the smoking gun, stared at the woman's body, a little green around the gills obviously nauseated by the scene. He swallowed convulsively. "How the hell am I gonna do that? It must be a mile back to the barn. Hey, stop. I need some help here! Xavier! You told us to stop her so I did." He watched in amazement as his compadres *departed leaving him in a strange place with a fresh corpse.*

"Felix! Arturo! Where are you going?" He looked down at Carole's body and kicked her. "Assholes," he spit out. He looked around for a place to stash the bitch.

He grabbed the woman by the cowboy boots. Dragging her away from the wood pile and toward the barn was sure harder than it looked. He stopped and looked around, noticed a door leading under the house. He looked around, again. A big box, destined for the dumpster, near the barn would make the perfect container. He slit the box down the side and rolled Carole into the box. He dragged her back toward the house. Opening the door under the house, he dragged the box in. Pulling and pushing, he jammed it in as far as he could. He brushed out the drag marks in the sand, closed the door, and slapped his hands against his jeans to remove the dust and sand. Quietly he cut through the fields back toward the old barn, congratulating himself on a job well done.

The crawlspace door stood in front of me. I stared at it until I could see the grain in the wood, the rust on the latch, and the body which lay beyond.

* * *

The fog slowly became a mist. The mist faded on the breeze, and I found myself in J.J.'s arms, his hand crushed in mine. I looked into those sea green eyes and watched as they crinkled at the corners.

"Are you back now?" His voice was soft and his touch gentle. I grabbed a handful of his shirt.

"J.J., I saw it," I gasped.

"I figured you saw something, but I was going to wait until you were ready."

I looked down at our clenched hands and gave him a watery smile. "Can't do it later, do it now. I might forget something like the wood pile. The woodpile! She broke her nails on the woodpile. Blood, oh God the blood! We ran and ran and they chased her down here!" I knew I was babbling, but I couldn't stop. I grabbed the clipboard and began sketching madly. I dropped, exhausted, onto the lawn. J.J. was right there. He yelled orders to check the woodpile take pictures and collect evidence. He told Moe to check the yard and the perimeter.

By this time I was crawling around and taking pictures of the plastic bag containing what I knew were some type of seeds with my cell phone in one hand and drawing with the other. Larry took pictures of the crawlspace entrance on his cell phone, and Moe had his out and clicked away at the back fence.

J.J. straightened and looked around." Why are we using cell phones to photograph a crime scene? What happened to the D700?"

The three closest deputies looked at the ground. J.J. cleared his throat.

"I'll ask again. Why is no one using the Sheriff's Department Crime Scene Investigations Camera?"

Again there was silence. J.J. turned to me.

"What the Hell are you doing on your hands and knees with a cell phone camera, for cripes sake?"

"Because I didn't see anyone else do it, and I wanted to make sure I got the plastic wrap in case it was important later on."

He sighed, looked around for his deputies, and made a general announcement. "Anyone get any pictures on a real camera yet? If not, let's get on it. It's starting to turn into a zoo around here, and we need to finish up. You-Moe, find the camera!"

Moe mumbled something and shuffled his feet. I turned back to the body and saw Mag with Mom's digital camera in hand, clicking away at the scene. How odd, I thought. She was not a cop, nor was she a forensic photographer, so what the heck was she doing over there?

"Hey Maggot, what do you think you're doing over there? Are you thinking of changing careers and going into police work or something?"

Click, click. "Heck *click* no!" Tongue in cheek, she narrowed her eyes. "Why would I give up the fame, glory, and financial independence that being a high school teacher brings? Besides, who would bash heads in my Biology class if I were to quit? Mom wants some pictures so she can show them to Jane, Mary, and Joy when she goes to coffee on Monday. She says they'll never believe someone croaked under her house."

I grabbed her arm and dragged her a short distance away. "Are you crazy?" I whispered to her. "This is a crime scene, not a neighborhood bar-be-cue! And nobody croaked under the house, she was murdered before she was stuffed in the crawl space." I yanked the camera away. "So stop with the camera, will you? These are not vacation pictures from Fort Lauderdale, and those little old ladies don't need any incentive to get their blood up!"

"I think it might be too late, Buzz–when I left the house, Mom was on the phone, bragging to someone that she was the first on her block to have her own croaker, and I don't think she was talking the amphibious type."

I felt a sensation of impending doom. If Mom called her friends, we were in trouble. I shoved the camera back into her hands. "Knock off the CSI stuff Mag, this is serious. I'd better warn J.J. He and Mee-Me went to see if there was a good camera in the meat wagon." I took off toward the driveway thinking of how close to the truth J.J.'s statement about the zoo was about to become.

Just then I saw another dust cloud coming up the driveway. Mag jumped up and down, gesturing toward the driveway with the camera. I stopped in my tracks.

"Hey, Buzz, that might be them now," she yelled. "Isn't that Joy Broussard's black Bonneville? Must be, all I see is blue hair over the dash. And whose red Crown Vic is that? Is that Mary Cromwell driving? Must be–look at all those police antennas. She must have been eavesdropping on the scanner again."

"Yeah, her and the rest of the geriatric SWAT Team. Mom probably didn't even have to call them."

Mag chuckled. "Well now, that's curious. I thought the state took Mary's license for the time she ended up in Volkert's living room with her old blue pickup, after Bobby

Haskin's wedding." With a shake of her head, she went back to clicking.

I sprinted across the driveway to warn J.J. and Meeme, but the huge black car barreling up the driveway beat me to him. J.J. took his life in his hands by stepping in front of Joy's car. I yelled, "J.J., get out of the way! She'll run you down–she can't see over the dash!"

He stood his ground, waving his arms and yelling. "Ladies, please! This is a crime scene. You do not want to be here! Go back home nowww–ohhh shit!"

He jumped out of the way and into the back of Dad's newly-scratched and dented pickup truck. He was still recovering his balance when the cars slid to a stop and the drivers' doors flew open.

J.J. jumped over the side of the truck and stood his ground in front of the ladies, explaining why they were not allowed to enter a crime scene.

His cries fell on deaf ears, and in the case of Mary Cromwell, *really* deaf ears. He had to jump out of the way again to avoid being run over by the stampede of three little old ladies wearing back packs and wielding casserole dishes and Jell-O salads. They waddled, shuffled, and toddled over to where the body still waited in its cardboard box. They stopped and stared as if they were paying their respects. Not wanting to interfere with such a solemn and personal moment, yet needing to know if they could shed light on Carole's death, I stepped within hearing distance and calmly eavesdropped.

"Would you look at that? Gerry wasn't lying!"

"A real live croaker, right under her house!"

"Just like John Wayne Gacy!"

"No, not just like John Wayne Gacy, you old fool. You think that Bill is stashing bodies under the house now?"

"Did you say that Bill stashed the body under the house

just like John Wayne Gacy?"

"No! Listen to me! John Wayne Gacy was from Illinois. Stuff like that doesn't happen in Wisconsin!"

"Can you say Ed Gein? Jeffery Dahmer?"

"Don't play know-it-all with me, Joy Broussard! I know my serial killers."

"Ahem, ladies?" I said.

They all raised their heads and looked at me with innocent expressions. They turned as one and bustled over to the picnic table by the back door. Looking as if they had rehearsed, they worked in complete harmony setting up a buffet on the picnic table.

Folding chairs appeared out of nowhere, and Moe, Shemp, and Curly abandoned the crime scene in favor of unsuccessfully setting up a canopy to keep the sun off the elderly partygoers. Larry was still fanning Al and patting her hand. Al was giving her best impression of the dying cockroach, a must in every Drama Queen's repertoire.

My mother chose that moment to bustle out the back door carrying paper plates, utensils, and napkins, followed by Dead Butts carrying soda, beer, and brats. He fired up the grill and to my amazement, began grilling lunch for everyone. Dad followed, grumbling about his truck, and carrying buns and condiments. He gave Ted a scathing look and said, "Hope he don't burn the sausage."

"Don't worry Bill," Mary chimed in. "Handling his sausage is probably the only thing my boy knows how to do well, heh, heh, heh!"

All grey heads turned toward the grill. Ted turned red and tried to look busy.

J.J. put his hands on his hips, looked at the debacle and shouted loud enough to startle even Mary. "What in the name of Sam Hill is going on here? Are you people going to have a tailgate party right here in Miller's back yard? Have you no respect for Miz Graff? Moe, Larry, did you find my crime scene camera?"

Mary popped out of her seat "Woo-Hoo, J.J.! I have just the thing here!" She proceeded to dump the contents of her backpack on the picnic table.

Self-sealing evidence bags, nitrile gloves, forceps, tweezers, and disposable scalpels clattered across the table. Crime scene tape, hemostats in three sizes, and another box followed. Inside were fiber brushes, an ink pad, silver and black fingerprint powder, clear lifting tape, silver tape, scissors, a magnifying glass, diaper wipes, a high powered clip light, and both black and white latent fingerprint cards.

J.J. looked at Mary like she was a nut. She smiled smugly. Digging deep into her backpack, she pulled out a new Nikon D3X digital SLR camera.

J.J. slapped his forehead and stumbled back a step. "Holy crap," he whispered reverently.

Mary plopped the camera into J.J.'s hands, closed his fingers around the case and said, "Okay Sheriff Green, you run along now and take your photos of Carole, God rest her soul."

"But Miz Cromwell, Mary, This is an eight-*thousand* dollar camera...before the lens!"

"Don't you worry none about that old camera James Green. I bought it to replace your old one, which by-the-way, my illustrious son damaged while taking pictures up at Parfrey's Glen during the 2008 flood."

"Uh, I'm almost afraid to ask."

"Then don't. But to make a long story short, your camera went bye-bye in the flood waters."

Mag nudged me. "Too bad sonny boy didn't follow the camera."

Mary cackled. "Turns out, he did! They had to air lift his sorry ass out of the Wisconsin River floodwaters! They asked him not to come back to help with clean-up."

J.J. took the camera out of the bag and popped off the lens cover. "Well thank you Mary. I shall guard this with my life."

I was fading fast. I always do after a vision as powerful as the one I just had, and all I wanted to do was to finish up and get home. "J.J., can we finish up here?"

"Oh, yeah." He spoke into his recorder. "R.O. is Sheriff James J. Green, twenty, September, 2009 at 1326. Investigation into the murder of Carole Graff." He clicked off the recorder and began to take pictures.

Jane's head spun around and she piped up, "Did you say that was Carole Graff over there? Damn! She still owes me two dollars and fifty three cents for those melons I bought her when they were on sale over at the Food Palace last week."

* * *

I jumped on that statement. "You saw her last week? When last week, Jane?"

"Uh, that would have been last week on Monday. I know because my son Joey was up from Chicago and planted the spiderwort and butterfly bush this past Wednesday that I bought from Carole last Monday."

I didn't mention to her that Joey was the son who lived in Albuquerque, and Harold was the son in Chicago. I also didn't mention that Graff's was closed on Mondays, so she probably got her plants on Tuesday, but she was on a roll, and I wasn't going to be the one to stop her.

"I told her about the melon sale and asked if she wanted a couple. She said sure, so I gave her the ones I had with me. Yes. I remember it as clear as a bell. We spoke when she loaded up the butterfly bush and the spiderwort."

"Hey, Jane, who's got an open fly and warts on her tush?" Mary yelled. She turned and yelled the same thing to

Ted, who was standing at the grill, less than two feet away from her. "Was that Carole, Sonny"

Ted turned and bared his teeth at his mother. "Not tush, you deaf old bat, BUSH! And don't call me Sonny." He angrily flipped the sausage.

Mary looked horrified. "Warts on her bush? Oh my! I never heard of that before, and since you're my son, I'll call you Sonny if I want."

Everyone laughed except Ted, who was becoming more embarrassed and angry by the minute. Mary prattled on. "It's those young singles, you know. 'Warty Bush' must be one of them new S.T.P.s they been talking about on Oprah." She shook her head. "Damn them kids and unprotected sex." We all stood open mouthed and staring, watching her polish off her beer.

Red faced and quivering like Jane's Jell-O mold, Ted gestured wildly with the tongs. "Ma, it's S.T.D., not P., for Christ's sake! They aren't talking about oil!"

"Well, how else did she get warts on her bush? Maybe they had one of them wild Mazola oil parties they talked about on Jerry Springer last week!"

"Not her bush, you wacky old broad, they were talking about flowers! FLOWERS! Geez, what does it take to make you hear?"

Her button eyes brightened. "Beer? Why thank you, Teddy dear, yes, I will have another." With that, she scuttled over to the cooler and snagged a Miller Lite.

Turning back to the grill, Ted stabbed a sausage and muttered, "Shoulda put her in a nursing home years ago."

"We heard that, Theodore Edward Puetz!" Ted turned to see four sets of faded eyes shooting daggers in his direction. Mary, Joy, Jane, and Mom stuck their chins out and glared at him until he ducked his head and apologized.

I poked Mag. "Taking on those four geriatric hellions

one at a time is not for the faint of heart, but I don't think even Ted is stupid enough to tackle them as a united front."

"You'd better believe it!"

Regaining my composure was more difficult than I thought as I watched Ted sputtering and Mary smiling slyly. I faced the ladies and began the interview process. Slowly a story emerged. I was able to piece together some of Carole's last days alive. I scribbled notes and recorded the conversation with J.J.'s mini recorder.

I was about to begin individual interviews when I was alerted to the ambulance arriving on scene. Shouts of "The meat wagon's here!" and "Here comes the body snatchers!" rose from the partygoers as the ambulance rolled to a stop. A bewildered Assistant Coroner, Ivan Sligorsky, gazed upon the scene before him.

Hands on hips, he said in his slow accented speech, "Hope you cooked up a brat for me, Ted." He nodded at the still incensed women. "Ladies, you are looking lovely today." They preened and he turned toward the body. "Malcolm, Sheriff Green, Miz Buzz."

Still looking at the body, Ivan held out his hand and Ted dropped a bratwurst in it. Taking a large bite, Ivan seemed immune to the smell of the corpse or the crowd. He finished the brat in three bites and methodically went about rifling through the Coroner's van, gathering materials he needed. Malcolm helped Ivan unfold a humongous body bag–big enough for box and all. He silently nodded to Malcolm, and the two of them, with the help of J.J. and me, moved the box onto the bag.

Ivan removed his gloves and held out a hand. Another bratwurst dropped. I heard a strange noise and looked at Ivan. He was observing an arm hanging out of the box and humming 'Sentimental Journey'.

I shook my head and smiled. Ivan is a special

character. Very large of stature, his lab jacket reaches about four inches above his wrists. He has a quiet way about him and speaks in a Russian accent. I think he plays up the gouly-stuff for the benefit of the little old ladies.

The seniors call him Igor and pronounced it 'Eye-Gore', after the Marty Feldman character from the movie classic, *Young Frankenstein.*

The beer flowed freely and the atmosphere had deteriorated to silly tittle-tattle and outrageous speculation from my mother and her cronies. I turned off the recorder and sat back to enjoy the repartee.

Jane chortled, "Hey, Igor, what hump? Ha-Ha-ha-ha!" She was joined by the others as they belted out lines from Young Frankenstein.

"What Knockers!"

"Ah, sweet mystery of life, at last I've found you..."

Mary looked her son dead in the eye and said, "The nonsensical ravings of a lunatic mind..."

He smiled back at her and said, "You Mother, are sooo Abby...Normal."

"Give him the sed-a-give," Mom yelled and they all cracked up over that one. Like I said, never take them all on at once, because you *will* lose.

Joy looked uneasy and suddenly leaned forward. In a stage whisper we could hear across the yard she said, "I'll bet it was that husband of hers, Glenn. I always thought he had shifty eyes."

Gerry clapped. "Maybe she was some gun moll for the Mob."

I rolled my eyes. "Geez, Mom, get real."

She put her nose in the air. "Al Capone had a house on Lake Geneva, and another over on St Mary's Road in Libertyville!"

Mary twirled the hair growing out of her facial mole.

She narrowed her eyes and poked out her chin. "I wonder if she was in one of them wild sex cults to get them warts down there."

"Mary," my mom shushed.

"Maybe someone got tired of her owing money to everyone in the county and put a bullet in her," Jane grumbled.

J.J. tried to help. "But Jane, did she owe anyone else two dollars?" Jane slapped her purse on her lap and pursed her lips primly.

Mom leaned forward in a conspiratorial manner. "Probably had a Mexican lover–remember she went there last month on vacation, you know."

"Mom, you watch too much television." I said *Now we're getting somewhere.*

Mary looked at her aghast, "Ain't no one gonna do the hinky-dinky with a woman with warts on her bush!"

"Oh, Mary," an exasperated Joy and Jane shushed.

Joy brightened up. "I remember now, Gerry, and you're right. She was gone on some plant exploration thing. She was gone the tenth, because I went in that day to buy mulch, and that snippy little Jill Greyson tried to tell me it wasn't on sale. I almost had to pay full price, and I had a coupon! Of course I demanded to see Carole, but Jilly told me that she had gone to Mexico." Joy put her head down but we all heard her mumbling to herself, "Sure, she could afford run off to Mexico on a whim but she didn't pay her bills before she left!"

"JOY!"

My mother picked delicately at her macaroni salad as she calmly added her two cents. "That mulch was not on sale that day Joy, the sale ended on the ninth, but you bullied that poor girl into giving you the sale price. Her mother told my niece's husband's brother that little Jilly cried all afternoon after you got done leaning on her like some mobster thug."

"I wonder if someone gets warts down there from some rare Mexican disease. You don't think she drank the water, do you?"

"Geez, Mary," they all yelled in unison.

Joy sat stiffly in her chair and sniffed. "She should have used all that extra money she made off of poor old women on fixed incomes to pay her debts, that's what I think! Lord knows you should have the decency to pay for your melons before you croak!"

Mary looked perplexed. "Who paid to see whose melons?"

Even I joined in this time. "MARY!"

Joy was no longer paying attention; she was getting on a roll. "Thug! Who does that Molly Greyson think she is, calling me a thug? I'll give you thug! I'm 78 years old. I'm more of a bug than a thug! I didn't push Jilly around!"

Mom piped up. "Bug my sweet patootie, Joy Renee Broussard. You're not only a thug, but a cheapskate too, and you know it! You should have paid full price instead of weaseling a lousy fifty cents off with an expired coupon and making that little girl cry!"

With her nose in the air, Mom got up and moved over by Al, pretending to be concerned over her delicate constitution. Al smiled weakly at her and laid her head on Mom's shoulder, playing up the drama. It was all I could do to keep myself from strangling her.

"Well, I never!" Highly insulted and fit to be tied, Joy stomped over to the picnic table, picked up her seven-layer salad, which Bill was in the process of digging into. She snatched it, Dad's spoon and all. Lettuce flew and a pea bounced off Dad's bald head. Joy stalked over to her Bonneville and tossed the salad through the back window.

Mom said out of the side of her mouth, "Joy's going to regret *that* move in the morning!" Mary and Jane nodded their heads in agreement.

Revving the engine, Joy peeled out of the driveway, spraying gravel across the front fender of Dad's new truck.

Dad jumped out of his chair (although he more resembled a beetle trying to crawl up the inside of a glass jar), looking like he wanted to kill something. "Damn, damn, damn old women! I am tired of you all playing free and loose with my new truck! You all can learn how to drive or stop coming over here to wreck my stuff!" He attacked the nearest thing to him Unfortunately, it was Ted.

Arms flailed and sauerkraut flew out of the bun as Dad poked Ted in the chest with his bratwurst. "My truck! My damn truck! You! You little sawed-off excuse of a political hack! Do your job and arrest that old broad! Go on," he poked him again. "Go get her! She wrecked what you didn't of my poor new truck. Throw her in jail and throw away the key! Get that crazy broad off the streets!"

Ted stumbled backward, trying to avoid the attack of the now-krautless sausage. Heedless of how idiotic he looked, dripping mustard, and sauerkraut hanging off his tie tack, he began to backpedal away from the livid 80 year old man. "But Bill, wait! I'll pay, wait! Stop! Sheriff Green! Mrs. Miller! Call him off!"

Not knowing whether to scream or cry, he mewled like a wounded kitten while scrambling backward away from my father. We all watched helplessly while his butt hit the food-laden picnic table full force. He floundered and teetered, realized he was trapped. He tried to regain his balance, tripped over his feet, and fell face first into the potato salad.

"Two salads down, two to go," yelled Mary, as her son picked a piece of celery out of his ear. "I haven't had this

46

much fun since me and the mister thought that the swinging singles ad we answered was a dance club! I remember when we walked into that place dressed in our square dance outfits; the place went up for grabs. That ruffled skirt of mine never got such a workout!"

"MARY," everyone yelled. She smiled her Mona Lisa smile and settled back into her chair, quiet for the first time all day.

Ted took advantage of the distraction and exited, stage left. He jumped into his squad and hightailed it out of there. Last seen was a cloud of dust settling in the driveway, and a trail of potato salad, kraut, and mustard scattered across the yard.

"Hey, Sheriff, we got everything all 'wrapped up' here!" Ivan waved his fifth brat in the air and smiled. He slammed the back of the ambulance closed.

J.J. scowled at him as he signed off on the paperwork. "Sick joke, Ivan. Get on downtown now so Malcolm can work his magic. Hey, Buzz, you're going in with me and Malcolm for the autopsy, aren't you?"

"Sure, J.J. You go ahead back to your office. Just let me make sure my folks are okay and I'll be right along."

"I don't think it's your folks you have to worry about. Ted just got beat up by an 80 year old man and a naked bratwurst."

"Uh, yeah, Dad's a little touchy about his truck."

J.J. ruffled the hair on top of my head. He knew I hated that. "See you later, pal. Thanks for the entertaining morning."

I sighed. "Later, J.J., Unfortunately it wasn't unusual by Miller standards."

J.J. smiled and shook his head. He pulled out behind Mee-Me's car. Moe, Larry, Curly, and Shemp quit the softball game they were involved in and sped off down the driveway after him. Mag printed the pictures she had taken on the computer and gave me a set for the investigation. I looked back on the scene as I pulled out of the driveway. Aside from the nasty smell hanging low in the air, it seemed like a friendly neighborhood gathering. If people only knew…

4

The unaccompanied drive back into town was the perfect way to restore the slim hold I had on my sanity. It gave me time to digest and disseminate the information I had gathered onto the whiteboard of my brain–not an easy task after just escaping the pandemonium of my parents' place. Something about the body tickled the back of my mind, but I couldn't quite grasp its significance. I decided to wait until after the autopsy to formulate a plan of action. I threw J.J.'s recorder and my notes into the investigation file (a.k.a. the glove box,) and continued on my way into town.

My timing was perfect because I pulled into the parking lot of the County Morgue just as the ambulance was leaving. Entering by the back door, I could see Mee-Me and Ivan finishing the prep work in the cold room. Autopsies never bothered me overmuch–some crimes scenes I'd been on were much worse–but I'm not a sandwich eater either. Ivan was, and took specific pleasure in grossing out some of the toughest he-men cops I ever worked with. I've watched Ivan perform his macabre magic on other cops many times. I remember when I worked with a fellow copper named Jeff Arsenal, chuckling along with him as some state boy barfed and fainted right there in the cold room.

Mee-Me offered to let me observe, but I declined, saying I'd rather check out the plastic I recovered from Carole's pocket. He suggested we look at it together while we had sole access to his lab. I agreed. Within five minutes we were both staring blankly at what appeared to be flower seeds wrapped in a paper towel. Under a microscope, we could see there were two kinds of seeds in the towel and neither resembled marijuana, but beyond that we were stumped. Malcolm folded his arms across his chest and pushed his glasses up onto his forehead.

"Why would Carole meticulously wrap a few seeds in her pocket? She owned a nursery with millions of seeds all over the place. Why would these be special?"

I went over a couple of possibilities. "Perhaps she was saving them to give to someone else. Maybe someone gave them to her. Let's try not to read anything into this that isn't there. She was a professional gardener, and probably had seeds in every room of the house."

I stared into the microscope again. "Look at the towel, Malcolm. Is that writing?"

The paper towel had striations on it, which could mean someone wrote on a piece of paper sitting on top of the towel at the time.

Malcolm peered through the scope and agreed. "It looks like a *u, t, h, e*, and maybe a capital *L*."

I wrote on a piece of paper: *luthier, lute, lutecium, Luther, Lutheran.*

"Hey, Malcolm, maybe Carole is a Lutheran." He bobbed his head enthusiastically. I laughed, waving my hands and shaking my head. "Hey, I'm just kidding!"

He stared at me blankly and I sighed in exasperation. "Malcolm, I was being facetious. Carole is *not* a Lutheran! This might, however, be a name. 'Luther' could be a possibility. Perhaps Theo L. Maybe he was a contact, or who she got the seeds from. Could it be part of a name of a town? Maybe it's the name of the seeds. We'll let the crime lab figure it out." I made a notation to send along my ideas with the seed sample.

It's got to be the seeds. If we identify the seeds, we'll be on our way.

Why was I concentrating on the seeds? Why was I not

zeroing in on the bullet wound? Probably because after looking at the shape the body was in, the bullet seemed like overkill.

"Maybe the reason I think Carole's murder is connected with the seeds is that Carole and Glenn do not have enemies in this town. They have a thriving business but are not millionaires.

"Their son does not get into trouble with the law, and there is no evidence that either Carole or Glenn was fooling around." In a small town in southeastern Wisconsin, we would know.

Between grapevine gossip and sauce talk at a local tavern, someone would have seen something and repeated it down at Sal's Diner.

"I don't know about life insurance or inheritances, but it looks, so far, like we have no other motive outside the business, so our next step is to look *inside* the business."

Malcolm looked up from his notes, "Yeah, you're right. Sorry I jumped the gun. Everyone wants to be a detective, you know."

I replied dryly, "It ain't as cool as it looks, Mal."

He looked like an eager puppy. "I'd really like to help, though. Maybe I can call the State of Wisconsin Crime Lab in Madison and ask if they know of anyone who could help us identify the seeds. I went to med school with the director up there." He jotted down another note to himself.

I cocked my head and thought a minute. "Do they really have guys that do that now? I would bet they don't have Forensic Botanists just lying around at the crime lab waiting for someone to call."

Malcolm sent me a telling look over the tops of his bifocals. I shut up. He continued. "We could also contact the university–they do everything there. In this day and age everyone borrows from everyone. I give the occasional lecture up there; they do some lab work for me that requires diagnostic capabilities, which are beyond my humble lab. The main thing is, we can't rule anything out, so if you agree this warrants a Forensic Botanist, I'll go ahead and try to find one. If this homicide involves the gardening industry, it would be good to make the acquaintance of the professional plant boys anyway."

Although J.J. was nowhere around, I gave Malcolm the go-ahead to make the calls and ship some of the samples if the state boys could identify them. I thanked him and told him to call me when he wanted me to pick up the autopsy report, and to let me know what the crime lab had to say.

"Oh, one more thing, Buzz. J.J. went out to the Graff place to break the news to Glenn. He said he'd call you later. Call me if you need me."

"Thanks Malcolm. Will do."

I was surprised to see Mag was in the parking lot, shifting back and forth on her feet next to my car, and looking grim.

I lifted a brow. "What's up, Magpie?"

She furrowed hers and glared at me. "Coffee," was all she said, and got into her car. 'Coffee' was a secret Miller Sisters word that was serious business. It could mean anything from, 'Yo Bitch, we have to talk', to 'I am devastated and need a shoulder', to 'I'm starving to death, let's eat'.

I thought I was probably the 'Yo Bitch' as we climbed into our respective vehicles. We automatically drove to the small diner a couple of blocks from the morgue. Actually, the place was a geographical oddity, in that Salvador's Diner (as it is called) is a couple of blocks from anywhere in White Bass Lake. It's the heart of the town in more ways than one.

The story goes that the owner, Sal Garcia, fell in love

and married an American exchange student (Amy) twenty-some years ago. Sal always wanted to be a chef in a five-star restaurant, but after meeting up with prejudice and snobbery in the culinary world, he lowered his sights just a little. He and Amy settled in White Bass Lake, bought the diner, raised three kids, and they run the best little breakfast and lunch place in the Midwest. It is a standing-room-only gold mine, especially when the summer people invade our little hamlet.

Sal bakes all his own pastries and experiments with different dishes. In front of a grill he is second to none. He is so fast that at times his hands are a blur. People come into his place just to watch him cook.

We timed him once, and he cooked breakfast for six people in less than five minutes: we are talking pancakes, potatoes, French toast, and omelets. He is, in short, simply amazing.

We go to Sal's for a number of reasons. First, they are all great people. Second, they don't care how long we sit and have coffee. Third, Sal's is 'gossip central' in White Bass Lake, so if you want to know anything about anyone, you need to be at Sal's. Fourth, Al never goes there, so we do.

I was banking on the gossip central aspect this morning, hoping to pick up more information on Carole's movements prior to her death.

Walking into Sal's is like walking into *Cheers*; *everyone knows your name.* The drawback to this is that everyone also knows your business, but that's the trade off of small town life for you. Mag and I came in through the back door like we always do. By the time we made it through the kitchen to the dining area, an eerie silence had settled over the room.

Sal, who usually yells 'hey' across the room, only

nodded silently and continued to chop and flip at the grill. Amy, who was behind the cash register stopped in mid-sentence to watch us cross the room to our regular table. The quiet was really giving me the willies, and I could see Mag felt the same way. By the time Donna silently served us coffee, I couldn't stand it any more.

"Yo, Sal–what's new, amigo? Is something wrong?"

Sal spun around yelling in Spanish and gesturing wildly with the spatula while bits of egg and ham flew across the room. A green pepper plopped into Mike O'Brien's cup. Unperturbed by these outbursts of Sal's, Mike just fished the pepper out with a spoon and never broke stride in his conversation. Sal looked fit to be tied and switched to English.

"What the hell you mean what's new? What the hell could be new in this town? Why should anyone tell me, anyway? What's new with me? I got friends who tell me nothing! I got enemies who tell me good stuff. What goes on at your folks' place out there? How come I'm the last to know?"

I accidentally chuckled, thinking that Sal's quick temper and flying egg shows were really quite funny. It pissed him off even more. It also meant that this particular tirade had been going on for some time–thus explaining the silence when we came in. Mag and I were definitely on Sal's shit list.

"Nothing much going on Sal, the folks are fine, we pulled a corpse out from under their house, you know, the usual."

Sal turned back to the grill. I looked at Amy. She just shrugged and made the crazy person sign around her ear. Sal, however, was not finished; he was only taking a breather. He spun and gestured with his spatula again. "I hear it's that lady with the flowers, Missus Graff. But I gotta hear it from someone else, because you don't come to my place and tell me."

Exasperated, I got up and went over to the snack bar, lowering my voice in hopes that Sal would lower his. "Sal, I just got into town. I had to stop at the morgue and then Mag and I came here. I haven't had time to come before now."

Sal flipped an order onto a plate and gave me an injured look. "I had to hear it from your snooty sister first. I was having a pretty good day before she came in."

"Al has that effect on a lot of people. I'm sorry Sal, it's just that–"

Sal let out a huge sigh. "Like I said, I was having a pretty good day until that Alexandra girl. She comes in and announces it to everyone like she's the star of the show or Headline news or something. Then she leaves and doesn't buy anything. She's not like you." He gestured with the spatula and I ducked. "You sure she's your sister?"

Mag and I nodded our heads reluctantly, admitting that indeed, Al was related. I contemplated telling him she was the milkman's daughter, or some pod child we found in the garden, but I didn't want the rumors to start flying. People who know Al would believe it.

I was silent for a moment wondering whether this scenario could get any more bizarre. Finally, the buzz of conversation resumed as the customers lost interest in us and Sal turned back to his grill. Mag and I walked back to our table.

Before I could say any more, my cell phone vibrated. A quick peek showed it was the morgue number. Mee-Me called to say he had contacted the crime lab, and they happened to have a Forensic Botanist in Milwaukee they would send out this afternoon. "Talk about one-stop shopping Buzz, what a coincidence to have a plant specialist so handy."

"I agree, Malcolm, what a happy coincidence." I thanked him and hung up, contemplating the odds that a Forensic Botanist was readily available and less than 50 miles away, with a free afternoon. Seemed a little fishy to say the least, and I don't do coincidence.

Realizing Mag had begun to speak, I pulled my attention back to the conversation. "And really Buzz, I think I should help you on this case,"

I could only stare at her, fighting off the instant nausea. She now had my full attention. "Oh God, Mag, why on earth would you feel compelled to do that? You do realize that this is a murder investigation, and with few exceptions, murderers are usually really bad guys, right?"

She stirred her coffee, added sugar, stirred her coffee, and added more sugar. My nausea increased as she explained. "Yeah, I get it, I'm not a moron, you know. Finding Carole at Mom's makes it kind of personal, like it's our duty to find out who killed her. I liked Carole, and she didn't deserve what happened to her. Besides, it's summer vacation at the high school and I'm not working, so I could like, be helping you full time. You know, investigate and stuff, I mean." She bit her lip and added sugar one more time.

"You already know I'm pretty good at research, and I've watched you work for a million years." She picked up her cup and sipped the sugar-laden coffee, grimaced, and pushed it away.

I felt it *my* duty to set her straight. No sister of mine was going to get tangled up in a murder investigation. Twenty three years of unexplained visions of every horrific thing one person could do to another, too much alcohol, nightmares, and bleeding ulcers was something I did not want to share with my little sister. "Mag, most of this stuff is real boring. If, by chance I do run into the bad guys, I mean if it gets ugly, I wouldn't want you in the firing line. Mom would kill me if you got hurt, and Dad would be pretty pissed, too."

She added more sugar to her coffee. "Not unless we scratched his stupid truck."

"Hah! You got me there, sis. Still, I'm not trying to be mean, but what do you know about police work? I certainly don't have time to train you, and like I said, it's not like television. What they do in an hour sometimes takes real cops months to figure out, if they ever do."

There, I thought, that ought to do it. The Maggot loathes boredom.

Unfortunately for me, it didn't work, and worse than that, she was on a roll. "But we have advantages, Buzz. No one would suspect me–I could be like, uh, undercover! That's it, undercover. I'm on vacation, and you're retired. No conflicts, no other cases, no boss, no muss, no fuss; we can devote all our time to finding out who croaked Carole! And don't cheese me on the police work, Miller. You spend a teaching career ferreting out cheaters, smokers, tokers, talkers, thieves, and vandals, and tell me teaching doesn't involve investigative work!"

I sighed. "Got me there, Maggot, okay, you're in. We're a team, but we do it my way. No Rambo shit, got it?" I got in her face. "And no pissing people off on purpose." She laughed. "Maggie, I'm serious. You have to develop some people skills, and fast.

"I can't be pulling your ass out of the fire because you used unnecessary force by lashing people with your tongue. Me, Lone Ranger, you, Tonto. Do we have a deal?" I held out my hand.

"Okay, Kemosabe, we got a deal." She grabbed my hand then rubbed her hands together. "Oh boy, when do we start?"

Something told me this was going to be a very bad idea. Mag was well-known as a loose cannon, and controlling her mouth might be a full time job. However, she was smart and had good instincts. She was cool under fire and she worked for free.

Taking a deep breath, looking left and right in a most conspiratorial fashion, I made a show of telling great secrets. "Well, so far you know what I know about the body and the evidence. J.J. went out to notify Glenn of Carole's death, and to ask why neither he nor Rob reported her missing. You and I will have to talk to them too, as well as the employees, but what J.J. finds out will tell us how we will proceed."

Mag lifted her chin and spoke with authority. "I will conduct my interviews with the utmost professionalism, even though that rat-bastard Glenn Graff probably murdered her anyway. What that jerk needs is a swift kick in the caboodles!"

"See, Mag, this is just the kind of behavior I was just talking about. What is up with you?"

"This is different, Buzz, you just don't get it!" She jumped up out of her chair and started digging in her pockets for money, mumbling to herself. She was visibly upset and creating an 'E.F. Hutton' moment in the noisy diner. While half the town looked on, the backs of Mag's knees hit her chair and tipped it over, causing her to lose her balance and fall backward.

She waved her arms in circles, trying in vain to keep her balance ala Al in Mom's backyard. She over-corrected and fell sideways into Burt Cheever's lap. Her change flew out of her hand and rained down on the room like pennies from Heaven. What was it with my sisters falling over and causing chaotic scenes?

I reached for her. It was like she wore strawberry

cream sleeves. My hands slid off her arms and I ended up with handfuls of whipped cream and no Mag.

She wavered for a second and began to fall again. Burt moved his already ruined strawberry pancakes aside. "Oh nooo," she wailed as she toppled sideways.

"Timberrrr," some smart ass across the room added.

Like a slow motion replay, we all watched Mag try to catch her balance. She twisted and did a swan dive face first right onto Burt's plate, squishing his strawberry pancakes out the side and spraying all of us with strawberries and whipped cream. Even Sal stopped slinging hash long enough to view the spectacle. He sighed, and reached for the pancake batter to replace Burt's order. He whistled for the kid in the back and told him to fill a bucket and bring a mop.

"Clean up in aisle five," was heard from the peanut gallery.

I jumped over the fallen chair, skidded through the strawberries and whipped cream on the floor, and grabbed Mag. She had pancake in her hair and a strawberry on her chin. She tried to explain to Burt how she must have had a seizure or been pushed, while still sitting on his lap. Burt looked as if it were more likely she'd had an attack of schizophrenia, and kept inching farther away from the table. I pulled her off his lap, apologized, and dragged her out of the diner, wishing a hole would swallow us up.

"Mag, what is with you and catastrophes lately? That's more Fred's M.O., not yours. What's up with you? One minute we were talking about interviewing the Graffs and the next you're spazzing out and scraping whipped cream off your butt. What the hell is the matter with you?"

She flicked a strawberry off her shoe, folded her arms across her chest and kicked the tire on my car. "That rat-bastard Glenn Graff is what the matter is. Like I said, he needs a good swift kick in the caboodles."

"Whoa, wait a minute Mag, we're not kicking anyone's caboodles, and why is Glenn a rat-bastard? I thought he was a Boy Scout."

It was easy to see Mag was extremely upset, but I found it particularly difficult to show empathy for someone waggling pancake encrusted eyebrows at me. While I tried not to laugh, she continued her tirade. "That's what he wants everyone to think, but he's a serial ass-pincher! A masher! A lecherous turd! He cornered me in the potting shed at the garden center, and I didn't think I'd escape with my virtue intact. What the hell is with jackasses like him? If someone would cheat on a nice lady like Carole, he'd probably kill her too, right?"

After getting over my initial shock, I looked behind us to make sure we were alone. Pancake and strawberries plopped off Mag's butt onto the sidewalk behind us. Trying for the lighter side, since I could no longer keep a straight face, I said, "Since when are you so concerned about your virtue?"

She grabbed my shirt. "Look Buzz, this is serious. You know I enjoy sex just as much as the next girl, uh, or…uh, maybe you don't know. But that doesn't matter because I don't do married men, and I like to say who and I like to say when, and where sure as hell is not among his wife, Carole's, grafted cactus plants!"

"He was going to nail you in the cactus plants? Ouch!"

"Yeah, Carole was off in Texas or New Mexico or somewhere, and that slimy toad thought it was a good time to express his unrequited love for me. If he'd have touched me one more time, I would have given him a new definition of 'Love Lies Bleeding', and I don't mean the common name of an Amaranth!"

"Wow, Mag, I had no idea. Speaking of ideas, how

long ago was this trip Carole took to Texas? The Geriatric Mod Squad said something at Mom's about Carole being in Mexico last week. What is she doing in the southwest? Visiting family all the time?"

Could her trips to the southwest, the mysterious seeds, and her untimely demise be connected? "Mag, you just might be on to something here."

Warming to the idea of intrigue, Mag momentarily forgot Glenn's perfidy and her sticky buns. "I thought she was from the east coast, but I do know she did a lot of work with rare and endangered plants. In fact, she was working with some research group on propagating rare species from the southwest. Glenn told me that much when he was chasing me around the potting shed."

"You really might have our first clue, Maggie girl. That was Mee-Me calling a minute ago, and he has already contacted the state crime lab.

"One of their plant gurus happens to be in Milwaukee at a conference. He or she will be stopping by today to look at some seeds I found in Carole's pocket, before they go back to Madison. If the good doctor isn't too much of a stuffed shirt, maybe he or she will go out to Graff's with us and do a little diggin' in the dirt; you know, looking for some *real* dirt."

"You do have an excellent turn of phrase, Buzz, but do you think I should still go with you because of Glenn and all? Maybe I should clean up and lay low. Besides, I don't feel like playing the nice-nice to some jerk and having to keep company with some boring algae man, or worse, some woman."

"Margaret Anne Genevieve Miller, since when has a man or woman ever intimidated you? Tell you what; if Glenn makes any kind of move toward you, I'll hold him down while you kick his caboodles, okay?

"We'll also have that bullet-brained plant geek with us and he can slap him with some seaweed or just bore Glenn to death with plankton and petunias. How's about that?"

She chuckled, and I knew that meant she felt better. Sticky, but better. "It's a deal, Buzz." We chatted for a couple more minutes, before Burt's breakfast began to dry on her skin and she started to itch. She decided to walk home and clean up. We agreed I'd pick her up when the hotshot from Madison arrived at the morgue. We parted ways. I couldn't help laughing while I watched Mag waddle home, pieces of Burt's breakfast falling off her in chunks and making her look like the killer pancake from Hell. Good thing she lived close by. Half the dogs and all the bees in the neighborhood would soon be following her around.

5

Dallas/Fort Worth the same day

The World Championship Appaloosa Horse Show is the elite competition of the finest halter and performance horses in the Appaloosa industry. Big names and big money abound. In this arena at least, Alejandro Montoya was truly an equal, rubbing elbows with Hollywood stars and world class trainers, as well as owners' families and their grooms.

The three men arrived at Fort Worth's Will Rogers Equestrian Center early in the evening on Thursday. Unloading the horses went without incident. Each mare was allowed time to stretch her legs before being placed in her respective stall. Princesa was feeling her oats as Alejandro trotted her down the blacktop drive and back. She tossed her head and kicked up her heels like she knew she was a champion. Many heads turned to watch Alejandro trot her toward the barn.

Alejandro looked up and down the aisles for Dr. Huerta. One of the broodmares had a slightly swollen tendon along her cannon bone, and it felt a little warm around the fetlock area of her left front leg. Alejandro thought he saw Huerta hurrying around a corner by the entrance to the coliseum. He carried the briefcase that had ridden up in the backseat of the pickup. Alejandro thought that was rather odd. He thought the registration papers and health certifications were in there, and the show office was in the opposite direction from where Dr. Huerta was headed. He called to him, but Huerta either did not hear, or ignored him.

Turning his attention back to the mare, Alejandro

broke open a cold pack and bandaged it in place over the swollen tendon. He helped Jose bed the mares down. They fed and watered them lightly to avoid colic after the long ride. Jose scuttled off to find them both something to eat, and Alejandro began setting up house in a double stall, which had been left empty in the middle of the line-up. It was totally enclosed for security and privacy by curtains, which hung on all four sides.

Señor Martinez had hired someone to have the stall decorations bought and set up in advance. Alejandro was happy to escape that tiresome task. He stood back and observed the results.

The red, black, and gold curtains, swags, and tassels covering the stalls were eye-catching and elegant. The white banner announcing 'Ranchero del Sol' and 'Princesa Dianna' draped across the aisle near the temporary tack room. Each stall had a name plaque and a listing of winnings and points. The tack room itself was large enough to accommodate living quarters for Alejandro and Jose, as well as tack, grooming, and medical supplies. Alejandro could have stayed in a motel, but he did not like leaving the horses at night. A curtain was pulled across one end to provide extra privacy for a dressing room.

Jose returned with supper, and he and Alejandro dined on burgers and fries. Speaking Spanish, Alejandro and Jose discussed the schedule for the next day. After supper, they fed the mares a little more and prepared to lock up for the night. After checking on the injured mare and replacing the cold pack with another, Alejandro turned to find Jose looking over his shoulder. "Jose, have you seen Dr Huerta since we arrived this afternoon?"

"No, Alejandro. The doctor, he is not in! Hah-hah, I made a little joke! I have not seen him since we arrived. Do we look for him now?"

"No, Jose, we get some sleep now. I'll check on the mare throughout the night. I iced her down earlier and I have her wrapped for the night. Right now the leg looks pretty good. If she is not considerably better by morning, I'll have an American vet check her out if Huerta doesn't show up."

Jose nodded and looked thoughtfully at the injured mare. "I will get a snack now. I will check on her before I go to sleep. You will be up with the birds anyway, and she will be good until then, no?"

"Yes, she will be good until then. Thank you, Jose, good night. Wake me if the leg looks worse, okay?"

Jose turned and walked back toward the cook tent in the parking lot. He waved over the back of his head and yelled, "Okay, boss!"

Alejandro checked on his charges one more time. He spoke in quiet tones and stroked each soft nose. They pressed against the stall doors, trying to get closer to him. He loved them all. They were such individual personalities; it was like having a room full of his own spoiled children. One despised what another loved. One could not be transported next to this one, but stood placidly beside another. One was at her best in the morning, and another kicked the stall apart if she was not coddled like an old lap dog before bedding down. Saying goodnight to each was a ritual he performed whether at home or on the road. It was comforting to both him and the horses.

Later, lying on his cot, Alejandro listened to the evening noises of the show barn: the rustling of hay, the occasional snort, the splash of water in a bucket, and the dulcet tones of horses nickering softly to each other in the night. Closing his eyes, Alejandro fell asleep to those restful sounds, thinking again about how good life was.

His peaceful world exploded around him about three in

the morning. He was blown out of his bed by splintering wood flying past his head. The pounding of thrashing hooves against the slats of the connecting stall sounded like some crazy offbeat cadence of a bad drum line. Someone was screaming, and it took a second to realize it was animal and not human. Alejandro leaped to his feet and tore out the door. A sense of foreboding spread through his limbs. With the whispered word *"Princesa"* on his lips he bolted into the aisle.

One look confirmed his worst fears. "Veterinario! Huerta! Doctor! Doctor," he yelled as he ran to the stall door next to the tack room. Blood streaked the walls as the wild-eyed mare rolled on her side, thrashing and screaming. Alejandro looked on in horror as his beautiful little filly bled from her nose, ears, and eyes. She suddenly stiffened. Her legs slammed straight out, her tendons popping. Just as Alejandro saw recognition of him in her eyes, her head reared back and she moaned long and hard in excruciating agony. Gasping, Alejandro stood by in helpless torment. Her muscles began to relax and she groaned again. She slowly quieted. Alejandro wrenched open the stall door.

Tears ran down his face as he stood over her and watched the light go out of her eyes.

"Princesa," he whispered again, and fell to his knees by her head. He collapsed next to her still form and gently placed her head in his lap. He tenderly stroked her cheek, whispering softly in Spanish. Tears flowed freely as his hand absently kept up its loving caress, for minutes or hours, he did not know or care.

"Sweet Jesus, Mary, and Joseph, what the Hell happened in here?" demanded the owner of a loud Texas drawl. The question snapped Alejandro out of his trance. He looked up. And up. Before he could ask, the big man stuck out his hand. "Donny Ray Little, Dee-Vee-Em. What the hell went on in here? It looks like a slaughter house around here!"

Donny Ray placed his hands on his hips, surveying the carnage inside the stall. He bent over the filly, lifted an eyelid, then felt for a pulse. He lifted her top lip and looked at her gums. Alejandro stayed where he was, holding the dead filly's head while the veterinarian tried to piece together what had transpired. Many people were gathered in the aisle gawking. He looked past the crowd and saw a veterinary medicine truck outside the barn entrance.

Alejandro gently placed Princesa's head back on the bed of shavings. He stepped out to look at the crowd. Wiping his eyes and nose on his sleeve, he sniffed. "Thank you for coming, Doctor, for all it's worth. Maybe you can help me make sense out of this. She was perfectly fine when we arrived; there were a number of people who witnessed how playful she was. She ate and she drank. All our mares eat the same feed, and none of the other mares were affected, so it can't be something foreign in the feed. Nothing abnormal in her bedtime manner, and she exhibited no deviate behaviors before…before…."

"I understand Mr.-Mr…?"

"Oh, I am sorry, and a little rattled. I am Montoya. Alejandro Montoya, head trainer for Eduardo Martinez, the filly's owner." Alejandro checked his watch. "Mr. Martinez is flying in this morning. In fact, he should have arrived already. Excuse me. I will call his cell phone." He dialed and got the voice mail. He left a message and hung up.

Donny Ray took off his cowboy hat and ran a hand through his hair. He looked down at Alejandro and gestured to the dead filly. "I hate to bring this up right now, but she really ought to be autopsied as soon as possible. The show committee will want to rule out communicable diseases as soon as possible, especially since she came from out-of-country. I'll need her health certificate, along with her Coggins test and any other health paperwork you have. The owner would have already signed a waiver so we don't have to wait for his arrival to get going on this. By the outward look of things there is something odd going on here. I understand you travel with your own veterinarian. If y'all will point me in the right direction, I'll see what he wants to do." He gestured to the gathering crowd.

Alejandro sadly looked at the filly. He turned back to Donny Ray. He also noticed security had been notified and the crowd was being pushed back. It was only a matter of time before the news media arrived. He understood about privacy and discretion, but he also had to trust someone. He made his decision.

"Dr. Little, I will be frank with you. I have not seen Dr Huerta since yesterday morning. I also cannot reach my boss. If you would be so kind, could you have the mare removed to your facility, and would you perform the autopsy? Even though Mr. Martinez cannot be reached at this time, I am sure he would not like his prize filly lying here like this."

"I agree, Montoya." Donny Ray pulled out his cell phone and made some calls. When he was finished, he assured Alejandro that all was taken care of. Alejandro headed for the tack room and changed out of his bloody clothes. Donny Ray's phone rang again. When he hung up, he caught up with Alejandro.

"Good thing you're still here, Montoya. The show office called and informed me that because of the unknown nature of the filly's death, the law mandates me to perform the autopsy. You and I both have to go to the show office and fill out the necessary paperwork. Good thing we made the right decision. Come on, amigo, we can go together."

Leaving the other horses in the care of Jose and the

show committee, Alejandro and Donny Ray made their way to the show office. Alejandro took care of the paperwork and gave a deposition of the events to the authorities. Hours later, Alejandro finally made it back to the stall area. Jose stood in front of the now empty stall, staring blankly at the ground.

"Jose, did Señor Martinez arrive here yet?"

"No, Alejandro, I no hear from him or from Dr. Huerta. It is very strange." He slumped against the door frame "I don't get it. She was okay when we arrived. The show people, they remove the broken stall after the police take photos. I helped clean up the...you know."

"Yes, Jose, I know. Well, we will not be allowed to show the other mares until they confirm cause of death, so we are finished here. We have to move these mares tomorrow morning. Let's find something to eat and call it a night." They ate supper and bedded down the other mares for the night.

Wondering what to do next, Alejandro patted his groom on the shoulder and went into the tack stall. He sat on the tack box, pulled out his cell phone. He again tried Martinez's number. He paced while the phone rang, but he reached the voice mail again.

In a rare display of anger and frustration, Alejandro spun around and kicked the tack box. Swearing in both English and Spanish, he picked up a currycomb and hurled it against the wall. He dropped back down on the tack box, put his head in his hands, and tried to think.

6

Back in White Bass Lake

The picture of Mag with the pancake sloughing off her butt stayed in my mind until I got back to my house. Still smiling, I absently gathered my notes from the glove box and took them to the house. Glancing at my shriveling plants in the window box, I sighed, thinking once again about Carole. Because I was so preoccupied, I did not prepare myself for when I opened the door, and promptly flew off my feet backward as I was hit full force in the chest by 160 pounds of doggie love.

"Wesley, for Heaven's sake, let me up!" I once again thanked my lucky stars I had talked the ex-husband into *not* putting a rail around the front porch. Had he done so, I would have crashed through it multiple times by now, and would have lain impaled and bleeding on the front lawn. As it was, I went ass over teakettle into the half dead impatiens at the base of the stairs. Good thing I left an old beanbag chair on the porch for the dogs–it cushioned the blow. While I dodged Wesley and his foot-long slimy tongue, I thought, where the heck is Hillary?

"Wes? Where's Hillary?" He sat up, looked west, east, and then up, grinning and waving his long black tail.

I laughed, rolled the three-year-old Newfoundland off me, and called for Hillary while I picked up my scattered notes. Wes decided it was playtime and helped me by proceeding to chew on my notebook. By the time I finished wrestling my book out of his gaping maw and wiping the doggie slobber off the cover onto my jeans, Hillary made her appearance.

She looked shyly around the doorjamb. I was struck as always by her quiet beauty and giving nature. She was a humane society acquisition, and at the time I got her, she rescued me more than I had rescued her.

Coming off an ugly divorce from an abusive alcoholic, I was scared and lonely, and decided I wanted a big, bad, killer watchdog. I went to the local animal shelter, thinking Doberman, Rottweiler, or Pit Bull, and came away with a quiet, female Bulldog who looked as damaged as I felt.

We healed together. I provided Hillary with a home and a purpose, and she provided me with unconditional love and undying loyalty. She used to go with me when I was still a full time investigator, and pulled my ass out of the fire on more than one occasion.

One time we were at a kennel a couple hours away and Hillary met up with the bad guy I had been chasing. She was badly wounded in the incident and I couldn't move her after surgery. I ended up leaving her at the kennel for a week to recuperate. When I came to pick her up, she was sleeping in a box with what appeared to be a little stuffed bear.

The bear lifted his head and I realized it was a Newfoundland puppy. The owners told me that her first night there, Hillary was whimpering in pain and loneliness. When they got up to check on her later, she was quiet and sleeping contently with the orphaned Newfie puppy. He was very gentle around her, so they just left him there. When I tried to leave with her, she began whimpering pathetically. After some discussion with the owners of the kennel, it was decided I would bring the Newfie home for a couple of weeks, so Hillary would have someone around while she was healing and I was at work. I fell in love with him just as quickly as Hillary did. Two weeks turned into four, and four turned into 'four-ever'. Wesley has now been a vital part of our family for over three years.

Hillary would not come out onto the porch. I knew she stayed back and gave me the injured look because Wesley had been naughty. She took all responsibility for his delinquent ways and he went blissfully through life wagging that long fluffy tail and grinning from ear to ear.

"Okay, Hill, what did he do this time?" She turned on cue and calmly walked into the kitchen. She looked over her shoulder to make sure I followed, and gave me the wounded look. Hands on hips, I examined the scene in front of me. The loaf of bread I had left on the counter that morning was nothing more than a few crumbs in plastic on the floor. The butter was completely missing, and the strawberry jelly jar I had thrown away was spotlessly clean and on its side next to the garbage can.

"Weeesley? Did you have a butter and jelly sandwich today?"

Grin, wag, grin. He let out a big sneeze–it was his only trick.

"You menace. That will not earn you points. Go outside and poop me a butter wrapper, would you?"

Grin, wag, grin. Jumping to his feet, the tail going 90 miles a minute, he danced to the back door, ready and willing to do as I bid. We all piled out the back door. Hillary trailed behind; she moved a little more slowly these days. She still had a slight limp from her injuries, and some days she was a little sore.

I grabbed the portable phone and a Diet Pepsi on the way out the door. As the dogs investigated the back yard, I sat in the big swing and checked my messages. One from Mom, two from Al and one from the pet shop Fred owned. Mom's was from this morning, asking if I'd come help her find the cowboy lamp. I now wished I had been in Kokomo or Ashland. I called Fred. She wasn't in, so I left a message.

Al, I ignored. No call from Malcolm or J.J., so I began to relax.

Watching the dogs play and root around was like watching tropical fish at the doctor's office. It had a calming effect on me and let the burdens of the day melt away. Wes brought me a slobbery ball, dropped it, and sneezed. I absently tossed it into the yard. I smiled as he bounded after it, barreling down the length of the fence like a runaway freight train.

I admit I got a little mushy feeling as I watched him retrieve the ball, drop it in front of Hillary, and patiently waited as he watched her bring it back to me. He bumped her with his head as they turned around and headed back out into the yard. He dropped her off about ten feet from my chair and took off down the fence line again, eager to repeat the game. I threw the ball again and let my mind wander.

I realized it was probably a good idea to involve Mag in the investigation after all. A partner was good for bouncing theories and ideas back and forth. I knew Mag well, and knew what to expect of her. How I was going to tell our parents that I was going to involve not one, but two of us in a homicide investigation, I had not a clue. I figured if it came down to it and Mom had a fit, we'd just lie. The biggest advantage of having my sister as a partner was that we could sit around in our underwear eating pizza and discussing the day.

Come to think of it, that was about the only thing I had liked about being married, too, but then I was married to a cop. Mom always said, if we wanted a man who did not cheat and was at home at night, *never* marry a cop, a lawyer, or a doctor; marry a nice farm boy instead. Did I listen? Hell no, and I have the physical and mental scars to prove it–but I digress. Mag would make a good partner, and she was not afraid to kick some major booty if the situation called for it. The problem was keeping her mouth under control; she can get people pissed off in three sentences or less. Oh well, I'll stop at the hardware store and buy some duct tape or something. I dug my toe into the ground and started up the swing, relaxing my mind and body. I floated into another vision.

Horses. A coliseum. People running. Carole running, scattering seeds over a cactus. In a boat on a river, the Sears Tower looms in the distance. A man, holding a horse over his head, the horse looks like the dying horse in my other vision. Who is that man? Carole entering a greenhouse, beckoning me to follow.

My feet are stuck, and the bad men chase her through the door. A huge gun materializes and points to my head. The trigger slowly pulls back. Tic, snick I hear the cylinders roll and I squeeze my eyes shut and scream for J.J. The blast fills my head and I am jolted back to reality.

Reality slammed into me with a physical force…then I noticed Wesley on my lap. I was breathing hard and tears streamed down my face. I raised a shaky hand and Wes stuck his head under it. I collapsed against him, buried my face in his fur, and cried until I was empty.

7

A shadow crossed over Alejandro as he sat on the tack box. He looked up thinking it was Jose. He opened his mouth to apologize to Jose for his outburst and froze. What looked like three large refrigerators stood in the doorway, blocking the light from the stall aisle. Alejandro blinked. The refrigerators took the shape of three very large Hispanic men. Knowing better than to stand up, Alejandro addressed the Frigidaire closest to him

"May I help you, gentlemen?"

A rumbling noise came from the direction of Fridge Number One. Alejandro realized he was speaking.

"You Huerta?"

"No, Montoya. Alejandro Montoya. I'm the head trainer. I have not seen Dr. Huerta since..." Pain blasted through his head as Fridge Number Three sent him flying off the tack box with a kick to the jaw.

He looked through pain-filled eyes at Number Three. "What was that for?"

Number One stepped closer, dragged him up by the shirt, yelled loudly, "Huerta! Where is he?"

Before he could answer, a knee nailed him hard between the legs. Sucking in air and gagging, Alejandro fell to the floor. The men kicked him repeatedly, but Alejandro was beyond pain. He weakly shook his head and whispered incoherently before passing out.

He came to at the sound of Jose's high-pitched screams. He dragged himself across the floor and silently lifted the tack box lid. Digging out the .38 caliber Smith he kept for emergencies, he crawled toward the door. He watched the thugs relentlessly beat the helpless Jose. He used the jamb to stand. Pain shot through his ribs.

A sound Alejandro did not even know he made must have alerted the 'Refrigerators Three' to his presence in the doorway. They turned as one hulking mass toward Alejandro, who stood with the cocked revolver aimed at the middle monster's family jewels.

The dead calm on Alejandro's bleeding face must have told them he was ready to commit murder.

He said in a lifeless voice, "Huerta is gone. Yesterday morning was the last time we saw him. We are employees of the Martinez ranch, not Huerta. Whatever business you have with him has nothing to do with us. Go now or he dies." Alejandro again gestured to the middle hulk.

Watching him with matching lethal eyes, they backed slowly away. Alejandro kept the revolver on them until they disappeared around the corner of the barn. He stood frozen, continuing to hold the pistol on the door until a mewling sound distracted him.

"Jose!" Alejandro fell to his knees and crawled to Jose, lying sprawled, broken, and barely breathing. "I will get help." As he flipped open his cell phone, barn security entered their aisle and saw the two of them on the floor. They rushed over, one called on the radio and the other kneeled by Jose. Alejandro looked on as if it were happening to someone else. He felt detached from the shouting of security, the screaming sirens, the scurrying of medical people and the rapid-fire questions of police.

Alejandro watched in numb silence as they took Jose away on a stretcher, not knowing if his friend was dead or alive. He allowed medical treatment but refused to go to the hospital and leave his horses.

The police badgered him about Huerta, asking again and again if Alejandro thought Huerta's 'disappearance' (as the police were calling it) had anything to do with the dead filly. He lost count of how many times he said, "I don't know."

The morning sun was up over Dallas by the time everyone cleared out, leaving Alejandro to wonder what the hell had happened. He was finished feeding the mares and had begun packing up the tack room when his cell phone rang.

"Montoya? Martinez here."

"Señor Martinez! I have been trying to contact you. I am so sorry to tell you..."

"Stop talking and listen to me, Montoya. I know about everything. I have men looking for Huerta. You will pack as soon as you can. Since we can not locate Huerta, you take the mares to Chicago as planned. The maps are in the truck, and I will wire you money. I will stay and take care of everything here, and call Chicago to tell them to expect you."

"But Señor Martinez, what about Princesa? She went with the American veterinarian. If you are in town, please, let us sit down and talk..."

"Stupido! I told you *no* Americans!" Martinez took a long breath and let it out. "Montoya, listen to me. Get packed. Take all the horses and get to Chicago. Now." Martinez hung up.

Stunned, Alejandro stared at his cell phone. A nicker from down the aisle galvanized him into action. Grabbing whatever was handy, he stuffed the horse trailer's dressing room full.

After loading the feed and the mares, he called Dr. Little's veterinary office.

Donny Ray answered the phone. "Little Animal Clinic, who's sick at your place?" Under different circumstances, Alejandro would have smiled.

"Dr. Little? Alejandro Montoya. I'm calling because I have orders from my boss to leave for Chicago right away. I wanted to touch base with you about the autopsy."

"Montoya? I've been trying to get you or that boss of yours on the phone all morning." He covered the phone momentarily and spoke with someone. Back on the phone, he said, "Listen, you got a minute to stop on over here? It's kind of a long story."

"Well, you see, Dr Little, my boss told me to leave for Chicago right away. I am to take the mares to the Gamble Appaloosa Farm north of Chicago and drop them off for breeding. I do not even know where he called from, and he hung up on me before I could find out. He told me he would take care of everything. Is there a problem with the mare?"

"Well, you could say that, mi amigo," the sarcasm heavy in his voice, "Your boss never called me back. I got up this morning to discover my place had been trashed and your horse has vanished."

8

I was startled out of my stupor by the clanging of the phone. The dogs piled off and trotted to the back door. Drawing on my reserves, I dragged myself back into the kitchen to answer the phone's incessant ringing.

"Buzz? Malcolm here. That forensic botanist from Madison just called back. He's on 94 East coming up on Highway 50, so he's about 30 minutes out. I thought I'd give you a ring so you could meet us here."

That sure didn't take long. Why was this big-shot-plant-geeknoid-algae-eater so eager to look at a couple of stupid seeds in Podunk, Wisconsin? This was a thought to contemplate at a later date. "Sure Mee-Me, I'll meet you at the morgue, and thanks. Just so you know, I'll be bringing Mag with me. She's going to help me out with some stuff on this case."

"Mag? Uh, okay. How about Fred, will she be here too?"

Slow down, Malcolm, I thought, you are way too eager to see Fred. "Why would... Oh. No, Mee-Me. She won't be coming. I think she's still at the shop."

I could almost hear his embarrassment. "That's good, uh, okay, I didn't mean–hey, Buzz, do you think you guys could call me Malcolm while the state guy is here? I mean, I think it makes me sound more like a professional and less like a French Poodle."

"Sure, Mee-me, er, Malcolm. I'll tell the Maggot to behave in front of 'Dr. Plantus Identifyus'. See you then–bye."

I hung up and called Mag. She was waiting in the

driveway when I got to her house, squeaky clean and raring to go. Boy, was she pumped! She complained non-stop all the way to the morgue.

We pulled in. I saw a black BMW no one in White Bass Lake would be caught dead in parked outside the door. Mag immediately went into a diatribe about Yuppie Scum who drove BMWs with university stickers in the back windows. She was just hitting her stride when we hit the door.

"Braggarts and Yuppie Scum, that's who drives Beemers. I'll bet this guy is some slick talking, Slim Shady suit wearing creep-noid. The kind of guy that Al would go out with. Speaking of old pain in the ass Al...uh, holy crap, I mean wow." Mag's tirade faded into nothing. I looked back at her, but she was staring beyond me.

Her mouth was slightly open, which was normal, but no sound came out–which was not. I turned around and froze, staring into the greenest eyes I had ever seen. I was momentarily speechless, my mind going fuzzy. I knew someone should say something, but my tongue was stuck to the roof of my mouth. Finally, Malcolm stepped in and filled the awkward silence.

"Buzz, Maggie, this is Ian Connor, the Forensic Botanist from Madison. He's going to take a look at those seeds you found, Buzz."

Being the consummate professional I am, I turned back to Ian, held out my hand and said, "Ah, eh-eh."

Mag jumped in front of me, nailing me with one of those lethal hips of hers. I flew sideways and bounced off the doorjamb. Mag skidded to a stop in front of Ian, and stuck her hand out, nearly knocking his coffee cup off the table. "Hi, Ian, I'm Mag, er, Margaret. Margret Miller. Maggie. Nice to meet you Ian. I'm working on this investigation. I'm not a cop, but I'm pretending for a while. I have a body, uh, not my body, but a dead one. Mine's not dead. Yet. Dead body, I mean. Uh, maybe we can compare notes–not on our bodies but on uh, oh–this is my sister Buzz. She's the cop. Or was."

More humiliated by her own nonsensical ravings than by the butt full of whipped cream she'd had this morning, she finally shut up, stepped back, and shoved me forward, breathing heavily and swearing softly at herself.

Ian blinked trying to make sense of Mag's babble. He stared past me at Mag, who stood looking at the floor, still swearing at herself. He calmly placed his cup on the stainless counter behind him. He stepped past me and took Mag's hand. She jumped. He looked into her eyes and said, "Glad to meet you, Mag, is it? Malcolm was just filling me in on what's been happening out this way. He thought perhaps I could service you–I mean be of service, you know, help. I hear you have some seeds which need identifying."

She stared at him as if mesmerized. "Uh, yeah, seeds. Buzz?"

Ian smiled and turned to me. We shook hands and I finally regained my composure. "Glad to meet you Ian. You will have to excuse Mag and me; you're not quite what we were expecting." At his quizzical expression, I tried to explain. "No! You're better. Uh, better than we expected, I mean. Different, in a good way." *Oh shit. Mr. Plant Guy thinks we're all insane.* "We're very glad you could come down on short notice. I hear you've had a long weekend. I hope we aren't keeping you from your family." *Subtle, Buzz, real subtle.*

Ian looked nonplussed, but smiled and shook my hand. "No, actually, my Mom lives not far from here, so I can stop and see her on my way back to Madison. I'm staying with her while I teach a class at UW Madison this fall called

'Court Presentation of Botany Forensics'."

He smiled again and showed off a beautiful set of white teeth. Too perfect, I thought. His physical beauty had momentarily stunned me, but I recovered sufficiently to converse successfully in English. Mag, unfortunately, had not. She still had that deer-in-the-headlights look about her, and was not yet speaking coherently, very un-Mag like. This might prove to be very interesting, I thought, something I could have a really good time with.

"Say, Ian, Mag is a teacher too. She teaches Biology at the local high school, which is why she is free to help us out on this investigation."

Mag stood there like a statue and I elbowed her hard. She squeaked, but her brain went dead and she lost her capacity for simple speech. I slowly exerted pressure on her toes with my foot.

"Yep, Mag graduated from UW Madison. I'd bet she could answer any questions you might have about anything up there. Isn't that right, Mag?"

He turned to Mag. I thought she was going to faint. Still standing on her foot, I nudged her at the same time he leaned forward and they almost bumped noses.

He smiled from about three inches away. "You teach Biology? Uh, that's great. I loved my Biology teacher in high school."

He took her hand and led her over to the chairs across the room. Mag continued to smile like a jackass and Ian kept up both ends of the conversation. Malcolm and I just stood there, looking on in awe.

Mag was not only quiet, she was not rude, not crude, nor was she socially unacceptable. It was truly a Kodak moment.

Malcolm, ever the party-pooper, must have gotten tired of waiting around, because he crossed the room and gently tapped Ian on the shoulder. "Uh, Dr. Connor? Did you want to take a look at those seeds now?"

Looking startled, Ian excused himself to Mag. He turned, blessed Mag with one last smile, and crossed the room to where we were standing. Gesturing to the seeds and microscope, Malcolm explained how they were found. Using what looked like a long, slim set of tweezers, Ian gently unfolded the paper towel and separated the seeds into a single layer. He picked up a tiny round seed and looked at it under a magnifying glass.

Completely absorbed in his task, he mumbled, "Papaveraceae," and placed it apart from the others. He picked up another seed of approximately the same size. After examining it, said the same word.

Mag finally came up for air, and at the sound of Ian's quiet voice, wandered over to see what was going on. "Did he say Papaveraceae? That's the poppy family. Are those all poppy seeds of some sort?"

"Not this one," said Ian as he held up a larger seed of an odd shape. "I'm not sure what this one is. I'd have to take it back to my lab and match it up. I have software and testing equipment that would give us positive identification while maintaining the integrity of the seed."

He jotted down some notes and made a simple sketch of the seed while he talked. "Did you know that the molecular biology guys could use randomly amplified polymorphic plant DNA (RAPD) to identify a specific plant? RAPD is rather like human DNA. It's like a genetic fingerprint, and has been admitted into court as evidence. If we need to, I can find out not only what kind of plant this is from, but what *specific* plant it came from."

"Wow," we all breathed.

Ian looked at us and chuckled. He placed the seed back onto the paper towel and said, "Gee, I wish all my students were as interested as you guys. Malcolm, what will it take to gain permission to take your evidence back with me to Madison for about 24 hours?"

Mee-Me clasped his hands in front of him and danced in place. "All we have to do is call J.J., our Sheriff, sign off on some paperwork, and we'll be good to go. We can pack this stuff up and go now if you want."

They proceeded to pack the seeds and Ian's equipment while I flipped open my phone and made the call to J.J. I wanted to know how the interview went with Glenn Graff anyway.

J.J. answered, told us to come on down to the office and take care of the paperwork for the release of evidence to the state crime lab, and he'd give us all a run down on what he had so far. I thanked him and told him I would do the same.

We finished up at the morgue and strolled out to the parking lot. Ian noticed Mag was headed for the passenger side of my car. He cleared his throat and suggested Mag ride with him so he did not get lost on the drive to J.J.'s office. Mag grinned like Wesley getting a belly rub and literally skipped over to the Beemer. *What a ninny. Mag never acts like that.* Disgusted, I wanted to throw Mag a dog bone. Disgusted, I ignored my ringing cell phone and got into my car. I drove the mile to the Colson County Sheriff's Department, never got lost, and didn't lose Ian.

We walked into the lobby of the Sheriff's office and were met by a barrage of questions, flashing bulbs, and microphones. I saw my mother talking to a reporter and felt sick. Another reporter was getting an education on warts and melons from Mary Cromwell. J.J. was trying to restore order to his lobby. I leaned over and whispered, "Malcolm, talk to them, they're all yours–hold back the seed information and any autopsy results. I'll call you tomorrow."

84

Malcolm smiled and cleared his throat. He straightened his tie, and smiling, walked into the fray.

I herded Ian and Mag toward J.J.'s office, snagging Mom on the way. She was still waving at the reporters when I dragged her into the office. I collapsed against the door and said, "Mom, what were you thinking, giving interviews to reporters?"

She looked imperiously down her nose at me and picked imaginary lint off her sleeve. "Now, Buzz, they just had a few questions for me, and I didn't want to waste my new hair."

"Your what?"

"My hair! Alexandra took Mary and me down to Pat's and we got new hairdos because Alex told us we'd probably get to be on television. We saw the Channel 12 truck out front here and figured they were here for us. Mary wants to tell the wart story on Dr Phil, but I told that wacky old bird Dr. Phil would have her committed. I'll bet old Joy will be jealous that we got to be on the tube and she didn't!" She got her first look at Ian. "Whoa! Is that Fabio? Why is a movie star talking to Margaret? Wait! Maybe we can finally marry her off–it's obvious she didn't open her mouth yet because he hasn't run away. Let's get him before she does!"

"Mom!"

"Oops! Sorry. Maybe he's one of those crime T.V. reporters." She tried to push past me. "Leave him to me, I'll tell him the whole story."

I was coming very close to losing it with her. "Mother, you were in the house making brownies the entire time, and Dr. Connor is a scientist, not a reporter, so leave him alone."

"He doesn't look like a doctor. Are you sure he's not a movie star? Look at those teeth. Those are movie star teeth."

My mother was going to embarrass us all in a minute. I

desperately searched for something with which to distract her. "Hey, Mom, Mag is going to help me investigate Carole's murder."

Mag sucked in a breath. I sat stunned. I couldn't believe I had blurted that out. Our mother froze in mid-sentence and slowly turned toward me. We might tease her about being loosely wrapped, but Air Ger is sharp as a tack.

I've faced violent felons who did not intimidate me like my mother can. I started to sweat. When she continued to stare me down, I began to squirm. Even Ian backed away from Mag as my mom turned the bad eye on her. Mom pursed her lips and straightened to her full height of five-foot-two.

She calmly picked up her purse and turned to Mee-Me. "Malcolm, would you please drive me home?" She whipped around and pointed the 'Mom finger' at Mag and me. "You two. I'll talk to you later. Wait until your father hears about this."

I was speechless. I was 12 years old again, and caught flinging mud pies at cars. Mag recovered first and yelled to Mom's retreating back, "I'm 35 years old, and if I want to chase down murderers with Buzz, I will!"

Mom stopped short of the door. I said, "Oh, good one, Mag. Now she'll probably put an Irish curse on us and we'll grow warts or nose hair or something even worse."

Ian stepped up. "She can't really put a curse on you guys. Lighten up."

Still shaking, I told him the story. "One time, Mom put an Irish curse on a strip mall. While the mall across the street was built two years later and has flourished, the cursed one lay there empty, and the developer went bust. A bank was at one end for a while, but even they moved out. What do you mean, can't put a curse on you? What kind of an Irishman are you, anyway?"

Ian stared slack-jawed at all of us. "Whoa, what is up with your mom? My mother told me you could tell someone with the 'sheeny'–the Irish magic–because they were just a little odd, like they weren't quite on the same plane as the rest of us–oh, I'm sorry Mrs. Miller, present company excluded, of course."

Nose in the air, Mom said, "Of course."

Mag and I looked at each other. We looked at Mom. The three of us burst out laughing. Mom recovered first. "They don't call me 'Air Ger' for nothing, young man! Of course we're *odd!*"

Ian breathed out slowly. "Wow, wait until I tell my mom."

Mag sighed and batted her eyes at Ian. "You mean you believe her? I think I'm in love."

Mom's round little face lit up like a Christmas tree. "I think I want to meet your mother, young man." She held the back of her hand to her mouth and said sotto voce, "You might want to know, Ian, that Buzzie has the sheeny too, but in a different way. She has gut feelings, precognitive dreams, and premonitions."

I fidgeted, turned, and looked out the window. "Mother, don't start. I'm not that reliable and you know it. Otherwise I would have seen…"

"Nonsense," she said, getting huffy. "That's why you made such a good detective then, and that's why you're going to help poor Carole now. Don't change the subject. I'm still peeved that you dragged Maggie into a murder.

"She's too dumb to fight her way out of a paper bag, let alone help solve a murder without getting herself croaked." She spun on her heel and stomped out the door, slamming it behind her.

Ian looked at the closed door, then looked at each of us for a long moment. "I am surrounded by fascinating females. What do we do next?"

I pulled back the blinds and peeped out the window, which led to the lobby. "J.J. is on his way in."

The door opened a second later. J.J. slipped through, locking it behind him. He stood inside the room breathing heavily.

"Thank God for Malcolm. He's a pro out there. The Putz came and dragged his mother out and the excitement died down almost immediately." He turned to us. "So, where were we? Ah, the paperwork. I had Edie get everything ready so you just have to sign off and go."

Opening a manila folder, he showed Ian where he wanted him to sign, and gave him the copies he'd need. Satisfied, he patted his belly and sat behind his old oak desk and addressed me. "I suppose you're headed out to Graff's now. You can catch Glenn there tonight, or you can wait until morning–he was hit pretty hard by Carole's death. I told him I'd give him a call if you were going out tonight."

I looked at my watch, and then Mag. "It's getting late now. We should probably take it easy tonight and talk with him in the morning."

I punched J.J. in the arm and headed out the door. "Night, pal."

He shot me in the butt with a rubber band. When I whirled on him, he was whistling, looking at the ceiling, and feigning innocence.

Ian and Mag snickered. J.J. said, "Night, Buzz. Night, Mag. Nice meeting you, Ian." They shook hands and we headed out the door.

9

Ian, Mag, and I stopped to talk in the Sheriff's Department parking lot. Ian seemed to be stalling and I wanted him to get on the road. He nonchalantly asked if he could tag along out to the Graff's place with us. Mag immediately grabbed his hand and hauled him across the parking lot to my car, babbling away nonsensically. I, on the other hand wondered once again about who this guy actually was, as he just didn't fit quite right into the puzzle. I liked it when things fit nicely, and Ian was a little...too convenient.

I tried for nonchalance and ended up sounding bitchy. "So, Ian, isn't your mom expecting you this evening? I forgot how long a drive it was. Where was it you said she lived?" I unlocked the car, trying again for an innocent demeanor and failed miserably.

Ian stopped in mid-stride and leveled a look at me. "She already knows better than to put an exact time on my arrival today. I warned her earlier that I didn't know what I would find here. To answer your second question, no, I didn't say where she lived. Will there be anything else, Detective?" He turned his back on me and climbed into my car.

I kicked Mag in the leg and jerked my head toward the back seat. We both knew it was a Miller Sister signal and it meant, 'Who The Hell Does This Guy Think He Is?' Mag just shrugged her shoulders and jumped in after Ian.

I stood there dumbfounded, staring at the rear door of my car for a moment. I shook off the willie I felt creeping up between my shoulder blades, told myself to get over it, and got into the driver's seat.

I was quiet and deep in thought on the way to the Graff residence. Mag would not shut up. Ian gave Chatty Cathy Maggot Brain in the back seat one syllable responses to her inexhaustible monologue, telling me he was also distracted.

Mag was so annoying that by the time we made the short trip out of town, I was fingering the duct tape on the front seat and wondering if Ian was ready to hold her down while I slapped it across her gaping maw.

I turned into Graff's greenhouse driveway, finally said, "Yo, Maggot, shut up and pay attention." Miracles upon miracles, she did.

I saw in the mirror that Ian was taking stock of the layout.

Immediately in front of us was the main building. The outside was lined with an attractive display of butterfly and burning bushes nestled among Japanese Maples and large planters. Cleome topped the annual racks where a profusion of colorful zinnias, verbena, scabiosa, and marigolds vied for attention. Petunias cascaded gently over a display of herbs and ground covers. The zebra grass on either side of the door gave an exotic appearance to the entrance to the main shop. The whole effect was welcoming and casual.

The door to the shop was open so we wandered inside. It was stocked full with pond displays, sale items, bulbs, and seed racks. Everything that would feed, fertilize, and keep bug-free anything in the garden was on display. The checkout areas were decked out with beautiful wind chimes ranging from tinkling bells to church gongs. The rich tones sang a melodic aria to the empty room. I thought it odd that the place would be open for business when Carole just died. I thought it even odder yet that not a single soul was around.

I called for Glenn. Mag cautiously peeked out the back door into the fenced-in yard, where racks and shelves were lined with hundreds of flats of plants. Seeing movement by one of the out-buildings, she poked her head back inside the main shop. "Hey, Buzz! I think I see Rob coming out of that last building. Yep, he's locking up and heading this way."

I rushed out into the yard just as Rob looked up and saw us. He stopped dead in his tracks like a deer caught in the headlights. I could tell he really wanted to be anywhere but here, but his indecision gave me time to hold him where he was. "Hi, Rob. Is your dad around?"

Looking like he wanted to bolt, he scuffed a toe in the dirt and watched the pebbles scatter at his feet. He looked disheveled and his pants were wet to the knees. Decision made, he walked slowly toward us, rubbing his hands on his damp jeans.

"Uh, no, he's gone. I mean, not *gone* gone, but not here now."

Little or no eye contact and nervous fidgeting are dead giveaways of a lie in progress. I stepped closer, which made him more nervous. I could see sweat beads gathering on his forehead and running down the side of his face. This was one scared young man. In my most soothing non-confrontational voice, I said, "Rob, I need to ask you a couple questions. Can we go back to the office, or if you were working in the last building, I could follow you back. We could talk while you work."

There was no hesitation as his head jerked up and ice blue eyes bored into mine. "No! Uh, I mean I was done out there anyway, Miz Buzz. Matter of fact, I was just coming up to close up the shop. With Her gone and all, folks figure we're closed anyway. No one comes around."

Mag piped up from the peanut gallery, "With 'Her' gone, Rob? Nice way to talk about your mom, Rob, her being freshly dead and all. And why did you lock the potting shed. Are you hiding something in there?"

Ian jabbed her in the ribs and dragged her off through the Rhododendron, while I scrambled for damage control. "Rob, I'm sorry'"

Rob looked ready to pass out and started backing away.

"Wait, Rob. Maggot is an uncouth ass. Hold on and talk to me for a second. We'll go somewhere else and talk. Rob!"

He continued to back away. He suddenly spun and trotted toward the back end. "I gotta go, uh, do stuff, Miz Buzz. My dad is counting on me and besides, he told me not to talk to anyone if they came around." He turned back toward me but kept a steady pace backward. "I don't think he meant like you and Sheriff J., but he said no one, so I gotta go now. You know, I got, uh, stuff." With that, he took off toward one of the many hooped greenhouses lining the back of the property and ran inside.

Whirling on my big-mouth sister with clenched fists and fire in my eyes I calmly said, "Good job, Maggot. You're fired."

I turned and stormed off toward the car.

Looking horrified she struggled to free herself from Ian's death grip. "Buzz, you can't fire me, I'm a volunteer!"

"Fine, then I'll kick your ass and dump your body on the side of the road. Mom will understand." Reaching the car, I got in, slammed the door, and revved the engine.

"Buzz, please, I was just trying to shake him up so he would crack under the pressure!" Near tears and begging, she climbed into the passenger seat, leaving Ian to fend for himself in the back.

"Mag, I told you this was not going to be like television. If you had half a brain you could have seen that kid was on the edge, and your little sarcastic shot about his mother pushed him over. You're fired."

She then exhibited the first good sense of the afternoon. She shut up.

Speeding back toward town, I went over the scene with Rob in slow motion. I was just past the part where Rob turned from the building when Ian interrupted my thoughts. "Say, Buzz, what do you think was in that building Rob was locking when we first saw him?"

Mag murmured, "The potting shed."

Ian looked irritated. "You don't keep a potting shed under lock and key."

She folded her arms and looked at the floor. "It's the potting shed."

I ignored Mag and thought about it for about a quarter mile. "It probably is the equipment shed, you know, mowers, weed eaters, rototillers, hedgers, edgers, the usual. Why do you ask?"

Wearing a sullen expression, Mag mumbled, "Potting shed, Buzz–potting shed."

Ian flashed Mag a confused look and leaned forward. I could see a small conspiratorial grin flash across his face. "I was thinking; what if there was something he didn't want us to see in there? Wouldn't that make him nervous? Maybe the sheriff could get a search warrant or something and take a look."

I laughed. "You and Mag make a good pair. You both watch too much television. Search warrants can take up to a couple of days to get." Ian quieted and sat back. I could almost hear him fuming, but I was beyond caring.

I thought about Ian's words on the way across town. Damn search warrants. What if I didn't wait for a search warrant and just popped over to the garden center unannounced? If I were caught I could say I was poking around looking for Glenn. If I found something, I could always pressure J.J. into obtaining a search warrant and picking up the evidence legally later. No harm, no foul, and no lawyer suppressing evidence for violating anyone's Fourth Amendment rights. "Buzz," I said to myself, "Sometimes you are a genius."

I pulled into the morgue parking lot in a much better mood. I turned off the engine and thought, keep it formal, Buzz, and send Plant Boy on his way and out of our lives, then get rid of Mag. "Thanks for coming out today, Ian. Please let me know what you find out about those seeds, will you? You can call me from wherever it is your mother lives, or better yet, just fax the information to the Sheriff."

Ian knew condescension when he heard it and there was nothing wrong with the boy's hearing. He shook my hand and through gritted teeth, assured me he would. He turned to Mag. "Want a lift home, Maggie?"

Her head jerked up and she was miraculously cured of her martyrdom. I felt a tingle of panic about sending her off with a virtual stranger, albeit a beautiful stranger. There was something about Ian that still did not settle well with me, and he knew it. He was hip to my feeble attempt to get rid of him quick and probably thought to use Mag to stall for more time.

His expression was guarded when he turned back to me. "Since it's getting late and I've been going for over 20 hours today, maybe you ladies could direct me to a decent motel. I'll pop for lunch first, since none of us have eaten, and then sleep until whenever. That way I can head out late tonight or early tomorrow fresh. To *Janesville*, Buzz, *where my mother lives*. In *Janesville*. For about 40 years now. In Janesville. About an hour away from here."

I bit my lip and grinned. "I get it, Ian. Janesville. Uh, thank you for enlightening me."

Mag practically jumped up and down. "I have a great idea! We can all go to Buzz's and order in pizza and discuss the case. She's already got a whiteboard set up with the stuff we have so far.

"We can catch it up with the Rob stuff and see if we have anything that adds two and two. Besides, over at Buzz's we'll be closer to the Interstate. There are a few good motels out there you can choose from."

Yeah, great idea, I thought, sighing heavily–again. Now he's invited to my house, invited to late lunch, what next? I had an evil thought. Maybe I could feed them both to Wesley…. "Uh, Mag, I thought Ian said he wanted to get on the road."

I furrowed my brow, dipped my head, and glared at her out of the tops of my eyes, a Miller Sister Signal that meant 'Shut Up And Go With Me On This'.

"We shouldn't hold him up. Ian is not interested in the investigation, only the seeds. We can catch up later, okay?"

Idiot Mag didn't get it, or ignored me and instead listened to her hormones. "But he offered to buy lunch, Buzz. Didn't you Ian? We're not keeping him too late, are we Ian?" She batted her eyes at him. I wanted to gag.

He laughed and said, "No, no. I'm flexible. Whatever you guys decide. I'd like to see how an investigation looks. It might be a good idea to go over the stuff while it is fresh though, don't you think, Buzz?"

He gave me the same face I gave Mag, only I picked up on it. I laughed out loud. "Okay I give. Pile back in. I'll drive. We'll get you back here later, Ian."

He sat back with a satisfied smile. "Lead on, MacDuff!"

10

Vanished! "The filly vanished?"

Alejandro felt the blood drain from his face. He put his cell phone on speaker then threw the last of his gear into the pickup truck. The sick feeling in his stomach was quickly turning into panic as what Donny Ray said sunk in. "Disappeared? Wrecked your clinic? Oh no! The refrigerator men; maybe it was those bad men who beat me up and put Jose in the hospital. Are you okay, Dr. Little?"

"Okay? Well, I wasn't beat up by any bad refrigerator salesmen, if that's what you're asking. Uh, Montoya, I think y'all better come down here and tell the police about your bad men. I don't know what the hell is going on here, but someone's got to pay for this mess. All I got left to show your mare was even here is one little old sample of blood in a busted vial. Under all this other garbage and busted shit, I might not even have a clinic left."

"Dr. Little, I have already told the police all I know. Something is very wrong here, and I think my boss knows more than he tells me."

"No shit, Montoya. When did you come to that brilliant conclusion? When they busted your lip, or my stuff?"

Alejandro slammed the back door and jumped into the truck. He started the engine. A terrible thought crossed his mind. "Dr. Little, please, can you do me a favor? Please run the blood if you can. Maybe we can find out what killed my Princesa. I might sound crazy, but I don't think I can trust anyone else. This whole thing is crazy. Can you call me when you have the results? You have my cell phone number, and I have yours. I will tell no one, and please, for your safety, I think you should tell no one of the blood sample."

Alejandro hesitated before addressing his greatest fear. "Dr. Little? Do you think that maybe those bad men were hired by my boss?"

Donny Ray thought a moment. "It looks pretty suspicious all right." He looked around his clinic and at the broken vial of blood on what was left of his desk. He gingerly picked it up and turned it in his fingers, studying the blood as if it would give him some answers. "On second thought, Montoya, y'all may be right, and maybe you'd best be heading out right now."

He heard the truck engine in the background. He scrounged around in the debris for his microscope and an unbroken slide. He found them both and set up the microscope on the stainless steel counter. He pulled up a stool and placed a drop of blood on the slide. "So tell me everything that happened last night while you light out of this town."

Heading northbound out of Dallas, Alejandro told Donny Ray what happened after the mare was taken away. He spared no detail as he described everything that had happened up until the time Donny Ray called him. The shocked veterinarian let out a huge sigh.

"Shee-it! It's no wonder you're getting out of town, Montoya. I ain't talking to no one until I find out what the Hell is going on around here. Don't worry about your friend. I'll check on him at the hospital and bring him back here when they let him go."

He spied his broken centrifuge under a surgical table across the room and swore to himself. Thank God most of this stuff was insured. He thought a second more. "Hell, Alejandro, I don't know who to trust either, but I'll tell you what. If I know one thing, I know that you loved that little mare. You've been the only one who's been straight with me so far, so I'll put my trust in you, too, amigo."

Tears of gratitude welled in Alejandro's eyes. He dashed them away before he drove off the road. "That is very kind of you to say, Dr. Little, but how can you run tests if you have no lab?"

"I got a real good friend who teaches over at Southern Methodist University. I know he'll let me use his lab, and no one will know anything about it. I'll stay over to his place for a few days in case those varmints come back for more."

Guilt lay heavily on Alejandro's shoulders. "I am sorry you have to leave your business, Dr. Little."

Donny Ray chuckled. "Hell, man, I can't do much here until after the cleanup is done anyway, and there was something about that little mare those guys didn't want me to find out. I'll give you a holler if and when I find something."

Relief spread through Alejandro and he swallowed the lump in his throat. "Gracias, Dr. Little, thank you very much. I owe you big. Princesa did mean the world to me, and I want whoever did this to her to suffer as she did. I appreciate anything you can do. Again, thank you, sir."

"Under the circumstances, Montoya, since we are now partners in crime, don't you think it's time you called me Donny Ray?"

This time, Alejandro did chuckle as he said, "Yes it is, Donny Ray, it certainly is. Talk to you soon, my friend." He disconnected the phone, stepped on the gas and sped toward Oklahoma.

11

Mag, Ian, and I were each busy with our own thoughts on the short drive over to my house. I went over things in my head again, but nothing seemed to add up. I was very curious about the seeds, but it didn't look like Ian was burning any rubber off his shoes trying to get back to Madison, Milwaukee, Timbuktu, or wherever the Hell he came from, to identify them. Maybe he thought the seeds were not that important to the case. He sure had a cavalier attitude about them. Maybe he already knew what they were. Maybe he had an ulterior motive for his procrastination. Whatever the maybe, it merited keeping him close, and keeping an eye on him.

Mag was another problem. She had really screwed up my chance for an interview with Rob, but it was in no way earth-shattering. Rather like losing the battle but not the war. I hate losing. It pisses me off. I also hate loose ends, and Rob was a dangler. I was also hoping Rob didn't lawyer up on us, in case he actually had something significant to say. Maybe I should have left Mag in the room with Rob and let her beat a confession out of him–oops! Another violation of an Amendment issue, but a nice thought.

Still deep in thought, I automatically turned onto my street without a resolution to the problem of whether or not to kick Mag off the team. This probably meant I would wienie out and give her another chance. Slowing down near my house, I noticed cars lined up along the curb of my street. I absently wondered who was having a party. I about crapped when I realized I was!

Cars filled my driveway and spilled over in front of the

neighbor's houses. I saw a small army of seniors, barking dogs, and squawking kids pile out of my front door, and food-lined folding tables near the front of my house. I looked for a place to park, almost missing a small opening between cars.

I cranked the wheel and bumped over the sidewalk, parked in the middle of my own front yard. Slowly exiting the car, I stood there, staring like an idiot. I braced myself when Wesley bounded over, grinning from ear to ear, and slobbered on my jeans. I bent to hug him, and he knocked me on my butt. It was the first time I'd felt normal in hours.

Mag's, "Oh, crap! Who called Rosie?" startled me out of my hug session with Wes. When I saw what she saw, I saw red.

"Dammit, Maggot! You called Rosie the Slut at the Times, didn't you? What's next? *Fox News*?" It was then I noticed the Channel 6 truck in my driveway. I about blew a gasket.

Mag backed away, holding up her hands (like that was going to stop mine from circling her neck). "Was not me, Kemosabe! I was with you, screwing up your chance to talk to Rob Graff, remember? I didn't call anyone, let alone Rosie the News Whore! Honest, Buzz, she's Alexandra's friend, not mine!" We stopped and stared at each other.

The answer came like a flash and we simultaneously hollered, "Al, you bitch!"

As if on cue, there stood Al in all her glory, using my rail-less front porch as a dais and wearing a pink sundress. She wore Tammy Faye makeup so her nose didn't shine on national television. She was also wearing a brilliant smile, and waving like the Queen of England for the cameras.

We speculated on whether Alexandra was going to do a 'Fish and Loaves' thing for the masses. (If you recall, Wesley ate the only bread I had. Other than that, there were three slices of drying bologna in the fridge.) She looked like she was preparing to accept her Academy Award for Best Performance by a Moron. One thing we did know: Al was in her element, so we ignored her.

I surveyed the pandemonium that was once my front yard with distaste.

"The whole damn town must be here."

At first I thought I had voiced my own opinion out loud, but then realized that, of all people, Ian had said it.

I stretched out my arms to encompass the entire chaotic scene. "Probably more than half. What's up, Big City Boy? This is the Small Town Grapevine at its finest. It's the Ninth wonder of the World!"

"What's the Eighth?"

I grumbled.

It didn't even faze him. Still wearing that deer-caught-in-the-headlights look, Ian turned to me. "I thought nothing could amaze me any more, but this is outrageous. Do you actually *know* all these people?"

I scoped out the crowd. "Yeah, pretty much. See that little old lady hiding behind the Russian Sage, wearing combat boots? That's Mrs. Simmons from two blocks over. Her cat pees on my patio furniture every morning. I always wondered where it pees in the winter. I keep hoping Mr. McCauley's Rottweiler will eat that nasty little sucker one of these days. That damn cat also pees on his doggie door. How insulting is that to a Rottie?"

I could feel his incredulous gaze on me, but I ignored him. Mag and Wesley came bounding up, each wearing identical grins. Wes woofed and sneezed. I automatically reached in the glove box and grabbed a Milk Bone.

Ian did a double take. "You reward your dog for sneezing?"

"Why, yes. It's his only trick, and he is very proud of

it."

Mag dropped the bomb. "I just talked to Mom."

"Oh no. Mom's here, too?"

Visions of hot dogs on the grill and the Geriatric Mod Squad shuffling around my notes and reading my whiteboard swam through my head. "I can't stand this. I'm going to your house. Are you guys with me?"

They nodded. I issued orders. "Mag–find Hillary. I'll load Wes in the car, grab our case notes, and we'll blow this carnival joint."

Mag and I took off on our separate missions. I remembered we left Ian standing at the car, and saw him wandering in my direction. He looked perplexed and definitely out of his element. "But what about your house? What about all these people? And all that food; ooo, I'm starving…"

He veered left and headed for the tables and stopped dead. "WHOA! Who is that gorgeous chick on your front porch?"

Mag spun around as if she was going to let fly, but just glared at him, and stomped off instead.

I elbowed Ian in the ribs and whispered, "Ix-nay on the ick-chay, Buster Brown. That is our sister Al, and a sore subject with Mag. If you value your life, don't go there. As for me, if you value your family jewels, don't go there. Just…don't go there, okay? Get in the car instead. My Mom or someone will lock up; they broke in easy enough, didn't they?"

Ian shrugged. "I guess so. Tell you what. Wes and I are going to grab a hot dog first. We'll meet you at the car." They trotted off in the direction of the food tables.

Circling around to the back door, I ran into the house, dodging Mom, Al, and the reporters. I grabbed my whiteboard and our notes and ran like the Devil was chasing me back to the car. Ian sat beside the car, munching on a hot dog while Wes looked at him with adoring eyes. I quirked a brow and he gave me a lopsided grin. "They started feeding me, how could I say no?"

Wes sneezed and Ian dropped the rest of his hot dog in Wes' mouth. He stood up and picked up a plate, mounded with food, off the trunk.

He gestured to Mag. "I was thinking about what you said about your sister. I don't get what the big deal is about your other sister. Sure, she's good to look at, Mag's much prettier in a fresher, outdoorsy sort of way. She oozes beauty from the inside out."

Ian paused, choosing his words. "Mag doesn't need war paint to knock 'em dead. The other sister is glam, a flash in the pan. Mag's kind of beauty stays with a woman as she ages."

I sat next to him and looked at Ian in astonishment. My whole attitude about him did a 360-degree turn. I leaned over and smooched him, and Wesley did the same. Actually, Wesley crawled up him and slobbered on top of his head, but Ian didn't notice and I didn't mention it.

He looked startled. I said, "It's a special guy who can see past the beast to the beauty of Maggie. You'll do, Ian Connor. You'll do just fine."

I smiled and turned Wes toward the car door. I thought Ian was much different than I had first imagined. I just wished he'd come clean about himself and his mission. Mission? Where did that thought come from? I looked back at and noticed he was looking toward the house. He smiled distractedly, watching for Mag and Hillary. Mom trotted over and shoved a grocery bag stuffed full of Ziploc containers into his hands. Ian smiled up at her, clearly smitten.

Mom patted him on the head and tottered back toward

the crowd. She stopped and looked at her hand. I giggled because I knew she had a handful of doggy slime from Ian's head. She glanced back at Ian, and looked at her hand again. Someone called her name and she shrugged, wiped her hand on her jeans, smiling as she went.

Al caught sight of Ian's smile from the porch and her face lit up. I could almost see her drooling. I also saw that predatory look of a starving cougar in her eye. She jumped off the porch and started pushing and elbowing her way through the crowd. I saw disaster and bloodshed written all over that scene.

"Uh-oh," I said, and opened the door to stuff Wesley in the back seat.

Mag came down the driveway carrying Hillary. She looked like Quasimodo as she awkwardly lurched through the yard while carrying the Bulldog. Another plastic grocery bag hung from her arm and banged against her hip. She and the dog were both panting as she staggered to a stop, "Uh-oh, what?"

I grabbed Hill and stuffed her into the back seat with Wes. Grabbing Mag by the shoulders I spun her around. I pointed to Al and two of her friends who had just joined the hunting party. I yelled in Mag's ear, "The carnivores are hunting and Ian is the red meat!"

Mag bounced up and down on the balls of her feet. Her hands started doing that fluttery thing they do when she's in a panic. "Oh, crap! We gotta get out of here!"

We each grabbed a hand and dragged Ian around the car. I stuffed him into the front seat, getting doggie slime all over my hand from his head. Mag dove into the back seat and Wes promptly sat on her head. Her door slammed shut. I jumped into the driver's seat and gunned the engine. Grass flew from under my spinning wheels as the car fought to gain hold.

I saw Al break into a run, falling off her high heels in the process. She kicked off her shoes and sprinted toward the car. I fishtailed toward the street, thinking only of escape. I had to drive down the sidewalk, dodging Mrs. Simmons and barely missing her cat (damn!) before I found another opening. I cranked the wheel to the left and bumped back out onto the street.

I swerved and careened around a corner. By this time I was singing the theme song from *Batman*. Ian and Mag joined in. With dogs barking and us wailing, I laid rubber on the street. We peeled off toward freedom.

We were a couple of blocks away, and my slobber-coated hand kept sliding off the wheel. I grabbed up an old Dairy Queen napkin and mopped up the Wesley spit. I handed Ian the napkin and casually mentioned, "Uh, Ian? Get your head."

Ian touched his head, his facial expressions ranging from grossed out to resignation. Welcome to the family, I thought, as he scraped the drool out of his hair. Wes looked on and grinned and Hillary looked at me as if she were the guilty party. Mag sat with her arms crossed, silently staring straight ahead–never a good sign.

I pulled into Mag's driveway and we sat for a moment. Mag distractedly opened her door. Wesley did not wait for her to exit, but clambered over the top of her and bounded into the yard. Mag lay half sprawled out of the car, her hands braced on the ground, her feet still inside the car. Hillary used Mag as a ramp and followed Wes at a much more dignified pace. Mag tucked her head and did a summersault out of the car.

She sat up and said brightly, "Hey, I just remembered. I still have a microscope!"

I was confused. "And this is important because why?"

Mag sashayed to the back of the car, talking over her

shoulder. "Because, my little brain child, Ian needs a microscope to look at the seeds, and I still have my mini lab set up in the guest room, which includes a super-dooper beauty of a scope. He can get a look at the seeds while we order pizza—I am not eating any more of Joy Broussard's Jell-O salads."

She looked at the grocery bags stuffed with food and said, "Heck, we don't need to order pizza, look at all this stuff!" She unloaded containers of burgers, brats, beans, green bean casserole, and potato salad, and hauled them into Mag's kitchen.

As she handed a container to Ian to open, she continued. "If you can hook up your laptop to my big terminal, or if you can access your computer from here, maybe you can get a jump on the seed identification thing."

She looked at her watch. "It's just three now. Marla, over at the school works all summer until four, so we can probably get into the science department for any materials we may need like slides or solution, or even a dead frog if we want."

Ian blinked, grabbed her up, spun her in a circle, and pasted a mongo-kiss right on her lips. "You are...incredible, Maggie." He set her down and she swayed.

"Good thing the counter is there to hold you up, Magpie."

She turned to me with a dazed look on her face.

"*Hmmm*? Uh yeah, I'm incredible."

Her bemused expression made me want to hurl. I left her there and headed back out to the car.

"Sure," I mumbled, "*Mag's* incredible." I sighed and reached inside the SUV. With an un-lady like grunt I hauled the whiteboard out and into the house.

I passed the kitchen on my way to Mag's office just as Ian turned a still dazed Mag around and cupped her face.

"So, beautiful, are you going to marry me or what?" He kissed her again and bounded out of the house to the car. She stumbled behind him and followed him out while the dogs brought up the rear of the party.

I had the whiteboard set up and my notes and recorder ready. *Where the heck is Romeo and Juliet?*

I looked out the front window and watched as Mag held the SUV's gate up and Ian dug his laptop out of the back. Ian trotted with the dogs back to the front door. He turned back to wait for Mag. She stared at him. He flashed her his lopsided smile and tilted his head. "Coming, Sweetheart?" Wesley took this as his engraved invitation to bound up onto the porch and scamper inside.

Mag stood inside the front door looking a little dazed. I stood next to her and we looked into the mirror on the wall. I could see we were wearing identical stunned expressions. I recovered first and smacked Mag in the back of the head. "Snap out of it, bride-to-be. Wesley just invaded your kitchen." Galvanized into action, Mag sprinted for the front door.

Later on, with a brat in one hand and a white board marker in the other, I looked at what we had so far. Not a hell of a lot. I retrieved the recorder and we went over the information as I had taken it when I first observed the body. I added and corrected as I went along:

I had noted general information I would need for my investigation. Graff, Carole Marie. Female, White, age 45-50 (exact D.O.B.?), brown hair, blue eyes, approximately 5'5" and 135 pounds. No jewelry visible, leather glove on one hand. I noted: *Where's the other glove?*

Beginning at the end, I wrote on the whiteboard that her boots were scuffed, small clumps of mud on the inside heel. Well worn–appear to be working boots. Grass and mud embedded by the toe of the left boot.

Was she dragged or was it from working outside? Looking closely I saw the grass on the toe was folded over the sole, some grass was broken off at this point. Scrape marks across the top of that same toe and down the side of the foot. I took note of the scrape marks on her jeans indicating that at some point, Carole was dragged over the ground (great deduction, Sherlock, how else did she get under your parents' house?). Off to the side, I scribbled notes as a million questions floated around in my head:

1) How did she get to Mom's house?

2) Dragged how far?

3) Why not carried or transported on wheels–re-check the yard for signs of scuffle.

4) One perpetrator working alone, or perhaps an unplanned murder?

5) What the heck as in her pocket?

6) Is J.J. coming by tonight?

Okay Buzz, focus. Pressing the button on the recorder I listened to my voice droning on. Mentally I began ticking off facts as I had observed them. Boots, then blue jeans, grass, mud stains, burdocks and chaff are visible on the bottom by the right ankle (the left had not been visible at this time), dirt and grass stains running parallel with the leg appeared on the thighs and knees. Jeans are not new, but not yet ready for the ragbag. Levi brand.

I thought I was placing too much faith in a couple of seeds, while Carole's body got colder by the minute. Ian had tentatively identified the seeds. He knew he had two varieties of poppy seeds–one being the opium poppy, the other, California poppy. Another he thought was a cactus seed, but he did not yet know which kind. The last he could not identify without his personal software.

The Rob Graff thing really had me going. I called Glenn's cell phone. He assured me that Rob was just having difficulty dealing with Carole's death.

He rambled on and on about Rob's great relationship with his mother, about Carole's movements the day before her death, almost as if he was reading a script. Something didn't ring true with the whole thing, especially with Rob's cryptic remark about 'her' lurking in the back of my mind. I thanked him and hung up.

On a whim, I called my friend, Janelle, down at the Clerk of Courts office and asked her to trace birth, death and marriage information on the three of them. Janelle called me back within the hour with some very interesting news. She did not find any local information on Glenn and Carole, which only meant that they were not married or born in our county. She then accessed the mainframe computer. She did not find either name on a marriage certificate, but found their names under births, to the same parents, but in South Dakota. After the initial wave of nausea passed through me, I asked Janelle to go on.

She said she contacted one of her friends at the IRS, and there was no record of a Robert J. Graff having been born, died, or married to either Carole or her husband Glenn. She told me one more interesting thing. Someone had requested Carole's birth and death certificates online yesterday, the day I found Carol's body.

Janelle said she could trace the customer by the credit card information and get back to me. I asked one last favor of Janelle, and that was to keep our conversation confidential. She told me she had not spoken to me in over a month and hung up.

Back to the drawing board, or the white board, in this instance. I told Ian and Mag what little I had learned, and Ian let out a big breath. He stood, hands on hips, and paced back and forth. The dogs followed his movements as if they were watching a slow motion ping-pong game. Ian bit a nail, he swiped at his face, and he paced some more. He came to a stop in front of the white board. He stared at it for almost a full minute before turning to us. "We need more help. We are getting nowhere fast."

"Duh?" I said

"No shit, Sherlock," Mag said

The dogs watched Ian with benign interest in case he had a hot dog in his pocket. Ian looked back at them and smiled. "Well, at least there are two other professionals besides me in this room." Wesley grinned at him and Hilary delicately passed gas.

Ian came over and squatted beside us. He fisted his hands in front of him and looked at the floor, gathering his thoughts. He inhaled and blew out a long breath. "If we can put the sarcasm on hold, ladies, I think I can help here. I have a couple of contacts I can get a hold of who may be able to shed some light on the Graff thing."

Contacts? Since when does a science teacher have 'contacts'? I stared at him and he stared back. I guessed this is what I felt all along was bothering me about him. The piece that didn't fit, the feelings my mom calls 'The Irish'. I sometimes hate it when I'm right. Ian Connor was a phony.

I wondered how much of himself he was willing to divulge at this point, or rather, how much he was willing to trust us with whatever his secrets were. I was getting angry and wished I had a TASER so I could pop him one in the ass.

I spoke first, trying for polite. I failed miserably and it came out as bitch.

"All right, cowboy. What the Hell is going on and who are you really? Don't give me the, 'I'm a plant-boy geek who *happens* to work for the University, and who *happened* to be in Milwaukee yesterday, and who just ***happened*** to be free this morning' to come to a podunk town to mix with the local idiots who are floundering around to do what? Make sure we keep floundering, or to do enough ground work so you guys can move in and take over. Or am I wrong and you're one of the bad guys?"

Ian squirmed uncomfortably and looked at Mag. She looked wounded. That really pissed me off. I was on a roll, and The Bitch turned into The Bitch of the Royal Potentate. I love it. "You know what else I think, plant boy? I think you reek of Fed. Before this morning's talk with Janelle, I thought the Graffs might have been Feds, but their trail is too sloppy; their cover too easy to blow."

I had a full head of steam going now. I put my arm around Mag's shoulders. "So you go ahead and make your little 'contacts', *Fed Boy*, and you ride off into the sunset, tooting your Yuppie Scum Beemer horn, and leave us the hell alone!"

As I let him stew on that I got even angrier. "So what do you guys suspect? Domestic Terrorism? Drugs? Trafficking of something else? Is Rob Graff in on it? Are they all illegal?"

I was thinking out loud now. "It's gotta be domestic, and it has to be big."

I glared at him. "And you came from Milwaukee, so my guess is you must be FBI. Were you all waiting for Mag or me to get hit before moving on this, or were you just entertaining yourself with the local color before pulling out?"

I heard a sob from Mag, who ran from the room. The dogs followed her. I heard the back door slam.

Ian glared at me.

"You Bitch."

"Wait a minute, asshole, before you start the requisite name calling. You're just pissed off that I caught on, so now instead of being intuitive or good at what I do, typical male feelings of inferiority provoke you into calling the female a Bitch." I laughed. "That's really rich. Well, have at it, Big Boy. I have better things to do than to be insulted by a scumbag like you."

I spun and made a grand exit. "And leave my sister alone!"

I slammed the back door for good measure. I found Mag and the dogs in the back yard all piled on the big swing. One of the beautiful things about having big dogs around you is that they stick by you when your world turns to crap, and they let you cry in their fur as long as you pay them off in snacks. At this moment, Mag had her arms around Wesley's neck, crying softly. Hilary was in her lap, taking on the burdens of the world. I squeezed in and made sure I was touching all three of them. With one foot I set us to rocking.

We rocked for a while in silence. "Mag, no matter what happens with Ian, we're still a team, and we still need to find out what happened to Carole."

Mag looked up, her tear-stained face wearing a hopeful expression. "Really, Buzz? I thought you'd dump me so I wouldn't be a burden to you anymore. What a dumb ass I am. I bought into everything Mr. Butthead said."

"Slow down, Mag. If you recall, Mr. Butthead didn't say much, which is why I initially had a problem with him. I speculated and guessed. I had a feeling about him and unfortunately I was right. But I was blowing smoke in there—I'd bet he's no bad guy. To give him his due, when it came to you, I didn't have any of those feelings like he was a phony, or giving us a line of crap. Maybe he isn't the pig I thought he was. Maybe he's just a little porker." She smiled. "At any rate, he should be pretty pissed at me about now."

I realized at that point what I said was true. Ian seemed like a pretty straight-up guy, except for when it came to who he worked for and what he was doing down here. Mag sniffed again and wiped her nose on Wesley's neck. Wes grinned and panted.

She thought long and hard before turning to me. "You know, I never did ask him what he was about. I just kind of ran out. You know how I cry ugly. I didn't want to subject him to that."

"Actually, Mag, I think crying ugly is a Miller trait. We all get that big old red nose, blotchy face, and swollen eyes. That's one reason why having big dogs is better than having a man. Look at Wes. He's got boogers in his hair, and he's happy as a clam. Dogs never care if you cry pretty or if your hair is a wreck. They are all about unconditional love. Give yourself a minute to get under control. Maybe you ought to go back in the house and see if you have a big dog you can love, or a small pig you can put on a spit."

"I love you, Buzz, thanks."

"I love you too, Maggot. Now get out of here."

Wes, Hilary, and I sat for a while, swinging in Mag's back yard. I thought about where we going to go from here on the case, and what part, if any, Ian would play. I relaxed and began to hum. The dogs settled in and fell asleep; each smiled and twitched as they romped in their doggie dreams.

12

For the next fifteen hours, Alejandro had nothing to do but think. He thought back about many things that had held little meaning at the time they happened. He thought how odd it was that some of those occurrences now took on a more sinister meaning.

He had many unanswered questions. Like why did Martinez insist they bring all mares to the championships, rather than the best horse for the job? Why was Eduardo Martinez late arriving, and why did he not check into his hotel? How did Martinez know what happened at the barns if Alejandro did not tell him? Why did Martinez hire people to find Huerta before he knew Huerta was missing? Were the thugs who beat up him and Jose possibly hired by Martinez? Why would Martinez send thugs to beat up Alejandro and Jose anyway? Why not just ask them if they knew where Dr. Huerta was? Hell, was Dr. Huerta even a doctor? Did someone think Alejandro knew too much? Did they think he had figured something out? Another terrible thought crossed his mind: was Alejandro Montoya supposed to die in Dallas?

Though he knew it was paranoid, he drove off the Interstate and onto small country roads to check on his horses. He could not deviate too far from his route because of the time element. He did not stop often, and he did not eat.

Martinez called him once to find out where he was. Alejandro told him he was in Joplin, Missouri, when in fact he was crossing the Mississippi into Illinois. He tried to ask Martinez questions about Huerta and Jose, but Martinez cut him off and hung up, leaving Alejandro even more confused and more frightened.

When Alejandro made it north of Chicago, he looked for a place to pull off the Interstate again. He saw what looked like a petting zoo off of Highway 176, and pulled into the parking lot. It was late in the afternoon and the place was closed.

Having little to do but think during the long hours on the road, he convinced himself there must be answers to some of his questions hidden in the horse trailer. He opened all the service doors to let in the night air for the mares. He pulled everything out of the dressing room and the truck. He spread it across three parking stalls, separating his belongings from those of Jose and Dr. Huerta.

Alejandro searched through the belongings, not knowing what he was looking for. He looked through the stacks of clothing and hygiene items, but found nothing suspicious looking. "I am now talking like a movie detective," he told the mares, "All those nights of watching CSI paid off."

He searched Huerta's veterinary bag, but found nothing more suspicious than birthing gloves, regular gloves, a large set of what looked like grilling tongs, and assorted wraps, needles, threads, and various other 'doctor' things. "Birthing gloves?" He thought about it. Perhaps to check for pregnancy down the road.

He was reloading the tack room with Dr. Huerta's hanging clothes when a small bubble envelope fell out of an inside jacket pocket. Alejandro picked it up and flipped it over. It was addressed to a Mrs. Carole Graff in White Bass Lake, Wisconsin. What held Alejandro's attention was the return address. It was from some Mexican research group he never heard of, but the address was the Martinez ranch!

Alejandro finished stuffing Huerta's and Jose's things

back in the tack room. He put his own things in the backseat of the truck. He threw the bubble envelope into the glove compartment of the truck. When he leaned across the seat, he noticed something was wedged under the passenger seat. He grabbed the flashlight.

Directing the light under the seat, he tugged on what appeared to be a briefcase. He yanked it out, stumbling backward when it tore loose. It flew out from under the seat, smacking him on the chin. He thought how ironic it was to have just injured the only spot on his entire body that did not already hurt. Rubbing his chin, he inspected the briefcase

It was dark brown leather and unfamiliar to him. He wondered if it could have belonged to Dr. Huerta. The thought came to him that one could mistake this bag for the one holding the registration and health papers for the mares. Alejandro remembered the last time he saw Huerta. He was jogging around the corner of the barn with a briefcase in his hand. Was this the briefcase he carried? Did he take the wrong briefcase? If so, then what was in this one? Dare he look inside something that did not belong to him? He thought that after all that had happened to him over the last 24 hours, hell, yes, he dared!

Just as he reached for the latch on the case, red and blue lights flashed on the main road. Alejandro stuffed the case back under the seat and walked around the trailer. He stroked and spoke to the mares before closing their doors. The squad pulled into the lot and caught Alejandro in the spotlight.

"Hey, Buddy, are you okay?" The funny Midwestern accent injected a friendly note into the question. Alejandro smiled as he turned toward the squad.

"I'm fine, officers. It seemed one of my horses was making a racket and I wanted to make sure they were all okay."

One officer was looking at the in-car computer. "Probably checking the plates," Alejandro thought. He hoped Martinez had everything up to date. The other officer looked in the trailer windows as he spoke.

"You got some nice horses in there. Where are you headed?"

"To the," he checked his notes, "Gamble Horse Farm in Gurnee, sir. I have brood mares to drop off." Not knowing where the next statement came from, he also blurted, "Then I need to make a stop in White Bass Lake across the border. I am on vacation, but I might be checking out a new job, too."

"White Bass Lake? Nice town. Good folks. I know the sheriff up there. Mr.?"

"Montoya, sir." He handed over his driver's license, thinking wouldn't it be his luck if Martinez reported his truck and trailer stolen?

The police officer strolled back to the squad and handed his license to the other cop. Alejandro thought fast. "I might see the sheriff when I get up to White Bass Lake, do you want me to send him your good wishes?"

The cop smiled. "Sure. You tell Sheriff Green that Mark Olsen from Mundelein says he owes me a doughnut. He'll understand." The other police officer stepped away from the squad and handed Alejandro his license.

"You can also tell that no-good weasel that he owes Harry Ballard a fish fry!" They both laughed at the 'inside' joke.

Alejandro discovered from the officers he was only two exits away from the one he needed. He thanked them both and climbed into the truck. He pulled back onto the Interstate and within twenty minutes was pulling into the front lot of Gamble's Horse Farm.

13

Ian and Mag strolled out of the house. I steeled myself against the determined look in hers and Ian's eyes. The dogs looked up and I could feel them tense as they followed my emotional lead. I absently stroked their heads, silently reassuring them I was not going to shoot anyone in the next five minutes–or so I thought. I watched Ian and Mag approach and noticed something else. Mag was not crying. What could he have possibly told her that would make everything all right? This could be a positive sign, but it also could mean he lied to her and she was now pissed off at me instead of Ian. Ah, life can be hell. There is nothing in the world compared to sibling anger.

The dogs and I sat rigidly where we were, and didn't offer anyone a place to sit. Good thing we all had big butts, I thought, because we took up the whole swing. Ian glared down at me, hands on his hips, and cleared his throat.

"Just for the record, my mother really *does* live in Janesville, and I *am* a Forensic Botanist, only I work out of the Milwaukee office of the FBI, and I only do occasional research for UW Madison. I have lectured there but I do not teach on a regular basis."

I hate it when I'm right, but at the same time relieved that he was not a real bad guy–he was only a jerk. That didn't exactly make him one of the good guys yet, but we were gaining on it. I didn't say a word, just kept staring at him. He shuffled his feet and continued.

"I had orders to maintain cover, even though it wasn't much of one. I had no choice. I was supposed to recover the seeds and find out what they were. I didn't count on Mag, and you, your mom, the dogs, the town–geez! Every time I turn around I am fascinated.

"I haven't even been doing my job. I've just been bumping along behind you and Mag, absorbing all this damn Americana. I do have one question, though.

"What the hell is it with all the Jell-O? Every time I turn around, someone is shoving a plate of Jell-O with some sort of 'stuff' inside at me! I have had peaches, pineapple, cottage cheese, Cool Whip, cabbage, carrots, and one I couldn't identify, but it tasted like a party loaf from a wedding I once went to."

Mag and I giggled. Ian jumped and looked panic stricken. "*That's* what your mother did when I asked her. What is so damn funny?"

Mag and I looked at each other, and I did the honors. "Spam."

He gulped. "Spam? In goddamn Jell-O?"

"Yep. Spam, pickle relish, mustard and some other stuff. Wes loves it; he gets it most birthdays and on other special occasions because we refuse to eat it."

Ian looked ill. "Only in the Midwest."

"I don't know. You could be right," I said. "It's my grandmother's recipe. She has 101 ways to make Jell-O."

Ian clutched his stomach. "Ugh. Enough about Jell-O! Let's get back to business for a minute." He pulled a small notebook out of his jeans pocket and flipped through it. "The FBI doesn't know much more than you already figured out. The facts as we know them are as follows: We do not know who the Graffs are. We think the blundering cover Janelle found was a calculated move. Our people found out just as much, but it turns out little Robby has a past. Our guys are looking into that past now. I say we let them–it's one less thing we have to worry about, and those guys do it for a living. The FBI computer geeks can come up with a fuzz ball in a hermetically sealed room. The Graffs, or whoever is paying their bills, probably think no one will dig deeper if they figure the target is stupid enough to leave a trail like they did and end up dead."

I interjected, "Either that or they were originally used for short term and targeted for removal anyway."

"Exactly." Ian paced a bit, reading his notes. He sipped his coffee. "The Bureau also thinks like you do, Buzz, that the seeds are connected with Carole's death somehow."

"I knew it," I said.

Ian nodded. "Turns out she was hooked up with a research group in Texas, who in turn is connected to another one out of Mexico which may or may not be real–I'll get more into to that later. This group initially looks like a rare plant species preservation group, as they find rare plants and propagate them so they can be moved to places where their habitat is not yet destroyed. The problem they face, or that they might be hip deep in, is one of illegal exportation of rare species, thereby shrinking their already diminished numbers. Plants such as these are shipped to the U.S. and other countries, for cultivation and sale in the elite market of rare species. Now with the Internet, that market is endless. Plants can be marked and shipped as Barbie Dolls, if the sellers have a mind to, and international markets are big money."

This time Mag jumped in. "Aw, come on. Do you mean to tell me that there are little plant geeks all over the world buying illegal plants and one of them offed Carole?"

Ian shrugged his shoulders. "Maybe, and maybe not. It's too early to tell. One plant Carole was working on has been illegal to export from Mexico for some time. The laws are still unclear as to whether the Mexican government is allowing the legal exportation of this rare little cactus even now."

He looked at his notes. "Mammillaria Luethyi could serve as a poster child for plant conservation. This is a small cactus, which only grows naturally in two small areas in the Mexican state of Coahuila. It clings to outcroppings of limestone.

"Two plant explorers re-discovered the cactus in 1996, and kept it a well-guarded secret until recently. According to Jonas Luethy, the guy it's named after, he did not receive a specimen until 2002."

He continued, "It was found that this cactus can be adapted to cultivar if grafted onto a more vigorous Mammillaria relative, but there has been no luck when trying to grow it from seed. They think it might have been because so few cultivars have been legally obtained. They do not know if cross-pollination even takes place. Here's where it gets interesting."

Mag said out of the corner of her mouth, "I've been waiting for it to get interesting for a while now." I elbowed her in the ribs.

Ian pretended he didn't hear her remark. "This research group has been smuggling first generation seeds out of their country and into ours, as they are easier to keep healthy and more easily hidden. Near as we can figure, Carole has been experimenting with the seeds up here, shipped through the Texas research group. She was working to be the first to raise this cactus from seed. Where her dealings with these people might have been a tad shady, we did not think it would warrant her murder. That is what brings me here. I needed to identify the seeds you found and report back."

He looked up at us. "That brings me to the last falsehood. Although I knew those were lutheyi seeds when I first looked at them at the morgue, what I didn't tell you is that the poppy seeds in the packet are opium poppies, and the others I am not familiar with."

I mulled over what Ian said. "So you already had a hunch that some of those seeds might be lutheyi seeds, right?" Ian had the decency to blush. "What the heck was she doing with opium poppies, and–oh no. Could Carole have either unwittingly stumbled upon or been trapped into being a pawn for something bigger, like drug trafficking?"

Ian thought for a moment and agreed this idea had possibilities. "Perhaps she didn't even know they were opium poppies, and thought all the seeds were lutheyi. After all, the package in her pocket was sealed."

A thought struck me and I dug in my pocket, frantically looking for a scrap of paper. "Oh my God, I think we have our first break!" I fumbled with the paper. "Lutheran, Luther, *lutheyi*; it fits! Look guys!"

I shoved the wrinkled scrap at Ian and Mag. "Malcolm and I saw what we thought were letters on the paper towel. We tried to make them out, but we only had a few to go with, but they fit–look!"

We discussed different theories as the sun sank over Mom and Dad's barn, in the distance. Since it was getting dark, we all gravitated toward the house. We ate some more leftovers and updated the whiteboard. Mag got some yarn and we taped our offshoot theories on the wall.

As I began filling the dog dishes with kibble, I paused at the sink. "So Ian, what are you doing later tonight?"

He raised an eyebrow and smiled. "Why, Miz Buzz, what did you have in mind?"

I strolled around the kitchen and poured a cup of coffee, feigning indifference. "I thought we might want to take a little drive in the country tonight. Check out the sheds…and the flower beds, with the Feds."

Ian said, "I'll wear my Keds. We'll knock 'em dead."

Mag joined in the game. "Who knows? We might be able to dig up a little dirt!"

I was laughing by this time. "As long as we don't get ourselves in a prickly situation looking for cactus!"

Ian looked at the two of us like we were bonkers. "What you two sick comics fail to realize is that what you are proposing is illegal. You know, like criminal trespassing? Breaking and entering? Criminal damage to property, illegal search and seizure?"

Still chuckling, I punched Ian in the arm. "Don't turn into a stick-in-the-mud law enforcement type on us now, Plant Boy. Tell me you weren't thinking along those same lines yourself. We're just giving you the opportunity of us helping you out and the pleasure of our company. You should be thrilled."

He shuddered. "What I am, is scared shitless."

Mag walked up behind him and stroked the back of his neck with one fingernail. With her lips close to his ear, she whispered, "Is there anything we can say or do to make you follow our illegal and unlawful order, Fed Boy?"

Ian looked at her wide-eyed and swallowed hard. "Yeah, two things. Can we get rid of Buzz for an hour or so? And hell, no, you can't go. It's too dangerous."

She pouted. "You're a hard man, Ian Connor."

He smiled slowly. "Not yet, Honey, but we didn't get rid of Buzz yet, either."

Short of throwing water on them, I didn't know how to regain control of the situation. "Yo, get a room later, you two. I am not going anywhere. Hey, Mag, knock it off and listen a minute."

When I regained their attention I said, "We need to know what's in that locked shed. We know Rob and Glenn will not open it for us. As a matter of fact, Rob said Glenn was 'gone' but he called me on the cell phone. I wonder from where?"

Ian picked up the thought. "We also need to consider

timing. Whatever is in there might be moved to prevent the issuance of a search warrant prior to its removal." He thought a moment more. "Buzz, you're right. Time is of the essence, so let's just do it and be done with it."

I felt a rush of satisfaction. "I agree. We are not going to be able to do it the legal way until three or four days from now, so let's just decide now to commit a felony and go for it. Ian, you stay here because this can cost you your career. Mag and I have known J.J. most of our lives, and my career is already finished."

He jumped out of the chair. "Are you nuts?"

"Yes. And your point being?"

"I'm Plant Boy, remember? Investigating plants *is* my career! You don't even know what to look for in that shed. Besides, I don't want to testify against either one of you after the arrests are made, so I am *going*. Oh my God, now I'm beginning to sound like you two!"

"Welcome to the family, Ian. Let's get packed and go."

14

Great, I thought, as I drove out of town. A plant geek, a schoolteacher, and a new member of the AARP are playing Matlock. We are going to either get arrested or killed. If the bad guys didn't kill us, Mom sure as hell would kill me for bringing Mag along. I shushed myself as we rolled into Graff's Garden Center. I cut the engine and the headlights and rolled quietly into the yard.

Mag's disembodied voice, coming from the back seat, blasted us like cannon fire into the new dawn. "Geez, Buzz! I didn't know that gravel could crunch this loud!"

I jumped and we had to peel Ian off the ceiling. In a stage whisper, I vented my spleen. "Geez, Maggot, why don't I just give you the bullhorn so you can yell it to everyone? Shut the hell up or start walking toward Mom's. And don't crunch the gravel when you leave!"

"Bitch," I heard as I quietly exited the car. I ignored her. I headed for the west fence. According to our plan, we each headed off in different directions. I reviewed our operation in my head, jogging in the direction of the house.

It was lucky for us the Graff's lands were neighbors of a sort to my parents' place. As kids, we had this entire end of the county's topography memorized. Any break in a fence, every empty barn loft, and every rusty gate was a landmark and a tool to enterprising farm kids with a little time and a little ingenuity. There should be an old break in the woven wire fence about half-way back to the property line we always rode our horses through. I headed there. On the chance the Graffs knew about the hole and had it mended, Mag headed for the broken-down service gate on the opposite fence line.

Since Ian did not know the territory he hung out at the entrance, seeing if he could quietly sneak in there. We were all to meet at the back door of the main building when we got through.

I thanked my lucky stars that the hole in the fence was right where it had always been. Wild rose and honeysuckle covered it, but I counted myself lucky. I only had to scramble through the bramble rather than haul my happy ass over the top. I stood for a moment breathing heavily and surveying the area.

I froze when I saw what appeared to be a light shining from the opposite position from where I stood. It swayed as it flashed . I thought, oh, shit, we're caught. "Five to ten rotting in the pen," I chanted to myself, making my way across the yard toward the closest building.

The light continued to sway drunkenly and flash intermittently. I stopped and hauled in a breath. "Wait a minute, that isn't the cops… Oh, shit. It's Mag," I whispered and took off at a run.

I skidded to a stop about twenty feet from the opposite fence line. Bent over, I panted, hands on my knees. If I weren't so pissed off I would have laughed my butt off at the sight my sister made dangling upside-down from the fence by one foot and furiously trying to S.O.S. us with the flashlight.

"Mag, you idiot! I should just leave you hanging there." I grabbed the flashlight out of her hand and shoved it light-side down into the weeds. I grabbed her by the belt and the back of the neck and tried to swing her back over the fence. She flopped around like a fresh-caught tuna on deck. I struggled with her and was finally able to shove her back over the fence. Her shoe flew off, her leg sprang free and she landed on her brains, on the opposite side of the fence. She sat with her cheeks puffed out and her eyes squeezed shut.

Ian trotted up next to me He took in the scene of me gasping and leaning on the fence, a shoeless Mag on the opposite side on her ass, the flashlight, the bent fence, and he slid to the ground, laughing. "Holy Mackerel!"

I looked at him and barked out a laugh. "Ian, you have no idea how apropos that is."

Mag slowly stood, rubbing her butt and looking martyred. She ignored us and scrounged for her shoe. Grumbling while she searched, she tripped over stalks. She winced as she stepped on rocks and field stubble. She finally located her shoe. She slid it on and stood, brushed off her pants. "Now what?"

Still steaming, I glared at her. "Now you go back to the car and stay there."

"I'm not one of the dogs. Don't tell me to sit and stay."

"Mag, I won't argue the point. Go back to the car. You can help tomorrow with something. You can be the lookout. I don't care what you do, but get out of my face and take you sore rear-end back to the car before I kick the shit out of it!"

"No way man! I am not going anywhere. I am a part of this team. This operation takes three people who know the plan. I'm 'Number Two'!"

In more ways than one, I thought. "Not anymore. You're fired. Go home."

"Just because I tried to take a short cut? That old gate is to hell and gone from here, and I didn't want to be late so I decided to hop the fence instead."

"Nice hopping, moron. Too bad you didn't look down the fence line a few feet more."

I walked about ten feet from where we stood and I leaned a hip on the old gate. It gave like an Irish Catholic on

Easter Sunday (and with less of a complaint, I might add). Mag lowered her head and minced through the opening.

I felt the storm gathering in me and was about to let fly on her when Ian touched my arm. "Come on, Buzz, no use arguing. She's in and we're wasting time. Let's just go."

I knew, of course, he was right. I tried to relax and focus. Deep breath, slow exhale. It didn't work.

Deep breath, slow exhale. I looked at Mag and felt my blood pressure begin to skyrocket again. I thought, "One more time for the Gipper, Buzz." Deep breath, slow– "Forget it." I said. "Let's go."

I gathered my pack and flashlight and led off. Mag jumped forward. Ian grabbed her shirt and hauled her back. "If you value your life, Maggie, stay the hell away from her for now." Mag eyed me and stooped to pick up her flashlight. She followed in Ian's wake.

"Hmmph," I thought, "Smart boy, and he learns fast, too."

We made our way through the back of the property, to the long buildings serving as greenhouses in the winter and propagation houses in the summer. We stayed as a group in case we ran into any trouble.

I stopped at the first shed and looked down the side. Running about 60 feet long and 40 feet across, the buildings were substantial and very conducive to a garden operation.

Ian moved past me and checked down the other side of the building. Mag was positioned at the door. After a nod from both Ian and me indicating the coast was clear, we listened for movement inside. Hearing none, Mag tried the latch. It gave and we were in.

We had no need for the flashlights since the glow from the rows of grow-lights illuminated the inside like a football stadium. Running the length of the building were three rows of waist-high shelving. Hundred of flats with thousands of plants of every kind imaginable sat happily under the grow-lights, photosynthesizing to their little hearts' content. The building had pipes crisscrossing throughout. From them rubber misters hung intermittently above the flats, periodically emitting a fine spray over their small charges.

Ian stood for a second, taking in slow deep breaths of that moist, earthy, greenhouse smell. He wore a look of ecstasy and murmured, "*Mmm*. Hi, kids. Papa's home."

I looked at him and then at Mag. "Oh, no. Mag, Plant Boy is getting high or getting off. Slap him or something."

Mag poked him in the ribs. "Yo, Ian. Back to reality here. How are we going to tell if what is here is really what is supposed to be here?"

Ian and I must have looked equally perplexed, because Mag regrouped and tried again.

"How are we going to be able to tell which plant is what specie?"

Ian looked over the flats in front of us. "Look. They're all marked. You and Buzz find where each new plant label begins. If there are any in that group that don't look like the rest, call me. According to the tags, these should all be common varieties of zones four-to-five-safe perennials. I can identify them in seconds. It's the odd ones we need to watch for. That's where you and Buzz come in. Now let's go!"

Mag and I began slowly, painstakingly reading the tags and making sure all the plants looked alike. Row after row and flat after flat, we searched until our eyes crossed. I wondered how Ian was doing and stopped for a moment. Looking up, the sight that met my eyes took my breath away. Ian literally flew through the flats. I poked Mag and gestured to Ian. We stared as his index finger zipped along the flats. The snapping of his finger against the plastic trays sounding like the staccato pop of twisted bubble wrap.

Murmurs of Calamagrostis, Pennisetum, and Miscanthus mingled with Echinacea, Hemerocallis, and Rudbeckia. On and on he went, those beautiful Latin names rolling off his tongue like a mystic chant. He rounded the corner and we stepped back out of his way lest we get run over. We followed in his wake until he reached the end of the third row. We were back at the front door when he looked up and blinked.

"Wow. You really *are* Plant Boy," Mag said in awe. She looked at him as if he wore a red cape. He looked at her like he was a starving man and she was lunch. She reached for Ian, and he leaned forward. They crashed together like waves against the rocks. I drew in a breath to yell at both of them and the watering system kicked on. They both jumped back like scalded cats. I hooted.

"Come on, Romeo and Juliet, get hinky later. We have three more of these buildings to go through. We now have a new plan of action. Ian, you lead, we follow. Together, Mag and I can't keep up with you. Mag, no playing patty-fingers with the genius here until we're safe and clear. Got it? Okay? Now focus." I put my hand on the door latch.

"Ready?" Nods all around.

"Okay–Go, go, go!" We piled out the door to the next building. Mag cracked open the door, looked in and nodded. We slipped through and Ian performed his magic. Mag and I started from the opposite end and worked our way toward Ian.

We came to Papaver, and I pointed to Mag and whispered, "Now these I remember." I gave my best 'Wicked Witch' impersonation of the word 'Poppies', drawing out the short 'o' sound and cackling at the end.

Ian stopped in mid-stride, and with furrowed brow and squinted eyes said, "What?"

At a loss for being caught doing something so stupid, I

groped for something to say. "Uh, look at these poppies–who would buy poppies that look like Bull Thistle?"

Ian still looked a little perplexed. "Poppies don't look like thistle. Who would buy thistle?" Mag tried to help. She pointed to the prickly little plants.

"Some crazy Scotsman, perhaps?"

Ian walked over to where we were standing. "Some crazy Cheesehead, maybe?"

"Hey–I resemble that remark. I'll have you know..."

Ian whirled on her and held up a hand. "Wait. Buzz, look at this! You might be on to something here. Not only do these not look like regular poppies, remember what I said about plants being different?"

I looked, and the hundreds of little nondescript plants meant nothing to me. I couldn't help but be a smart ass.

"What, oh Mighty Doctorus o Plantus? What did you find among the Plantus In-a-flattus?"

Ian picked up a prickly poppy plant. He looked down his nose and cleared his throat. "Argemone mexicana, or Mexican Poppy, to you lay people. I'd explain, but we have to keep moving. Mag, be careful and grab a couple of those. Also, get a sample from each of the other labeled poppy plants. I'll finish the rest of the greenhouse."

I pulled and Mag bagged each labeled specimen in Ziplocs, stashing them in her backpack. Ian came around with a couple more plants, and we bagged them as well.

Excited and on a roll, we exited the building and went on to the next one. Locked. Crap.

Now, I have many skills; some were acquired from law enforcement, and some learned along life's many roads. One of those latter types of skills is picking locks. Lock picking is another one of those television fantasy skills. In the time it takes them to commit a murder, gather evidence, try, convict, and sentence the bad guy on T.V., I'm still picking open a damn lock. Given enough time, however, I can pick even some of the more difficult locks. This particular specimen however, was an easy pick. I dug into my backpack for the perfect tools for the job. With all the finesse of the professional I am, I cut that sucker off in two seconds flat with the bolt cutters I'd brought along.

The clank of the bolt cutters cut through the silent darkness like a cherry bomb in a cemetery. We all froze, looking for movement from the direction of the house. It remained quiet and dark.

An eerie feeling crept over me when I touched the door to the building. I shook it off and Mag whispered, "Yo, Buzz, are you okay? Did you just have a sheeney?"

I nodded. I reached for the handle again. Slight vertigo and a little nausea swept through me. "It's bad, Mag. Whatever it is, it's not going to go well, so you stay here. So far the sheeneys haven't lied on this case–I just can't get a handle on what's behind Door Number One."

"You're having a what?" Ian whispered back.

"A shiver, a willie, what ever you call that creepy feeling that crawls up the back of your neck. Were you not listening to our mother? It's a touch of the Irish magic. With Buzz, it usually means a premonition when she's awake."

Ian looked wary. "I, uh, okay. Now what?"

They both turned back and looked at me.

I pulled back from the eerie feeling. "We be careful, and we keep Mag out of trouble. Let's go. There's something about this building–I don't know. We'll talk later. Ready everyone?" Silent nods. "Be careful. Let's go."

We crept through the door and stopped, surveying the scene before us. It was definitely a grafting room, with what seemed like acres of plants under lights. The only ones I recognized were the cactus. The back half of the building was separated from the front by an opaque, heavy plastic curtain. It was dimly lit and only shadows could be seen from our side.

Ian moved directly to a small little plant grafted onto a cactus and picked it up. It was dark with an upside-down pine cone cluster on top. It was topped with a cluster of lovely magenta flowers with white centers.

"Beautiful," I breathed.

"Ditto," said Mag.

"Leuthyi," a smug Ian announced.

"What?"

As Ian tucked a specimen into his backpack. "One thing puzzles me, though. Look at all these grafted plants. If Carole was trying to cultivate from seed, why spend all this time grafting? If the intent was *not* to cultivate from seed, why the big deal with the seeds in her pocket? We need to look for seed pots like these in the other sheds. Mag and I can do that. Buzz, how about if you look behind 'Door Number Two'?" He gestured toward the plastic sheeting.

I moved to the back of the building while Mag and Ian searched among the tables. I reached for the plastic sheeting and hesitated. I touched the plastic and shivered. It felt, I don't know, evil or something. "You guys had better come back here."

Mag took one look at me and headed in my direction. "Oh, oh. Bad news, I'll bet." She grabbed Ian's hand and trotted over to me. She touched my shoulder. We all took a deep breath and heaved the heavy curtain back.

The smell hit us first, and we staggered as one. Until you've smelled one, the smell of a drug lab is indescribable in the rancid stench of the cooking and filtering of multiple chemicals. My own head spun as the smell smacked me in the face. Mag choked and leaned against the side of the barn. Ian stood frozen, staring over my shoulder into the room. In his outstretched hand was a big bad Glock 23, .40

caliber monster.

I suppose had we been a little quieter or a little more alert, I would have noticed three burly Hispanics standing over the red blob of a human form. They were blocking the only exit on this side of the building. As it was, they were as startled as we were, which gave me a split second to shove Mag to the floor and join Ian with a drawn weapon.

Beforehand, we had decided to let Ian do all the talking if we happened to run into bad guys because, he had the most official sounding title. Somehow 'Biology teacher, put you weapons down!' did not have quite the punch we were looking for.

The bad guys just stared at us—or should I say at Ian. I realized the impression he must have made on them. He was wearing the only black shirt we could find at Mag's house; a tight v-neck cashmere sweater with ostrich feathers around the cuffs…and I knew we were in deep trouble.

15

"FBI! Put your weapons on the floor, place your hands on top of your heads, and back away toward the wall!"

All three moved not a muscle and continued to stare at us, or rather at Ian. Mag tried to stand, but I stood on her upper arm until I heard her whimper. Never wavering, Ian moved to the left, closer to the trio. I followed his lead, and held, my sights set on the one closest to the door. If I had to drop someone, I'd shoot him first and perhaps slow the exit of the others. Ian tried a different tactic.

"FBI! ¡*Pone su arma en el suelo!*"

The bad guys just stared at him. Ian and I looked at each other. I shrugged my shoulders. "So much for Spanish 101."

Mag said from the floor, "Maybe they're Portuguese." I kicked her.

Suddenly all hell broke loose. The gorilla by the door swung his gun up. I dropped him with a shot to the chest. Ian ducked as the second thug fired a round over his head. I feinted right and tripped over Mag, who was still lying on the floor. As I went down, I felt the air whoosh by my ear as a round missed me by a fraction of an inch. Lying on top of Mag, I grabbed her face and kissed her forehead before I reloaded.

"Thanks. Don't move!"

I heard Ian still firing on my left, so I crawled under the tables to the right to get a better angle. I saw stout legs with toes and knees still pointed in Ian's direction. I popped my head up to make sure Ian and I didn't create crossfire. Man Number Three moved and now stood less than three feet away from me, still firing in Ian's direction. I calmly leaned forward and very gently nudged my Smith against his head. His eyes grew wide and he held his arms away from his body. He held an automatic in his right hand. I sure hoped he understood English.

"Now stand there like a good boy and I won't have to blow your ass clear back to Mexico, pal. Now, *DROP THE GUN!*" He did without argument.

I heard a scream cut off and held my breath. A second later Ian's voice yelled, "I'm okay, Buzz. Number Two is down." Ian popped back up and trained his weapon on the guy I had. He changed out his clip and I heard the step-and-drag of his feet across the pea gravel on the floor.

My bad guy's eyes grew even larger as he looked for the others and realized he was now quite alone, I hummed softly, 'One is the loneliest number...' I stepped back out of striking range and gestured with my weapon. "Hands on your head and kneel, amigo."

He kept his beady eyes on mine, his hands slowly rose to the top of his head. I was just beginning to get that satisfied feeling in my gut that things were looking up when the asshole lunged for me.

In retrospect, I suppose he eyed up my grey hairs and my fluffy stature. Combine that with his macho arrogance, and it gave him the confidence he needed to get stupid. He lunged. I brought my other hand up. I barely had time to register the sound of a cantaloupe dropping on a hot sidewalk before I saw him pitch forward onto his stomach like he had been run over by a Mack truck.

I looked dumbly at my feet, which were now covered by a profusely bleeding head. I looked up and saw Mag holding a shovel, grinning like she just broke Barry Bond's home run record. I glanced to my left and saw Ian, both hands still on his weapon. It was pointed like mine was at the space where the big man on the floor had been standing. Ian and I both stared open mouthed at Mag. We both began yelling at once.

"I could have shot you, you stupid idiot!"

"You could have been killed!"

"I could have shot you and then Mom would have killed me anyway! Mag, you're fired. Again! For Good this time!" I stomped off a few feet, adrenalin pumping and breathing hard.

I barely heard Ian speaking quietly to Mag. When I turned back I heard him say, "And I agree with Buzz Mag, You're fired...but it was a really great shot."

Mag stood with her arms crossed, staring at the ceiling. She looked around the room. Dropping the shovel she was still holding, Mag turned and left the drug room. She sauntered past the plastic curtain into the greenhouse area. Ian and I were flummoxed. We looked at each other and looked back at the plastic curtain. We looked at each other again. Old 'Slugger' walked back into the room carrying baling twine in one hand and pruners in the other. She stopped in front of us, held up the twine, and snipped the pruners into the empty air. "Anyone care to tie him up? Since he's the only one you guys left alive, I think we should probably save him for J.J."

That galvanized us into action. Ian and I each grabbed a hand. Ian pulled out cuffs from somewhere and secured his hands. I shackled his legs with the baling twine rodeo style–three wraps and a knot. Mag calmly called J.J. on her cell phone. Only then did we turn toward whoever it was they had been torturing.

Ian rolled the body over. We all said, "Rob," as we recognized him under all the gore. Fighting the urge to gag, Mag once again pulled out her trusty cell phone and called 911 for an ambulance. I checked for a pulse and made sure he was breathing. Ian untied him and laid him flat. I checked for mortal wounds. Ian tried several times to get Rob to speak, but he drifted in and out of consciousness and did not say a word.

Mag kept watch on Rob's vitals. Ian and I sifted through the rubble, trying to make sense of the situation. I pulled out my cell phone and took pictures of both rooms and Rob.

Ian called his district office. He walked toward the front of the building, quietly arguing with someone on the phone.

Cars began to arrive on scene. Ian went out front to direct the emergency personnel back to the correct building. As more people arrived I slipped out the back door to check out the last building. Mag followed, told me this was the potting shed where Glenn cornered her. I thought fleetingly, "Where the hell is Glenn, anyway?"

The door was cracked and I opened it slowly. We peeked around the corner and groped for a light switch. The room illuminated and Mag said. "What's up with this? Holy shit, Buzz, we're not in Kansas anymore!"

Gone was the potting shed and in its place was a well appointed stable. Four stalls, rubber floors, cross ties, a tack room, a wash rack, and feed room. It was stocked and looked like it waited for guests.

"Mag, wasn't this the building we saw Rob leave and lock the last time we were here?"

She ran her hand over a stall door and nodded at me. "Sure was. Why on earth would they turn this into a horse barn when they have no horses? Where'd they get all the hay? They have no fields and someone in town would have mentioned the new barn and stocking it."

I continued down the aisle "You're right, unless they brought it in or bought it locally–" I stopped suddenly, a queasy feeling coming over me. Mag must have felt it too, because we looked at each other and began babbling.

"Oh crap." I said.

Mag looked over the hay. "You don't think..."

"Mom and Dad?"

"Who else?"

I stood looking inside the stall. "Why didn't they say something?"

"Dad was too concerned about his stupid truck getting dinged."

"Mom was too busy making damn brownies for Dead Butts."

We stopped. A look of horror crossed Mag's face as we came to the same conclusion. Mag spoke first.

"Aw, shit. Is that how Carole ended up under their house? Do you think she found out about the drug room? I'm thinking she wasn't at the farm to pick up hay. This is so confusing!"

"I know. This makes no sense. Come on, we have to get back to your house and regroup. Let's see if we can sneak out of here." I stopped again. "Oh, damn. What are we going to tell J.J.? Oh, man, I am in deep shit with J.J. I don't suppose he would overlook a couple of dead bodies and a break-in, would he?"

"Fat chance," Mag laughed without humor, "I don't think he likes us that well."

We found Ian where we left him, on the phone in front of the drug building. We hid out by the door and signaled that he come hither. He held up an index finger, signaling for us to wait. I turned, saw J.J. coming down the aisle like a steam engine, and elbowed Mag in the ribs. We slid out of sight behind the door before he could get hold of us, and ran around the front to grab Ian. We ended up dragging him through the potted plants, out the front gate and across the

139

parking lot. He was still on the phone when we stuffed him into the back seat. I took off over the lawn because the driveway was clogged with vehicles. There was no way in hell I was waiting around for J.J. to realize we had skipped. I appeased my conscience by justifying that he had his plate full enough for now, and he knew where to find us. Oh, man, was there going to be hell to pay for this one!

16

The sun was sliding toward the western horizon when Alejandro found the Gamble Appaloosa Horse Farm. It looked to him as if someone had taken a small ranch and crunched it into a tiny area. The two-story house sat near the road, off to the left. What would have been the back yard and pastures were fenced enclosures looking more like dog runs than turn-out yards. A large parking area began about thirty feet east of the house where six or seven horse trailers were parked. Two large barns were situated end-to-end, each had to measure well over 100 feet in length. The back barn had an extension off to the side, which Alejandro figured was an indoor arena for winter riding. Other outbuildings lay to the east of the barns, with a gravel road cutting down the middle.

A thin, wiry man with black hair and a pocked face met Alejandro in the front parking area. He ignored Alejandro's greeting, acting as if he did not even hear him.

"So much for Midwestern hospitality," Alejandro sighed.

The little man silently directed Alejandro toward the road running down the east side of the barn. Alejandro drove until he found a gap between the barns where he was halted by another man.

Several stern-faced cowboys stood waiting. Alejandro raised a hand in greeting and only one responded with a curt nod. There was none of the joking, convivial atmosphere Alejandro was used to seeing when in the company of cowboys. The entire operation here made him nervous.

He wondered, momentarily, if he should just turn

around and leave. He turned off the engine, but before he could exit the truck, they had the trailer doors open and were unloading the mares. No one spoke to him as they led the mares into the second barn. A lanky older cowboy came back out of the barn and told Alejandro he was to collect the papers for the mares.

"Sure," Alejandro said as he reached into the glove compartment for the sealed envelope he had been given in Mexico.

Thinking it was weird that no one asked where Dr. Huerta was, Alejandro closed up the empty trailer. He turned to ask one of the cowboys a question and found himself alone. He poked his head inside the back barn and noticed his four mares were still tied in the aisle. All the farm hands were gone. He thought how odd it was that after the long ride in the trailer the horses would be standing in an aisle rather than bedded down in stalls.

He stood alone next to his truck, hands on hips. He thought about the atypical behavior of the employees. The breeder had not come out to greet him. No one offered to show him around, something that happened on every horse farm no matter where you went. The older cowboy never opened the envelope to check the papers against the proper mare. The horses were still tied in the aisle. Were they staying or going? The peculiar goings-on since he arrived were sparking Alejandro's T.V. detective alter ego's imagination.

Alejandro drove around to the front parking area and backed the truck and trailer among the several other rigs in front of the barns. He needed to find a bathroom and get directions to White Bass Lake, in that order. He looked around inside the front barn for an office or a restroom. A burly looking fellow in a flannel shirt stepped in front of him and said, "Hey, Mex. You got no business here. Get the hell out."

Startled again at the harsh treatment, Alejandro stood staring at the man.

"I was looking for a restroom, sir. I just brought in those four…"

"They ain't your concern no more, Paco, and I don't give a shit if you piss yourself. Get out before I throw you out!"

Alejandro backed away from the man. He was about to turn when a commotion toward the back barn made both of them look. Alejandro caught a glimpse of one of his mares fighting against her halter, refusing to be loaded onto another trailer.

He turned around and headed out the front door before the rude man noticed that Alejandro saw the mare. He looked over his shoulder and saw the man hurry toward the other barn. Alejandro ducked behind the barn door and watched as all four mares were loaded into the trailer. He sagged against the barn door and scratched his head.

"Where the heck are they going now?" he murmured. "If the mares are here for breeding, why are they leaving?" He headed for his truck, thought about the rude man and froze. "What if they are horse thieves? People still steal horses in Mexico, why not here too?"

He fumbled for his cell phone while starting the engine of the truck. His decision made, Alejandro the detective pulled out behind the other horse trailer and followed while he dialed Eduardo Martinez's cell phone. He got the voice mail and snapped the phone shut. The other rig turned right and headed north on Route 45. Alejandro waited for a few vehicles to fall in behind the other trailer and then pulled out and followed. Wondering what the heck he was doing, he grabbed a pen and wrote that he turned right so he would remember how to get back.

He tried to remember landmarks and street signs, but it was dusk and the traffic was heavy. When he saw the 'Welcome to Wisconsin' sign, he started to worry. A couple of miles down the road, the rig in front turned left. Alejandro followed.

He couldn't believe his eyes when he passed a sign that said 'White Bass Lake–4 miles'. He backed off the rig in front, as the traffic had thinned.

The darkness was now on his side, but he wanted to be safe. He figured he could double back to White Bass Lake and find somewhere to stay the night if they didn't go too far.

About a mile out of town the rig in front signaled and turned. When Alejandro caught up, he realized they had pulled into a driveway. He looked up at the sign illuminated in his headlights and his heart froze in his chest. Could 'Graff's Garden Center' be a coincidence with the 'Carole Graff' addressed envelope? He did not think so. He drove couple hundred yards further down and pulled off the side of the road onto the wide shoulder.

He killed the engine and let out a deep breath. Was he up for this? He thought about Princesa and the detective in him said, "Absolutely!"

Alejandro exited the truck quietly and hiked back to the entrance to the garden center. He made his way down the side of the driveway, careful to keep off to the side so his feet did not crunch in the gravel. Nearing the main building, he saw the trailer enter through a gate to the right. They left the gate open and Alejandro slipped through. He hid among the plant displays and watched the truck pull around the end of the last building.

A thrill of anticipation shimmied up his spine. *I knew I would make a good T.V. detective.*

He crept stealthily around the opposite side of the

building, hesitating when he heard the noise of the horses being unloaded. Crawling on hands and knees to the end of the building, he watched two cowboys finish unloading his mares. He took a couple of steps back and looked through a window. Crouching down, he thought, "Now what?" He heard one of the cowboys speak.

"That's it, Jack. Now we wait."

Wait for whom or what, Alejandro wondered. Not wanting to give himself away, he sat with his back against the building and settled in. The long hours in the truck finally began taking their toll, and he felt himself drifting off. His last conscious thought was, "Television detectives are right about one thing, stakeouts really suck."

* * *

Jarred awake by the sound of an approaching vehicle, Alejandro quickly lay flat just before the headlights swept over his hiding place. *Oh God. More people. What if they saw my rig?* The vehicle parked at the back of the building along side the others. He heard doors slam and the crunch of gravel as several people walked to the barn. He stood, and again peeked through the window. What he saw made his blood turn cold.

"Huerta and Martinez," he breathed. He could not believe it. Huerta was not dead–hell, he wasn't even missing! Alejandro pulled back from the window and ran a hand through his hair. He rubbed the sleep from his face and peered through the window again. His head was whirling with a thousand questions. He waited until he heard more conversation and risked another look. Sure enough, Huerta was there, opening up one of those doctor bags. Eduardo Martinez looked on as Huerta pulled out what appeared to be a plastic bag. Alejandro realized it was a birthing glove, like the one he found in the medical bag. Huerta slid the glove over his arm and up to his armpit. The elastic at the top held it in place.

The rude man in the flannel shirt from the Gamble farm led one of the mares out to the cross ties. She stumbled and Alejandro noticed her lower lip hung down and her eyes were almost closed. *Sedated. Why is she doped up?*

Flannel Shirt hooked her in the cross ties and Huerta moved around to her rear end. Flannel Shirt lifted her tail and Huerta reached into her vagina. Alejandro looked on in horror. The mare moaned as Huerta's arm disappeared inside.

Alejandro's revulsion increased as Huerta's arm slowly emerged holding what appeared to be a large brick. He handed the brick off to another man and repeated the process. Alejandro could stand no more and took off at a run toward the next barn. He threw up in the grass next to the building, and slumped to the ground, tears forming in his eyes.

He heard the rattle of wood and metal as someone opened the door to the horse barn. Alejandro ran around the end of the building and yanked on the door handle. It gave and Alejandro slipped in, leaving the door cracked open. The tiny beam of light was enough to make out shapes in the darkness. Alejandro wove his way around tables and came to a plastic wall.

The acrid smell of the place burned his nostrils. He was about to feel his way around it when he heard noises outside the building. He quickly hit the floor and felt his way under a table. The lights flickered on. Alejandro held his breath.

"See, Carl? I told you no one was out here. Geez, you're paranoid."

"I swear I heard something, Jack, and you saw for yourself that the door was open."

"Anybody coulda left that door cracked. Ain't nobody here, Carl. Come on, we gotta go get the load and check it."

Almost hysterical, Alejandro tried to slow his breathing and think. He looked for somewhere to hide. He saw a shelf under a table behind a huge barn fan, and crawled, combat style, across the floor to get there. Once he crammed his body into the tiny space, he remembered he never did find a bathroom.

"Don't think about it," he told himself, so of course it was all he could think about. Just about the time he was near to bursting, the door creaked open.

The two villains came back in, carrying two bricks a piece. They dropped them on a table opposite to where Alejandro lay hidden.

Just my luck. On television the crooks never have their backs to the detective. He heard tearing and saw movement of the two cowboys. He spotted a hand shaking back and forth, and the truth hit him like a two-by-four across the head.

Drugs! I know it is drugs, because I saw something like this on CSI! The reality staggered him. They were smuggling drugs inside the mares from Mexico to the Midwest! He felt the bile rising in his throat. Oh God, he had to get out of here. Now. He was going to choke. If they caught him he was dead. He might be dead anyway if they saw his truck. *Breathe! In and out. Slow down, in and out. Don't panic. And don't pee. For God's sake, don't pee!*

He jerked his attention back to the drug men. One of the two men chose that moment to hurry out the door. The man called Jack went to the door. Alejandro heard, "Carl! Carl, you forgot the other brick...Carl!"

Hoping Jack followed Carl out the door Alejandro rolled off the shelf and crawled toward a plastic curtain. As quietly as he could, he lifted it so he could slither underneath. Breathing hard, he scrambled against the wall, clutching his knees.

Alejandro, shaking and sweating, crawled on all fours toward the end of the aisle.

He made it to the door and checked over his shoulder to make sure the coast was clear. He reached for the handle and pulled. The clank of the metal latch echoed through the building. Alejandro automatically froze. He heard talking from the other end of the building and took the opportunity to slip through the door under cover of the noise. He quietly closed it and scrambled around the corner of the building. He stood and inched his way back to the corner. Wiping the sweat out of his eyes, he checked left and right looking for danger. Seeing none, he ran, hunched over, darting from display to display until he was near the front gate.

Shit! He spotted a man leaning on a gate post.

He crouched down, trying to think of a way out. He was stuck. He scooted back and hid among the pots of bushes near the main building. Alejandro waited. Nothing happened.

The man at the gate chain-smoked and occasionally spoke into a walkie-talkie. He stubbed out a cigarette and suddenly headed in Alejandro's direction.

Alejandro panicked and began hyperventilating. He was about to bolt, but calmed himself in time. He made himself as small as possible and listened for the man's footsteps. The sound of the man's feet came nearer. Alejandro began to pray. The man walked within a couple of feet of where Alejandro lay in a ball. Alejandro watched the man stop next to the building and begin to urinate.

"This might be your only chance, Montoya," he muttered. He took a deep breath, half stood, and picked his way out of the bushes, his eyes never leaving the guy by the building. He took a deep breath and held it. He tip-toed past the gate post, took off at a dead run toward the main road. His legs pistoned beneath him as he flew toward his truck.

He thought he heard someone yell "Hey you!" in the distance, but it could have been his imagination.

"Don't look back, just run for the truck," he chanted over and over, speeding down the drive. He tore around the corner post and sprinted toward the truck. He could barely breathe by the time he got to it.

He jumped in the truck turned the key in frantic haste, and the engine roared to life. He slammed the truck into drive. Sod flew out from behind the dual wheels as he tromped on the accelerator. He had no idea where he was going, nor did he care.

His only thought was to get far, far away. He stopped only to relieve himself (finally!) as he zigzagged cross country. He came across a sign that said Interstate 43– Milwaukee/Beloit. He chose to go north.

"Milwaukee it is. I could use a beer anyway," he said to the truck. Nearing the city, he saw signs for the airport and had another idea. He took 894 East and found Mitchell Field. He pulled into long term parking and disconnected the horse trailer. He drove back out the exit and got back on the expressway south. He picked up a map at a gas station and found White Bass Lake. Sitting in the truck, munching on a breakfast burrito, he mapped out the best way back.

"What the hell," I'm certainly not going back to Mexico. I guess my questions about Martinez knowing about it are answered. That was why he would not return my calls." Speaking of cell phones, he pulled his out and made a call to Donny Ray. He left a message.

"Donny Ray? Alejandro Montoya. Check for drugs. Illegal drugs." He flipped his phone closed and plugged it into the cigarette lighter to charge.

He crumpled the wrappers from his breakfast and stuffed them into the bag. Throwing the map on the passenger's seat, he pulled back onto the Interstate before he could change his mind.

"What was the name of the sheriff down there? J.R.? R.J.? J.J? That's right, J.J." The last name? Weasel? No, that's what the copper in Illinois called him. Copper…his name was a color! He went through the entire rainbow and still could not remember the last name.

He saw the exit for White Bass Lake and had a moment of weakness. He almost drove past, but came to his senses at the last second. He heard someone lay on the horn when he cut them off trying to make the ramp. Gravel flew when he hit the shoulder and then righted the truck. He skidded to a stop and dropped his head on the wheel. He took a deep breath. Confirming his resolve, he turned right and headed toward White Bass Lake.

17

Alejandro drove into the pretty little town of White Bass Lake a little after six in the morning. He was sweaty and dusty from the previous evening's nightmare, and couldn't find a motel closer than the Interstate. He checked into a bed and breakfast on the outskirts of town. Fresh from the shower, he went back out the door.

He set out looking for the police department, and after going a couple of blocks, came to what was obviously the local hangout. There were more cars in the parking lot of the local diner than there were on the streets, so Alejandro pulled in and parked. He hoped the people in the diner were friendlier than the Midwesterners he had met thus far.

The bell on the door tinkled as he stepped into the diner. The talk around him stopped: *Here I go again.* He looked at the floor as he walked to the counter and sat. The crowd noise resumed.

A hand slapped his shoulder. Alejandro jumped out of his skin and yelped.

"¡*Hola amigo,*" Sal shouted in his ear. "Welcome to White Bass Lake! You look like a Bear fan. You don't like those Packers, do you?"

About a third of the crowd yelled "Go Bears!" and the rest booed.

Swallowing his heart, Alejandro looked up A small Latino man looked him in the eye, even though Alejandro was sitting and the man was standing. The man grabbed his hand and pumped it, grinning like they were long lost brothers. He continued to shake Alejandro's hand, waited for him to respond.

"Uh, I'm Alejandro Montoya. It's very nice to meet a friendly face."

"Sal Garcia." He nodded toward the crowded diner now hotly debating football, and chuckled. "I like to get them going in the morning. Hey, just a warning: watch out for her."

He winked and pointed to the waitress closing in on Alejandro. "I fired her this morning, but she won't go away." He smiled as he turned back toward the grill, whistling.

Donna stopped by Alejandro's right shoulder and slammed down a coffee cup in front of him. She poured him a cup even though he hadn't asked for one. Of average height, she was big busted and showed off her 'Sal's Diner' tee shirt to its best advantage. Hair in a pony tail, she had a work-worn face, but her lovely brown eyes danced with merriment.

"He fired me twice last week, too. Don't believe nothing that guy tells you. He lies, especially about who really runs this place. We tried to sell him on eBay, but no one would make a bid!" Laughing heartily at her own joke, she patted Alejandro on the shoulder and moved on.

Alejandro was bowled over by the warm welcome and the hum of friendly conversation from the people around him. He listened to Donna teasing and joking her way through construction workers and families, seniors and vacationers. He smiled, relaxing for the first time in days. *Now this is more of what I expected when I came up here.*

Amy came up to him from behind the counter and asked what he wanted to eat. Guessing most people didn't use a menu, Alejandro ordered bacon and scrambled eggs. He watched in fascination as Sal's hands flew across the grill. Donna refilled his coffee and gestured to Sal. "Showoff," she said out of the corner of her mouth.

Sal was still grinning when he turned from the grill and slid the steaming plate in front of Alejandro. "So what brings you to White Bass Lake, my friend. The fishing? I could tell you where the best places to fish are. I once caught a 14-inch walleye right off my pier over there." He gestured in the general vicinity of the lake.

"He lies about fish too," floated up from the crowded diner.

Alejandro smiled and leaned forward. "To tell you the truth, I haven't been fishing in quite a while. I'm originally from Arizona. I'm just passing through on this trip. I told a friend I would pass a message on to the sheriff for him when I stopped here. Could you tell me where to find him?"

Sal looked over his shoulder at the clock. It was 7:40.

"J.J. usually stops in around eight unless he gets a call. Lately the bad guys have been keeping him pretty busy, so if he doesn't come in, I'll give you directions to the office."

Alejandro also looked at the clock. "Well, if you don't mind, I'll have another cup of coffee and wait."

"Be my guest, amigo. Stay as long as you like." Sal whistled the Chicago Bears *Fight Song* as he began the next order.

Alejandro sipped his coffee and listened to the friendly banter between Sal and Donna. Snippets of conversation reached him as the ebb and flow of people talking swirled around him. He suddenly sat up when he heard the name 'Carole', and then 'Graff'. He tried to concentrate on the voices behind him.

"...don't know what Buzz...Carole's body...coroner"

Oh my God. Body? Does that mean she is dead? Alejandro leaned in the direction of the conversation.

"...Not a teacher. He's...BI...out there."

"BI out there." What did that mean? That the FBI was involved, or did he hear that in a different conversation?

Perhaps if he turned in his chair, he could see who was talking. He turned on his stool, sipping his coffee.

Sitting near him were two little old ladies having coffee and dessert.

"No, Joy, I'll get the check. I know you're tapped out. When Carole Graff up and died, she took the Broussard Family Fortune with her."

"Who knows if I'll need that missing money some day?"

Alejandro froze. Did Carole Graff steal money too? Maybe he should look in that bubble envelope before he turned it over to the sheriff. He listened some more.

"That money-grabbing hussy. How dare she make off with your life savings?"

"Gerry Miller, there is no need for sarcasm. If Carole had settled her debts in a timely manner, she wouldn't have died owing everyone money!"

"Joy, for the last time, she owed you a couple bucks for some cantaloupe, which, may I remind you, you *volunteered* to buy! It was not like Carole knew she was going to croak. She was murdered."

Ohhh, shit–murdered. Alejandro turned back toward the counter and tried to think. Now what was he to do? Should he go to the sheriff or not? Would they think he killed that lady and arrest him? He had to think. Alejandro reached into his pocket to shove some bills on the counter, but was saved from having to make the decision to contact the sheriff when Sal yelled across the diner.

"Morning, J.J. There's someone here wants to talk to you."

Alejandro sank back onto his stool as Sheriff Green walked through the now silent diner to the counter. J.J. sat on the stool next to Alejandro and winked at Amy when a full coffee cup appeared at his elbow.

He held out his hand to Alejandro, the crow's feet at the corners of his eyes crinkling as he smiled. His open and friendly demeanor and casual greeting did much to put Alejandro at ease.

"J.J. Green. How'r ya doin'?"

"Alejandro Montoya. I'm fine, thank you."

"New Mexico?"

"Close. Arizona."

J.J. sighed. "Story of my life. Close but no cigar. I'm usually pretty good at accents, though. So, Alejandro Montoya, what brings you to our little burg?"

"Well, first, I am to bring you greetings from two police officers I met from Mundelein in Illinois."

"Ha! That would be Olsen and Ballard. I can imagine what kind of message those two sent. We all went through the academy together in Champaign a lifetime ago. Don't tell me; fish fry and doughnuts?" Alejandro nodded his head. "Figures, they have no imagination. So where did you run into those two flatfoots?"

"Well, Sheriff Green, to tell you that is to tell you my whole story. I believe you would not want it told in front of half the town." He leaned forward and lowered his voice. "I think it has to do with Mrs. Carole Graff."

J.J. eyed him for a full 15 seconds, then stood. "If you're ready then, let's go back to the office and we'll talk." Amy handed J.J. a Styrofoam container. J.J. sighed happily.

"Amy, you are a gift from God."

She giggled, "That's what I keep telling Sal. Maybe you should tell him too!"

"Hey, Sal! You got a keeper here," J.J. yelled across the diner as he paid for his breakfast.

Sal looked up and grinned. "Don't I know it! See you J.J.. Come again, Alejandro. Go Bears!"

"GO BEARS," half the diner responded as they exited.

Alejandro was still shaking his head in wonder over his experience in the little diner when he reached his truck. By mutual consent, Alejandro followed J.J. to his office. Once there, he retrieved the bubble wrap envelope and his courage, and walked into J.J.'s office.

J.J. was on the phone, but signaled for Alejandro to have a seat. Alejandro looked around the spartan office and heard J.J. say, "Okay, Buzz, we'll see you in a minute."

Alejandro lifted his brows in question. "Buzz?"

"Buzz Miller, do you know her?"

"I heard a lady by the name of Gerry argue with her friend in the diner and the name Buzz was mentioned in conjunction with Carole Graff. Listening to those ladies is how I came to think Carole Graff might be dead. Is she?"

J.J. looked at the younger man across from him. He sat on the edge of his chair, clutching an envelope in his hand. His wide eyes and frightened demeanor told J.J. there were no nefarious reasons for his questions. If Alejandro Montoya was involved in this mess, it was on the periphery or as a pawn; he'd stake his job on it.

"Okay, Alejandro, let's take this from the top. Before we get further into this, I need to tell you that I am going to record our interview. This is a criminal investigation, and I need to keep my facts straight." He picked up the small recorder and spoke into it.

"November Four, Two Thousand Seven, Nine Eleven A.M. James J. Green, Sheriff. In regard to the homicide investigation of Carol Graff, interview with Montoya, Alejandro, Male, Hispanic D.O.B..." He looked at Alejandro.

"Eleven, Eleven, Seventy Four."

J.J. continued. "November 11, 1974. Mr. Montoya, what is your stake in this? How did you become acquainted with Carole Graff?"

Alejandro looked at the envelope in his hand and slowly pushed it across the desk toward J.J. He picked it up and looked at the address. He raised an eyebrow and gave Alejandro an assessing look.

"You see, Sheriff Green, I am a horse trainer for Eduardo Martinez from the Mexican state of Coahuila. I brought five mares up from Mexico to the Appaloosa World Championships in Dallas/Fort Worth last Tuesday."

Alejandro had recounted his story from the time they left the ranchero until the point where he unloaded the mares and Dr. Huerta disappeared, when there was a knock on the door.

Before J.J. could say, "Come in," a huge ginning bear bounded through the door, straight to J.J.'s lap, followed by an ugly little bulldog, a middle aged woman with glasses and flyaway graying hair (that would be me), another, younger woman, pretty, dark blonde and looking angry, a man about the same age, nice suit, looked wealthy, wearing a tense expression, and the little old lady named Gerry he'd seen] in the diner.

* * *

J.J. flipped off the recorder and calmly said, "Hey, Buzz, what's with the circus?"

I grinned. "Circus? You got that right. Complete with dancing bears," I pointed to Wes, who was spinning and grinning, "and fire breathers!" I pointed to Mag, who was still pissed.

Mom piped up, "Don't forget the clowns." She laughed as she pointed to the three deputies who poked their heads through the door. Moe, Larry, and Curly gave her injured looks and backed out, closing the door again. With everyone talking at once, it was hard to hear anyone.

J.J. yelled his favorite line from *Cool Hand Luke*. "What we have here, Buzz, is a failure to communicate!" He straightened from his desk and tried to look stern and official.

"Buzz, I asked you to come down here because you're heading up this investigation. What I didn't ask for, no offense Miz Miller, was your mom, and your sister. Dr. Connor...I assume you are here at Buzz's request, though I'll be damned if I know why."

He held his hands out, palms down. "Now I don't want anyone taking offense, but–" Everyone promptly began talking at once. Alejandro looked scared. Wesley walked up and shook doggy slime on him. Alejandro looked as if he was waiting for us to come to blows, or for the sheriff to start shooting. The other deputies should have heard the noise and come barreling in, but they wisely stayed away.

Hands flying, dogs barking, people shouting to be heard over the others. Alejandro looked overwhelmed and ready to bolt out the door. I figured a little order was needed. I put my index fingers to my lips and let out an ear-splitting whistle, compliments of one of my dad's important childhood lessons.

"Yo, everyone–knock it off!"

Even the dogs shut up.

"J.J., to answer your questions, Mag is working on the case with me and she should be in on everything. Turns out our friend Dr. Connor isn't *just* a plant biologist at the university. His day job is working for the FBI." Jaws dropped, and heads turned in his direction.

"Mom saw us when she and Joy came out of the diner and followed us over. She wouldn't take no for an answer, so I thought maybe you could threaten her with obstruction, disorderly conduct, or something. Wes and Hilary are just a bonus."

Wesley licked J.J.'s hand and placed his head on his arm, gazing up adoringly at him. J.J. sighed, rubbing his ears.

"If you will all excuse me for a moment?" He eyeballed Ian and said, "You, Mr. FBI-Let's-Not-Tell-the-Local-Sheriff-I'm-in-Town, follow me.

"You," pointing to Alejandro, "Stay put. You," pointing at Mom, "Go home or I'll call Bill to come get you."

He jerked a thumb in my direction. "Buzz, you're with me. Mag, meet Alejandro. Alejandro, meet Mag. Stay here– both of you."

With that he stomped out of the room. Clenching his jaw, Ian followed. I shrugged my shoulders at Mag and in sign language said, 'later'. All that angry testosterone was pretty intimidating and I trailed far behind both of them.

18

J.J. had a full head of steam going. He bulldozed his way past dispatch down the hall to the break room. One look cleared everyone out, and J.J. slammed the door. He calmly crossed the room and poured himself a cup of coffee. He plunked himself down in a plastic chair, put his feet up on the table, and crossed his arms over his belly. He narrowed his eyes and sent an evil look toward Ian.

"So who are you really and what are you doing down here?"

Ian strolled over to the coffee pot and picked up a Styrofoam cup. He filled it and turned, hoisting himself up onto the counter. He set the coffee down next to him and leaned forward, folding his hands between his legs. I stood there looking stupid.

"J.J.," I began. He immediately held up his hand.

"Buzz, if you please, first things first. Let me get this out of the way, and don't start making excuses. I'll deal with *you* next."

I slid into a chair like a whipped pup and waited for Ian to start.

"Sheriff Green, I'm Ian Connor. I am a forensic botanist for the FBI, Milwaukee Field Office. I do occasional work for the State Crime Lab and for the university. A friend of mine over at the crime lab called me to ask for help, but since this might be connected to another case the FBI is involved in, I had orders to remain undercover until I found out who the players were down here, and if this case could possibly be connected to the other."

J.J. looked at him for a long moment. "Why didn't you use our local lab at the morgue if you needed a lab? Why run off with the evidence to Keokuk or wherever you took it?"

"I had to use the Milwaukee labs because they had the software I needed. I have a couple of findings I know you'll be interested in hearing about.

"Sheriff Green, I am not one of those asshole Fed guys who comes onto a scene and throws his weight around. I want to–no, I *need*–to work with you and your people on this. We're meeting at Mag's house for an update after we're through here."

J.J gave me an 'I don't get it' look, so I jumped into the conversation.

"Yeah, J.J. We're grilling out and we have everything from salads to desserts. We can all get fat and solve a crime together."

J.J. winced. "As long as your mother made the brownies and Mag didn't cook at all." Ian held his stomach and made gakking noises.

"It's Chez Buzz all the way–well, Wesley helped a little, but you can hardly tell."

J.J. straightened up and headed for the door. "Okay. I'm in. Right now let's go see if your sister performed her *Mag*-ic on our star witness, or if she drove him over the edge." He turned to me and grabbed the front of my shirt. He jerked me forward and got in my face. "Don't think I've forgotten about your stunt from the other night. We still have a date to talk about it. I'll call you–*then* I'll yell at you." He let me go and stalked away.

I saluted him with my middle finger. "O-Tay Mr. Sherwiff. I'll be waiting by the phone until you call. Pant, pant."

"I heard that, Smartass," he said, as he barreled into his

office and slammed the door.

We followed him in, Mom was gone, and Mag had already begun the interview. She stopped Alejandro and turned off the recorder. She looked up and smiled.

"Great timing, folks. Alejandro needs a bathroom break and I'm thirsty. Grab a seat and we'll get right back at it."

She gestured to J.J.'s office as she whisked out the door like she'd been interviewing subjects all her life. J.J. turned to me and pointed at the door.

"Okay, who is that, and what has she done with your sister?"

I was still staring after Mag, somewhat bewildered. "I don't know, J.J., but something sure is different. Hey, Ian, didn't we lose the old Mag somewhere back at the drug lab?"

J.J. loomed over me. "Are you telling me that Mag was at the Graff's place with you? Are you out of your frigging mind? She could have been killed, Buzz; then where would you be?"

He whirled on Ian. "And you! You're supposed to be a professional! Where in that fancy FBI handbook does it say it's okay to take a Biology teacher on a shootout with some very bad men?" He threw up his hands and stalked toward his desk. He collapsed in his chair and rubbed his hand back and forth across his brow. "Wait. Hold on a minute. We'll deal with this later. I need Montoya's story right now."

He glared at me. "I'll just add this to my list of grievances for tomorrow's pow-wow."

He crossed his arms and spun his chair so he faced the window. One could almost see the green smoke coming out of his ears. Ian stood and made as if he were going to confront him. I grabbed his arm, shook my head and mouthed, 'later'. We all turned at the sound of the door knob rattling.

Mag reentered the room, oblivious to the tirade that had just occurred. Alejandro followed behind her, and took his seat. Mag picked up the recorder, hesitated. She looked at the recorder and then held it out to J.J. "I'm sorry, J.J. I didn't want to butt in, but Alejandro wanted to tell his story. I thought I would record it so he didn't have to repeat it again."

J.J. held up his hands. "No, Mag, that's just fine. You started, you finish. You talk Alejandro through it and we'll see if I have to have him explain further. I'll be right here if you get stuck."

Mag shrugged her shoulders and grinned sheepishly. She turned on the recorder and set it on the table near Alejandro. She took a deep breath.

"Mr. Montoya, your last statement before we took a break was," she consulted the paper in front of her, 'And then I ran out of the tack room and saw blood all over the stall'.

Alejandro looked at her with tears in his eyes. She put a calming hand on his arm and said, "Take your time, Alejandro. This must be very painful for you."

He nodded and drew in a shaky breath. He wiped his eyes with the back of his hand.

"Yes, I ran out of the tack room and saw my Princesa thrashing in the stall, screaming in agony."

He continued his grisly tale. For the next two hours, we sat transfixed by the gruesome and shocking events that eventually led him to Sal's diner and the meeting with J.J. His voice died with the last of his narrative. His look touched each of us as the silence in the room lingered.

Ian was the first to comment. "Wow. Drugs inside the mares. Does that not beat all?"

I was beside myself. "Those rotten, no good rat-bastards! Can you imagine what would happen to those poor horses if one of those bricks came open...OH MY GOD!"

They all stared at me. One by one it hit each of them. Alejandro sat for a second with a stricken look on his face. He jumped up out of his chair and shouted as he streaked toward the door, "I need my cell phone! Oh my God! I have to call Texas!" He ran to his truck and ripped the cell phone out of its charger. He frantically searched his address book and punched Donny Ray's number. He reached the voice mailbox, and near hysteria, left a message. "Donny Ray, Montoya here. Check that sample for drugs. Illegal drugs! I know that is what killed the mare, and that is why they stole the body before you could autopsy! Call me as soon as you can, and be careful. If they find out you know, I think they will come for you." He also read J.J.'s number off the business card he had taken from the lobby. He flipped the phone shut and slumped against the truck door.

J.J. put an arm around his shoulders and steered him back to his office. He sat silently in the chair and stared straight ahead. We were all silent, trying to put it all into perspective.

J.J.'s voice was like cannon fire in the stillness of the room. "Well, that about wraps it up for now, folks. It's getting on toward afternoon and we should call it quits for today. Alejandro, what kind of plans did you have for the next few days?"

Alejandro started and looked thoughtful. "Actually, I was hoping to stay around a while. I had thoughts of looking for a new job if I liked it here, and I do. I certainly cannot go home."

J.J. nodded and picked up the phone. He asked Alejandro, "You're staying over at Journey's End Bed and Breakfast, right?" At Alejandro's nod, J.J. finished dialing.

"Hi, Cheryl? Yeah, it's J.J. Listen, One of your guests is staying on for a few more days. Send his bill for the week to the Sheriff's Department, okay? Yeah, he's working with me on something through the end of the week. Uh-huh, Montoya, Alejan...Yep, you got it, and thanks, Cheryl. Talk to you later–what?" He turned his back to us and spoke in a quiet voice. "Oh, uh, yeah, I guess so. Saturday? I'll see if I can make it, uh, okay, you too. Bye now."

He hung up the phone and Alejandro spoke right away. "Sheriff Green, you don't have to pay my bills. I have money and credit cards. I'm okay–really."

J.J. interrupted him. "Look, as long as you're here working with me, I'll pick up the tab on the room. We still have a lot of work to do on this. Number One priority is to try to get ahold of that boss of yours–Martinez. Next, we retrieve the horse trailer from the airport. We can probably park it out at Miller's farm." He grinned at me, "That will give your mom something else to lord over her friends."

Mag jumped on her cell phone and called Mom. She nodded and waved that it was okay to J.J., and continued talking.

J.J. pressed the intercom on his desk. "Edie? Find Tom, Dick, and Harry. Get them in here pronto."

"Right away, Sheriff Green," came the disembodied voice of Edie, the dispatcher.

Ian raised a brow and looked at Mag and me. I whispered, "You know, the guys we call Moe, Larry, and Curly. Remember, at my place? I don't know their real names. Everyone calls them something different."

"Oh, uh, right. I wonder what J.J. wants with those guys?" Ian whispered out of the corner of his mouth. "Oh, never mind." Speaking louder, he said, "Hey, I need to call this latest development into Milwaukee. I don't want to call Texas until I know who the good guys are in this play. J.J., what do you think? I'll leave it your decision, but I have to let my superiors in on this."

J.J. scratched his head. "I guess you have a point. The only guy we can trust down there right now is a country veterinarian. We need to make sure he's protected, so we gotta trust somebody down there. I'll work on it."

Just then, the three deputies stumbled through the door. "There you are." J.J. said. "There's a change of assignments this afternoon. You," he pointed at Moe, "go with Montoya up to Mitchell field. He has a horse trailer parked in long term. Pay the bill, then take the trailer over to Miller's, and park it behind the barn out of the way.

"You," pointing to Curly, "you get the evidence collection kit and meet me back here in 20 minutes.

"And you" pointing to Larry, "are on patrol. Go fetch Squad Two and gas it up. I'll be at Graff's if you need backup."

He turned to me and his phone rang. He flipped it open. "Sheriff Green. Yes? He did? Thank you, I'll be right down." He slapped the phone closed and narrowed his eyes in our direction. "Change of plans, everyone. That was the hospital. Rob is coming around and I need to be there when he wakes up. I'll have to take a rain check on Chez Buzz." He poked me in the chest. "But you and I are going to talk. Tomorrow. Got it?"

I rubbed my sternum. "Uh, yeah, got it, Chief."

J.J. turned once again to Curly. "Forget the evidence kit for now. I need you at the hospital. They're moving Rob out of ICU, and I am going to put you on the door. I want you to stand watch and not let *anyone* in that room. Questions? Good. Let's get at it." He chucked my chin as he swept past. We all breathed a little easier.

Ian broke the silence. "Well, why don't we get going? I want to try to beat rush hour traffic." He consulted his

166

watch. "It doesn't look like I'm going to at this point, but I need to get on the road. Is that okay with you and Mag?"

We nodded like a couple of dumb sheep and followed him out the door.

19

The drive back to Mag's was quick and uneventful. Over coffee, we compiled the notes and transferred them to the whiteboard. I uploaded the pictures onto Mag's computer and made prints to add to our report on the evening's events.

I also tried to come up with a believable story to tell J.J. There seemed to be no good way to tell him we planned and executed an illegal break-in, killed two guys, injured a third, and ran off before the cops could question us. I expected warrants would be issued for us by morning.

Nothing seemed to bother Ian as he went through the backpacks and retrieved all the materials we took from the greenhouses. We sat on the living room floor and separated each item by type.

Mag dug in her bag and produced a Ziploc which held a small metal tin with some sort of gook in it. Ian grabbed it from her. "Mag, is this what I think it is?"

She stuck her nose in the air. "If you think I grabbed it from the drug room, you'd be right! I scraped a couple more things too. In all the chaos, I didn't think anyone would miss them."

Ian looked perplexed. "Scraped?"

Mag laughed. "Lifted, took, absconded with, stole, pinched, copped, pilfered, filched, appropriated. What term do you prefer?"

Ian sighed. "I *got* it. Scraped. Geez, leave it to the school teacher. Here–let me have them."

I sighed. Better add stealing evidence and obstruction to our crimes. Ian was elated. He looked like a kid with his first Tonka truck. He grabbed the bags from Mag and took off for the kitchen. He poked and prodded, held them up to the light and shook them up. He ripped open his backpack and pulled out a hygiene travel bag. I was about to make a smart comment when he unzipped it and pulled out several glass bottles and a few vials. He set everything out on the breakfast bar.

I mentally took a step back.

"Ian, do you carry drug testing kits around with you?"

He didn't say a word but grinned like Wesley with a T-bone, held up a little test tube and twiddled it at us. He laid out the bottles in order and like a mad scientist, began testing. So totally absorbed in his task was he that he never heard Mag and me discuss tomorrow's strategy while we put out the leftovers. He suddenly looked up from the table and held up a vial.

"Eureka!"

Mag and I both jumped. Mag took the vial (which had turned blue) from him, looked at it and shoved it back at him. "Eureka? Eureka what? So you were able to confirm that I snagged drugs from a drug lab. Whoopee, Ian. Wesley could have told us that. How is this significant to Carole and the investigation? Do you think she was murdered with drugs or because of them?"

Ian stuffed all his testing paraphernalia back in the travel bag. "Even not knowing her, I would guess because of." He closed up the plastic bags and labeled them. Mag brought him a box and he packed everything away carefully. He talked while he worked.

"It might pertain and it might not. Either way I have got to get this stuff to a lab where I can work on it. I don't want to get into it right now, but this may be related to more than just the garden center murder.

"I'll see if I can get this connected up to a drug

trafficking route we've been working on. I can also find out if they are dealing straight cocaine and heroin, or if this lab was making designer drugs. The guys at the M. B. Lab can find out every ingredient in this stuff. It's really quite amazing."

He must have interpreted our perplexed expressions correctly. He might as well have been speaking in a foreign language. He wrote furiously on a notepad.

"I'm leaving you the office number, my work cell, and my personal cell numbers. If anything happens while I'm gone, call me. I'm also leaving my mother's number in case I get that far. I called her around 1:30 this morning and told her I wasn't coming in. I'll be back as soon as I can, probably as early as tomorrow night. The office can call me, or fax the results here.

"I'm sure J.J. will help us out with that."

I stopped listening after he told us he called his mother. "You called your mom at 1:30 in the morning? Mine would have been yelling for 911!"

"Yeah, along about now, at daybreak she would have started worrying." He zipped his bag shut and looked from Mag to me. He rubbed his hands together and smiled. "Now all I need is a ride back to my car and I'm off."

I got up and dumped my coffee cup in the sink. "I got you covered. I have to go home anyway and it's on the way. Wes, Hill, let's go." The dogs clambered out the front door. I turned to Mag.

"Oh, and Mag? You're hired again. Nice work."

"Thanks, Buzz. Some vacation, huh?"

"Yeah, some vacation. See ya in the morning."

"Night, Buzz."

"Night, Maggot."

By the time I got the dogs settled, Ian was ready to go.

"I appreciate what you guys did tonight," he said.

"You're good, Buzz. You can be my partner any time."

"Thanks, Ian." I rubbed my hip. "I'll sure be a hurting unit tomorrow! I'm really worried about Mag, though. She flew by the seat of her pants tonight and got lucky. I don't want her to start getting all cocky and thinking it goes down this easy all the time. I don't want her hurt or, Heaven forbid, killed."

Ian chuckled. "I don't think she's going to run off and join the police force or anything, Buzz, so don't worry. I'll see what the lab boys can find out and I'll give you a call later on today."

"It's a deal, partner." I was about to back out of the driveway when Mag yanked the back door open. I slammed on the brakes and the dogs and Ian flew forward.

"What the hell?"

Mag grinned and held up a Thermos. "I'm going to Milwaukee. Uh, Ian might fall asleep and needs someone to keep him awake. I can also help him with the plants. I can be a very useful mammal when I want to be."

I looked at Ian, who was looking at Mag. I noticed both wore big sloppy grins on their faces. I sighed.

"Get in, Mag." She flew through the door. She nudged Wesley over, but he just grunted and pushed back. Mag happily rode across town sandwiched against the car door by a big hairy butt.

I pulled into the morgue parking lot. Ian opened the rear door and Mag exploded out into the parking lot–ass over tea kettle.

Wesley's butt hung out of the car, his fluffy tail waving slowly back and forth. We got everything transferred to the Beemer. Ian turned and stuck out his hand. I shook it. He said, "Later, Buzz. Get some sleep."

"You too, Plant Boy. Be careful driving."

Ian laughed. "Thanks, Buzz. Mag brought along some

of that truck driver coffee she made. Milwaukee's only a 40 minute drive, but I'll probably be good until noon." He checked his watch. "Damn, got to get going, rush hour is coming on fast." They jumped in the Beemer, both waving as he took off down the empty street.

I walked back to my car. Wes had jumped into the driver's seat and was grinning and panting like he was driving home. I wedged my butt in next to his and heaved him over far enough to reach the ignition. I rubbed his ears and sighed. He let out a big doggy sigh and flopped down. Tail waving, he leaned into my hand and grinned.

"Come on, kids, let's go home." Even Hilary grinned at that.

20

Ian sped toward Milwaukee thinking of the connections to a case the FBI had been working on for almost a year. If he could connect the seeds to the ones Jeff Fuller from the Molecular Biology Lab had traced from Mexico across the southern states, they could work on how the drugs jumped from the south, to the northern Midwest. There was no trail leading north, yet the drugs had turned up in Chicago and Milwaukee, then Portage, La Crosse, and Minneapolis, on up through Duluth into Canada.

Mag stretched and yawned loudly. "You're very quiet Ian. Tell me what you're thinking."

He glanced at her. "If these seeds and the cocaine connect up to another case we're working on, we'll have a new connection on where the drugs are going. We need to find out how the heck the drugs jumped from the south to the north, without traces of them in between. Right now, they're traced through Texas, Mobile, Atlanta, Charlotte, Philly, Buffalo, and into Canada, but nothing up this way. The Mexico connection is why I think they might be linked. I just can't figure out how to connect the dots in between."

"Ian, didn't Alejandro talk about the men pulling the bricks out of the horses? Wouldn't that make the connection?"

"I guess in all the confusion I never gave it a thought. Holy Cow Mag, do you think they could transport that much cocaine that way?"

"I suppose they could if they sent it pure and cut it up here."

He blew out a breath. "Wow. At any rate, we'll take the

poppy plants we confiscated to the Molecular Biology boys. They can put them through what's called *amplified fragment length polymorphism,* or AFLP. AFLP is based on polymerase chain reaction, or PCR, just like the RAPD test I explained to you and Buzz, but it's more sensitive than RAPD and can tell us even more."

Knowing Mag would follow, he explained. "Jeff Fuller, the head of MB, took cuttings from some marijuana plants we confiscated during a bust. Using the polymorphic markers in the plant DNA, he was able to find patterns of marijuana fields cloned off the mother plants.

"We mapped the plantings, and you could see the sweep of the cloned plants across the western states. Through the seeds, he was able to link specific shipments of marijuana to weed the DEA recovered off of a suspect during a bust in a different part of the country. This gave us another point where the drugs entered the country.

"Then the marijuana chaff recovered from a non-related building in yet another area, linked the rest of the operation to the shipment, and was followed back to the original grower in Central America. It was the biggest coup we've ever made, and hopefully the beginning of the end of the drug cartels."

Mag stared at him, riveted to his story. "Holy cow! I had no idea that you could trace a plant back to the source like that. So that's what you'll be doing with the drugs we have. How cool is that!"

She shifted closer to Ian and took in a shaky breath. "Ian, do you have any idea how, uh, stimulating it is to listen when someone speaks with so much passion about something?"

Ian gulped and stared at her. The car began to drift toward the right shoulder. Ian jerked the car back into the lane and stared out the windshield. "Uh, Mag, do you mean stimulate as in inspiring, or, uh, stimulate as in uh....arousing?"

She unbuckled her seatbelt and scooted over so her breast pressed against his arm. She ran a finger along the top of his ear, her moist breath caressing his neck. "Let's just say that if we weren't in big city traffic right now," she ran her other hand up his thigh and settled it between his legs, "I would be jumping on you like Japanese beetles on your prize dahlias, Plant Boy."

She stuck her tongue in his ear and ran her hand over his zipper. She wiggled her fingers and her eyes grew big. "Holy Gigantus Peeniscus! I can't ever again call you Plant *Boy* with a straight face! Bad Boy maybe..."

Ian turned pink. "Come on, Mag, knock it off. It's no big deal."

She continued to tease him. "No big deal? Why the heck do you bother carrying a gun? You could just beat them to death with that thing! Talk about your Lethal Weapons..."

Ian squirmed and turned dark red. "Mag, I mean it! We're in traffic, now stop. And don't poke fun at him...uh, at it...at me. Oh, shit, I don't know what to call him!"

Mag flashed him a brilliant smile and continued to play. "Just say, 'Happy Birthday, Mag!'"

Ian gritted his teeth and gripped the wheel with both hands. "Mag, we have an audience. I'm awake, so let's talk about something else, okay?" He glanced out the window at smiling faces.

"And, would you please uh, move your hand while you're at it?"

Mag kept stroking and kissing Ian's neck. She began singing softly in his ear, "Bad boy, bad boy, whatcha gonna do when I come for you bad boy, bad boy?"

Ian sucked in a breath. "If you don't knock it off,

Missy, I'm going to pull off this road and show you what this bad boy can do!"

Mag flopped back into her seat and sighed. "Killjoy! I was just keeping you awake like I'm supposed to. Who said I couldn't enjoy myself while I do my job?"

Ian narrowed his eyes at her, and she rolled her eyes back at him. She pouted and looked out the window. Staring back at her was a truck driver grinning from ear-to-ear and giving her the thumbs up. She realized he had been watching them while traffic was slow. She blushed and slowly slid down in her seat. Another truck drove past them and blew the air horn. Ian chuckled at Mag's mortification. Mag moaned and pulled a jacket over her head. Horns blared, truckers waved, and people whistled as they passed Ian's car. Humiliated, Mag slid a glance at Ian. He was laughing silently, his shoulders twitching.

Mag huffed and threw the jacket in the back seat. "What the heck was that all about, I wonder? And what is so funny?"

Ian laughed out loud, "CBs, Mag. Everyone within a five mile radius probably knows what was going on in here."

Mag stuck her nose in the air and smoothed her hair. "How immature. Why didn't they just take videos while they were at it?"

Ian sobered and signaled for an exit ramp. "Actually, sweetheart, I did see someone with a cell phone recording as they passed us back about three miles. Let's just hope we're not the stars of some cheesy joke that ends up in your mother's email."

Mag grabbed the dash and stared wide-eyed out the windshield while she absorbed the impact of what Ian just said. "Oh, my God. Ian, you don't really think…"

He stopped for a red light and patted her knee. "No,

Maggie, I don't. Seriously, though, I want you to know that when we do make love, it's going to be just you and me in a big old bed and not half of Milwaukee in a BMW during rush hour. Does that sound okay to you?"

She covered his hand with her own and sighed softly. "Perfect, Ian, just perfect."

21

Ian kissed the end of her nose and drove to his condo. Mag walked through the front door and was immediately struck dumb. There was vegetation everywhere. The condo was a corner unit and had both a southern and western exposure. He had an atrium of sorts in the corner and made full use of all that sun. Bird sounds chirped in the background. Tiny frogs sat on lily pads, and koi undulated slowly across the small pond. A waterfall trickled among the flora and fauna, and a huge bamboo ceiling fan turned slowly, the giant paddles creating a soft breeze which rustled through the leaves. "Wow, Ian, that really sounds authentic."

Ian held a finger to his lips, shushing her. Into the apartment, Ian raised his voice. "Anyone home?"

Immediately the Banana Palm said, in a high voice, "No one here but us chickens!" and then, "Cluck, cluck, cluck!"

Mag frowned. "I thought you said you lived alone. Who's the comedian?"

She started off toward the door. Ian grabbed her hand. "Wait. Watch this." He walked to the refrigerator and took out a mango. He sliced it in half, leaned on the breakfast bar, and made slurpy sounds. "*Mmmm*, chow time!"

The Banana Palm screeched and in a gravelly voice said, "Now wait just a cotton pickin' minute, you varmint!"

Mag watch wide-eyed as a huge Cockatoo flew out of the Banana Palm and skidded across the breakfast bar. He grabbed the mango and began munching. Ian stroked the bird and Mag watched in fascination as he ripped chunks out of the mango with his impressive beak.

Ian said, "Yum!"

"Yum, yum, yum," Bird squawked.

She backed into Ian, not wanting to lose a finger. "What's his name?" she whispered in awe.

"Kitty," he whispered back.

"KITTY, KITTY! HERE KITTY, KITTY, KITTY!" The bird screeched. *"HEEEEERE KITTY!"*

Mag stared at Ian. He shrugged. "That's all he would say when I first got him, so that's what I called him."

"HERE KITTY, KITTY, KITTY!" Kitty alternately tore into the mango and hollered for the non-existent cat.

Ian flinched. "But I don't call him that often. Most of the time I just call him Dumb Bird. Hey, Dumb Bird, don't talk with your mouth full."

"DUMB BIRD!"

Ian sighed. "Maggie, why don't you relax for a bit? I need to make some calls and get organized. The small bathroom is down the hall to the left, second door. The master bedroom is to the right. It has its own bathroom. You might like that one better. I'll be on the left behind 'Door Number One'. Just walk in when you feel like it."

He kissed her nose and picked up his laptop. He mumbled to himself and went into his office. She stood looking down the empty hallway. She glanced at Kitty, slurping away on what was left of the mango, then again at the empty hallway. She could hear Ian talking on the phone. Picking up her overnighter, she wandered down the hall.

She poked her head into the first bathroom and sighed. The walls were done in sand-washed burnt orange. Different species of cacti lined the many shelves. Interspersed were desert succulents and other arid climate plants. The walk-in shower was done in light beige, and accent splashes of blues, pinks, and reds made the room look like the desert at sunset.

She stood in the doorway and stared. Ian's words came back to her about liking the other bathroom better, but she didn't know how she possibly could. She said aloud, "You really think you know a guy..."

She wandered down the hall and stepped into Ian's bedroom. His personal space reflected a quiet glen. The massive four-poster looked as if it was made of fallen trees.

The design was asymmetrical, but the beauty of the natural hollows and ridges of the wood created by Mother Nature could never be duplicated by man. Mag ran her hand over the dark wood, which had been waxed to a beautiful luster. A green, beige, and chocolate comforter was a perfect compliment to the cream walls. Instead of curtains, she saw a high shelf set with ivies, vinca, and other trailing plants. A huge bamboo paddle fan delicately moved the air. The gentle breeze carried the exotic scent of flowers. Aside from the bed and a matching night table, no other furniture graced the room. Mag walked across the knotty pine floor. She peeked behind a door and found a walk-in closet the size of her living room.

She walked to the only other door in the room. She opened the door and understood what Ian meant by she 'might like this bathroom better'. Orchids of every color and size were scattered throughout the room. Flowering plants were on shelves, some hung in baskets, and others were planted in a natural environment in a raised bed. A large skylight loomed above a six-person Jacuzzi. The raised flower bed rimmed the wall side of the Jacuzzi. Tropical flowers she'd only seen in pictures gave off an intoxicating scent that made her feel light headed. "Oh my God. I don't know this guy at all. Or maybe I do."

Moving as if she were in a trance, Mag turned the jets on low and checked the heat. She lit the five pillar candles on a tray beside the faucets and dimmed the lights.

"Well, he did say relax. I hope he meant make myself at home, too. He'll probably be hours anyway."

She grabbed a huge fluffy bath sheet and placed it on the hot rail. As the steam rose in the bathroom, the smell of the plants seemed to grow more intense. Mag hugged herself and spun in a circle. She ripped off all her clothes.

She picked up a stereo remote and turned on some Chris Botti. She stepped across the stone floor and lowered herself into the warm, swirling, water. She leaned back and kept time with one toe, letting the music seep into her soul.

The water, the scents, the music, and the muted candle light assaulted Mag's senses until she was as limp as a rag doll. She whispered, "I think I'm in luuuv!" Eyes closed, she let her head loll back against the pool pillow.

* * *

Finished with his calls, Ian found her there. He stood looking down at her, thinking she was the most beautiful thing he had ever seen. He fell head over heels in that moment. Instead of feeling like he should be running to the nearest exit, the weirdest feeling of well being and rightness swept over him. Overwhelmed with emotion, he stood rooted to the spot, watching her.

Mag came slowly back to consciousness and realized she was no longer alone. She looked up and raised one hand toward him. "So, handsome man, what are you waiting for?"

Ian slowly smiled at her and she thought her heart would stop. He touched his palm to hers and they both felt the faint tingle. Feeling suave and debonair, he shed his clothes at nearly the speed of light. He paused for a second and she thought she had never seen anything as beautiful as this man. He threw his leg over the side of the Jacuzzi, his eyes never leaving hers. His toe caught on the faucet and pain shot through his foot. He bent to grab his foot and let out a howl of pain. He slipped and cannon-balled into the Jacuzzi right on top of Mag.

They both came up sputtering. Mag burst into peals of laughter, grabbed for a hand-hold and sank under the churning water. Ian hit his sore toe on the bottom of the tub and sucked in a lungful of water when he tried to take a breath and yell.

With him coughing and gasping, and her laughing so hard she hurt, she made the astute observation that they had to be the absolute last of the red hot lovers. The hilarity of the situation finally hit him and he laughed along with her. "Less like Carey Grant and more like Clem Kadiddlehopper, wouldn't you say?"

She nodded and agreed. "Yeah. Come here, Clem, and I'll show you some kadiddle hoppin' you'll never forget!"

She stretched her body along the length of his. He gathered her close and held her to him. The water flowed over them as the emotion flowed through them. They couldn't tell where one ended and the other began. He ran a finger lightly down the side of her face and cupped her chin. The kiss he gave her was so sweet, tears welled in her eyes. He trembled with emotion as he ran his hands up her thighs, over her derrière and up the slope of her back. His hand came to rest at the back of her neck and he supported her head as he deepened the kiss.

She gave as good as she got, and Ian finally snapped. Suddenly his hands and mouth were everywhere. She responded in kind. They came together on a tidal wave of passion that took them higher than either of them had ever been. She came apart in his arms. He felt her spasm around him and he tumbled after her.

As the emotion ebbed, they settled back in the tub, fingertips touching, eyes closed. They drifted on sensation and transcended to a new understanding of what 'making love' could mean.

"Wow."

"Wow."

"Hey, Ian?"

"Yes?"

"Do you really have to go to the office this afternoon?"

"Yes, Mag. They were expecting this stuff about an hour ago."

"Damn."

"Why damn?"

"I wanted to try out that beautiful bed."

Ian sighed heavily. "Me, too, but how about if you catch a nap in it and we'll try it out when I get home?"

"I don't have to go with you?"

"No, Mag. I'm dropping the stuff off at the correct departments and leaving instructions. Neither of us has slept. You take a nap, because when I come back to you and the big tree bed, neither of us are going to sleep, okay?"

"*Mmmm-hmmm.* I suppose we have to get out of this tub eventually, too."

"Yep. Right now, Princess. Let's go. I'm not going to have you fall asleep in here and drown on me while I'm gone."

She laughed and they clambered out of the Jacuzzi. Ian grabbed the towels on the hot bar and they wandered back into the bedroom. Ian fluffed her hair and dried her back. She ran the warm towel down his front and ran her tongue back up. He waited until she got nipple high before he grabbed her and tossed her on the bed. He pulled back the comforter on the bed and Mag slid in. He covered her naked body, kissed her nose and said, "Don't move until I get home."

Mag giggled and said, "Not a chance, Mister."

He laughed and went to the closet to get dressed. He came out in blue jeans and an FBI polo shirt. He checked his wallet and picked up his keys. He was set to go, but loathed leaving her. He turned to kiss her good bye and stopped. Mag was out like a light, sleeping like an angel. He left quietly by the front door.

Ian called the field office on his way downtown. Jeff Fuller had a team waiting when he arrived. Jeff took over explaining to Ian how responsibilities would be delegated.

"The M.B. lab will get the majority of the evidence. My guys will be able to do the RAPD, and the AFLP. Ned Thompson will work with cocaine and analyze the stable isotope and trace alkaloid data. The Palynology boys will take the seeds and check for anemophilous pollen, to see if they can hook up the seeds with one of the confiscated shipments from the south. There should be plenty of pollen in the wrappings surrounding the seeds. If all goes as we think it will, it will give us a jump on tracking the drug traffic to the north and back to the source."

Ian held up a vial of off-white powder. "Jeff, your molecular biology guys are going to have their hands full. Do you want me to do the breakdown analysis on this to see exactly what is in this stuff?"

"Already got it covered. I am personally going to do the analysis on this and the other samples to find out if they're making designer drugs, or cutting it for the streets. You're busy enough doing the field work, so get out of here. I have the phone and fax numbers of that Sheriff down in White Bass Lake. I'm going on your recommendation that we're not dealing with some hick Bozo, and I'll send everything I have to you through him."

Ian nodded. "Sheriff Green is a smart and savvy professional. We should have more guys like him out there."

Jeff doled out samples and paperwork to the lab techs. He moved nervously, and Ian could tell he was anxious to get started. He became more engrossed with each sample and spoke to Ian with a distracted air. "Uh, thanks for the drugs, Ian, and uh, we'll get right on those plants." He waved a hand in the air in Ian's general direction. "I'm sure you want to get into your bed as soon as possible, so you go on home and don't even think about this place. I'll call your cell tomorrow."

Ian sent him a crafty looking smile and said, "Jeff, you're a man after my own heart. I will take that as an order and make haste toward home and bed." He did an about face and practically sprinted for the door. He sang *Bad to the Bone* on his way to the car, glad it was mid-day and the traffic wasn't too bad. He stopped for milk, eggs, and ice cream on the way home, and practically danced through the door to his condo. He set everything on the counter and tip-toed to the bedroom. Mag was sprawled on her stomach across one side. Ian kneeled on the bed and kissed her ear.

She didn't even move. He nuzzled her neck and she said, "Mmmpf yum nar Eee-annnn!"

"Hey, Maggie," he said in dulcet tones, "Are you hungry, or do you just want to play?"

"*Hmmmm*." She rolled over. Away from Ian.

Ian flopped on his back and put his hand over his eyes. "I can't believe this! I guess I have my answer, though." He looked over at Mag and linked his fingers behind his head. "Well, sweetheart, I'm starving, how about you?"

Mag did not move.

"I agree. I'll make the eggs. Otherwise, my belly will keep me awake."

He went into the kitchen and pulled out the frying pan. He scrounged in the freezer and found some ham. He threw it in the microwave to thaw, and poured himself a glass of milk.

He checked Kitty's automatic waterer and filled his food bowl. The microwave dinged and he rubbed his hands together. "Aha!"

Kitty heard the bell and yelled, "Surf's up!"

He bowed to Kitty. "Meet Chez Ian at his finest. Take note, Dumb Bird!"

"Dumb Bird," Kitty replied.

Ian chuckled, "Well, at least we agree on something!" He plopped some butter, eggs, and the ham into the frying pan. He splashed a little milk from his glass into the pan, took a swig, and whisked the mixture together with a fork.

Putting the flame on low, he looked in the fridge. He eyeballed a block of moldy cheese, shrugged, then cut away the green stuff. He grated some in the pan and sprinkled in a pinch of garlic. Grabbing a paper plate, he dumped out half of the concoction and carried it to the breakfast bar. He wiped the remnants of mango off the counter top with a bleach cloth and sat down to eat.

Ian polished off the eggs and eyed up the leftovers in the pan. He figured he'd leave those for Mag. He put foil over the pan and put the whole thing in the refrigerator. He stood and patted his belly. "Now that's some fine vittles! And no dishes to wash. That's my kind of cookin' too!"

Ian took his remaining milk with him into the office. He fired up his computer and typed out his report. Opening up a drawer, he grabbed a Snickers Bar and munched on it while he read his notes. His eyes grew heavy and his head began nodding.

Yawning hugely, Ian shut down his computer. He stretched and yawned again, then stumbled toward the bedroom. Dropping his clothes where he stood, he slid under the covers next to Mag. She mumbled in her sleep and snuggled her butt up against him. He threw an arm around her, inhaled her sweet scent, and tumbled off the face of the earth.

Six hours later Ian cracked his eyes open. He smiled, stretched, and felt around for Mag. His eyes flew open when he reached out and touched empty space. He shook his head and looked around. Orienting himself, he became aware of two things. One, there were people talking in the other room, and two, Mag's clothes were still where she left them.

Ian shot out of bed and into his closet. He grabbed a pair of sweat pants and shoved his legs into them. He was down the hall and in the living room in four strides. The sight that met him made his heart do a *ba-da-bump* in his chest. Mag sat on the sofa with a bowl of popcorn in her lap. Kitty sat at her shoulder sharing her popcorn, dropping pieces all over her and the immediate vicinity. She was wearing a pair of his flannel pajama bottoms and his Northland College jersey. She and Kitty were watching *The Philadelphia Story* on video.

She looked up at him and smiled. "Hey, cowboy, you from around these parts?"

He ruffled his hair, stretched, and scratched his belly. "Why didn't you wake me? Did the phone ring?"

"Yep. Some woman called for you. I told her you'd be verrrry busy for the next fifty years or so. I'm afraid she won't be calling back."

"Won't you be embarrassed when that woman turns out to be my mom?"

"Naw, this woman sounded young. She didn't have a 'Mom' voice. You got any stray girlfriends lying about, Plant Boy?"

"You goof ball! It was probably my sister."

She gulped. The popcorn stuck in her throat. "You have a sister? Oh no, it's coming back to me now. Sister, Shannon. Twenty-five and finishing up vet school at UW

Madison, right?"

Sudden banging on the front door sent Kitty flapping toward the banana tree.

"Iiian!" *Bang, bang, bang, bang!* She pounded hard enough to shake the pictures on the wall. "Ian! I know you're home. Open this door you evil Son of a Gun!"

"Good thing I never gave her a key," Ian said as he turned the knob. A whirlwind blew through the front door and swept through the kitchen. She came to a stop next to the sofa. She took in Mag's attire and her bare feet on the table. She looked at the movie as Jimmy Stewart stumbled drunkenly out of the car at Carey Grant's carriage house. She took in the popcorn all over the place and turned to Ian. One look at his hair standing on end and her usually perfectly pressed brother dressed only in a pair of sweat pants, and she turned a sweet shade of cotton candy pink.

"Uh, Ian, this is the weekend I was going to stay here. Remember, no school? Spend the weekend doing the town? Uh, have you changed my plans?" She wiggled her eyebrows and grew more agitated. "Amber and Emily are supposed to meet me here in a couple of hours. Mom told me you were here, but I didn't believe her. I came in early to see for myself. *IAN!"* She grabbed his arm, "You have to go."

She looked at Mag. "You must be Maggie. Are you going to be my sister? Mom says Ian finally sounds serious. She can not *wait* to meet you. You guys aren't staying, are you?"

Mag laughed. She thought Shannon was adorable. Ian thought she was a pushy pain in the ass. "Shan, we're just stopping over. We will be gone in an hour or so. We need to get back to White Bass Lake tonight, but I overslept. You're early, Shannie Girl, but have no fear, Louisa is due any minute to clean up, I'm going to throw some things in a duffel and we are out of here."

She smiled–all straight white teeth. "You are the best brother in the world!" She bounced over and kissed him on the cheek. She chuckled and patted Mag on the shoulder. "Fifty years or so, huh?"

At Mag's groan she laughed and said, "Don't worry about it–I thought it was sweet. I like you, Maggie Miller." She hugged Mag and bounced back out the door to get her luggage.

A small round woman bustled through the open door. She waved a hanky and said, "Oh, Mister Ian, you are still here. Are you staying?" She looked around. "Do you want me to start now or come back?"

Ian hugged her. "Louisa, you can begin whenever you want. I'll be out of your way in a minute. Mag? Are you about ready?" Mag numbly nodded her head. "Good. You just keep those clothes on–you can change when we get to your house. Is that okay with you?"

Mag nodded again. Ian took off down the hall and Kitty flew after him. "I'll get our stuff, Mag. You can get rid of the popcorn bowl and find your shoes. Will that be okay?" Mag once again nodded her head.

Shannon turned to a dazed Mag. "It was great meeting you, Mag. Sorry I'm kicking you out, but we've been planning this for weeks."

Mag put her shoes on and stood. "No, that's fine. We probably should have left already anyway." She yawned.

Coming back into the room, Ian waggled his eyebrows and winked at Mag. "It *has* been a real long two days and neither of us has had much sleep."

Shannon cringed and held up a hand. "Stop! Too much information! I'll change the sheets."

Mag blushed and tried to correct herself. "No, what I mean is that you don't have to change the sheets. We didn't, uh, in the bed..." She turned even redder and looked beseechingly at Ian as he waltzed back into the kitchen.

Ian grinned at both women. "No, but you might want to change the water in the hot tub!"

"Oh Ewwwe, you sick jerk! Maggie, how can you stand this knob?"

Mag made for the front door. "I'll take that as a rhetorical question and get out of here. Nice meeting you, Shannon."

"You, too."

Ian set Kitty to flight, and he flapped off into the atrium. The Banana Palm leaves shook when he landed. Ian kissed Shannon on the cheek and headed for the door. He carried an unzipped duffel stuffed full of clothes and his files.

"See you later, brat. Hey, you get to feed the Kitty–don't forget, no pizza this time, and tell your friends to either empty their beer glasses or drink out of a can. I don't want to come home to a drunken bird with pizza breath."

"Okay, okay. Kitty food only. Got it. Thanks again for your place!"

"Here Kitty, Kitty, Kitty," came from the Banana Palm as Ian followed Mag out the door.

22

While Ian and Mag were busy falling in love on their way to Milwaukee, I sat staring at the whiteboard in my living room, trying to connect the dots. I decided to check my answering machine, and saw the red light flashing. I punched the message button.

"Hi Buzz, this is Malcolm. I'm calling on official Coroner business. It's regarding Carole. I have the results of the autopsy sans the toxicology report. Either call me or stop in when you have time. Thanks."

I looked at the date. Shit. He'd called early this morning. I grabbed my keys and headed for the door, punching in Mee-me's number. He answered and I told him I was coming in. Next I punched in J.J.'s cell. I got his voice mail and left a message for him to call me.

I drove to the Coroner's Office by way of downtown. I noticed my mother's car at Sal's–didn't want her seeing me. She loves to badger Malcolm about who's in the cold storage. I turned right and went around the block in case she was looking out the window. I noticed Mary's and Joy's cars were also in the parking lot. I couldn't help but wonder what kind of mischief Mom and her cronies were stirring up. Dad's problem, not mine, I reminded myself as I pulled into the medical building's parking lot.

Mee-me met me at the door and we went into his office. He sat behind his desk and slid the report across to me. He rearranged his blotter, straightened his pencils and pens, pulled at his tie, and kept glancing at the clock.

"Malcolm, are you feeling okay this morning?"

He cleared his throat and fidgeted. He pushed his

glasses up his nose and cleared his throat again. "I, uh, nothing, Buzz. Excuse me a minute, take your time."

He got up and bolted from the room. I sat there momentarily thinking about how strange it was for Malcolm to just get up and leave like that. It was also strange that he did not ask after Fred.

I got up to follow him. I opened the door and almost ran into him. "Malcolm, for God's sake, what the hell is wrong with you?"

He stared at me for a moment and brushed by me, picking up the autopsy report. He shook it at me. "This, Buzz. This is what's bothering me; the results. I went over Carole with a fine tooth comb. The bullet killed her, but she had the crap knocked out of her before she was shot."

Tongue-in cheek, I teased him. "Is that what the report says in *professional terms?*"

"Don't laugh at me, Buzz. A nice lady like that shouldn't have to go that way." He flipped open the report and pointed. "Look here, I found wood chips and bark in her hair where she bled from the back of the skull. I sent Ivan over to check around the trees near your folk's house. He came back with a log from the woodpile with hair, blood, and broken fingernails that match up to Carole. There were also embedded fibers in the log which initially match her tee shirt in color and type."

I looked at the autopsy photos and the log. I felt a little ill and took a cleansing breath. "With the fingernails embedded in the wood, she was probably either scrambling to get away or she picked up the log to fight back." I again looked down at the pictures. "It looks like they beat the living daylights out of her with that log."

Mee-me showed me the police photos. "J.J. actually came up with the theory. I just matched up the wounds. I think he's right because it looks to me like they shot her by the wood pile when she tried to escape. She was killed over at your Mom and Dad's, Buzz."

I tried not to panic. "I see that. What the heck was she doing over at Mom and Dad's that night? What does that say about our murderer, and what about the gak under what finger nails she had left?"

"J.J. had me scrape the nails and I sent that off with the rest of it to the crime lab for DNA testing. I also need to tell you that one of the dead guys from your night out at the Graff's place had interesting scratch marks on his jaw and chin. I sent a sample of his DNA to the crime lab too. I'm thinking we're going to get a match."

I thought about that piece of information for a minute. "Well, doesn't that just wrap this murder up all nice and tidy?"

Malcolm bit his lip and cleared his throat again. "With a pink bow on top. So does that mean this is over?"

I walked over and placed the file on Mee-me's desk. I didn't know how much I should reveal about the drug connection. "Not by a long shot. What bothers me is that there are still so many unanswered questions about this case. I don't want J.J. to close the book on this, but I'm afraid he doesn't have enough evidence of a secondary crime to delve further into it, so it's over. Now I find out that I killed the guy who probably killed her."

I ticked off the humiliating points on my fingers. "The victim is dead, the perp is dead, the whole damn thing is dead. When J.J. finds out I killed his defendant, I'm probably dead too."

Malcolm bustled over to his desk. "That's why I wanted to talk to you first. Word has it that J.J. is pretty pissed at you for, um, you know…your midnight rendezvous with your killer amigos and all."

He jerked his head toward the cold room where,

through the window I could see good old Ivan smiling and nodding at me, pointing to the bad guy he was cutting on.

I let out an exasperated sigh. "Does everyone know about that? No, don't tell me. I already know the answer. And what do you mean you wanted *me* to know first? Didn't you already show J.J. these results?" Malcolm slowly shook his head, biting his lip and stepping away from me.

"Oh, shit. Malcolm, I gotta get out of here! You never saw me! Call J.J. and give him the report." I grabbed my keys off the desk and hustled out of his office. I was jogging down the hall and calling over my shoulder, "Malcolm, call J.J. right away. I don't want him to think th–" I ran full bodied into a brick wall. I bounced off and looked up at J.J. scowling down at me. In full defensive stance, legs apart, and hands on hips, he blocked my only way out. He took a step forward and I took one back. He stepped toward me again and I retreated.

He walked me backward until we came even with Malcolm's office where he grabbed me by the sleeve and dragged me with him. He dumped me in a chair as he stormed behind Malcolm's desk. He tapped the autopsy report. Very casually, he asked, "So, what's the *Buzz, Buzz?* Was anyone going to invite me to this party? And what is it that you don't want me to think?"

He pulled his reading glasses out of his pocket and put them on. He looked at me from over the top. "Before you even ask, Jane Knight was behind you when you made that right turn to avoid your mother. She went straight to Sal's to tell her. I was having coffee at the time and heard you were here. I couldn't imagine that you and Malcolm were having a tête-à-tête with Fred still in the picture. The only other thing you have in common is the murder, and the autopsy report." He banged a fist on the desk. "*MY* autopsy report!" I flinched and Malcolm shrank back and fled down the hall.

I figured the best defense was a good offense. "I called you and left a message to call me. I wanted you to come with me to read the report. How was I supposed to know you hadn't seen it?

"I was in the process of telling Malcolm to call you because I didn't want you thinking exactly what you are thinking."

He stopped reading and again looked at me over the tops of those damn glasses. "And what is it, my darling Buzz that I am thinking?"

I blinked at the absurd address, and realized J.J. was angrier than I had ever seen him. Oh well, honesty was even better than a good offense. What was he going to do, shoot me? "That I was being low-down, sneaky, and going behind your back. That I somehow coerced Malcolm into letting me see the report first. That I was sneaking off when I ran into you and I was going to run off half-cocked into some situation out of which you would have to come and rescue my sorry ass."

He stared at the ceiling, his steepled fingers tapping on his lip. "Yep, that about sums it up. So what did you and Malcolm find out?"

I glared at him. He could be so damn annoying! "That it was Colonel Mustard, in the library, with the wrench!"

He barked out a laugh. "Damn, and here I thought it was going to be the knife. Quit trying to soften me up Buzz. It's hard to stay mad at you when you do stuff like that."

"Not after I tell you that the guy who murdered Carole is probably the same guy I killed out at the greenhouse."

I heard J.J. suck in a long breath through his teeth. He pursed his lips and slapped his palms down on Malcolm's desk. He pushed himself to his feet, shoving Malcolm's chair against the wall. "Well, I guess that's it."

He picked up the autopsy report and slid it inside his

jacket. I jumped to my feet. He walked around the desk and rested his hand on the back of my neck.

I jumped about a foot in the air and he patted me between the shoulder blades. Absently, he rubbed my neck. "Come on, Buzz, let's get out of here."

Damn, that felt good. No wonder the dogs love it so much. In a daze, I asked, "*Mmmm*, are you talking to me?"

He sighed and lightly grabbed the back of my neck. He steered me down the hall. I stumbled going out the door. "No, I'm talking to the mouse in your pocket! Of course I mean you."

I grinned and tested the waters. "Am I under arrest now, Officer? Am I going to ride in your big police car now? Are you going to guide my head through the door after you cuff me? Am I going to ride in the back with the puke and the bugs? That's one sure way to piss me off."

He shifted his arm around my shoulders and laughed. "Damn it Buzz, you sure know how to castrate a guy with words, don't you? I just thought maybe we'd get a cup of coffee or just go to your house so I can yell at you in private and play with the dogs."

I was so relieved I had tears in my eyes. He noticed before I could look away. "Hey, now, no need to get sloppy over a cup of joe, pal. We could go to my house, but you've got the bonus of having the dogs."

I sniffed and wiped my nose on my sleeve. "J.J., you and I go back a long way and I would have hated to do something stupid enough to jeopardize our friendship. Besides, my dogs would disown me if you didn't come over any more."

He laughed again and squeezed my shoulders. "Kid, it would take a lot more than a misplaced bullet to wreck what we have. Hell, we're practically like an old married couple as it is." He kissed the top of my head.

23

I smiled and got a tingly-mushy feeling. It scared the living shit out of me. *Not J.J.,* I yelled at myself. I ducked out from under his arm and jabbed him in the ribs with my elbow.

"Yeah, hot shot, and we'll be front page news if Gossip Central sees you hugging on me in public, so knock it off."

He grinned and shoved me sideways. "Oh, God, could you imagine? Your mom would be picking out china this afternoon! Mag would bitch constantly 'cause she had to wear a dress. Fred would rip hers when she fell off her shoes walking up the aisle, and Al would make sure she was in all the pictures! Ha-ha!" He stumbled against the squad in a fit of laughter. "Can you picture Wesley knocking the cake over? Ha-ha, it's a good thing we never went that route!"

The truth hurts, they say, and the warm fuzzy feeling I was afraid of vanished into thin air. When the laughter didn't stop I became downright grumpy. "Yeah, yeah, it's a good thing you escaped with your life, now come on turkey-butt; you owe me coffee." I marched off to my own car and slammed the door.

J.J. sobered and trotted over to the driver's window. I lowered it a crack. He seemed to think that was funny too and I almost ran over his toes just to shut him up. "Come on, Buzz. You know it was funny. Lighten up! I have an idea. Why don't you follow me over to my house and I'll drop the squad off? That way no one will see it parked in your driveway."

At my scowl he said, "Who started on Gossip

Central?"

I sighed. "Okay, Cowboy, let's go. You buy the pizza and I'll pull out the good china and the Irish linen."

He clasped his hands over his heart and sighed loudly to the Heavens. "The paper plates and the paper towels. What more could a man ask for in his lifetime. A beer, perhaps?" He waggled his eyebrows.

I laughed. "Beer I got."

"You are the perfect woman, Buzz Miller."

"Just don't let it get around. I don't have time to fight them all off."

He was still chuckling as he got into his squad. I followed him across town to his house. He parked the squad, grabbed a duffel bag out of the back, and jumped into my car. I took off and he peeled off his uniform shirt. I looked at him. He grinned and tossed it into the back seat. I turned on my street and he pulled his tee shirt out of his pants and dispensed with it in the same manner.

It shocked the crap out of me, but I tried for nonchalance. "Damn, you look pretty good for an old guy, Green!"

He poked at his biceps. "I don't know, Buzz, I keep finding soft spots that won't go away."

I held up a hand. "Let's not get into your love life, J.J.. This is a family show." I laughed at my own joke.

He stuck his nose in the air. "When I said soft spots, I was *not* referring to Mr. Ed."

I hooted. "Mr. Ed? Who the hell would name his penis Mr. Ed?"

He sang, "*A horse is a horse, of course, of course...*"

I banged my head against the headrest and moaned in disbelief. "Please spare me, Oh Keeper of the Equine Erectus!"

"Laugh now, Oh Ye of Little Faith. Once you sneak a

peek at Mr. Ed...."

I pulled into the driveway wiping the tears out of my eyes. I was still laughing as I turned off the car.

"Oh, give me a break, James Joseph Green. First of all, I have no intention of peeking at the One-Trick Pony. Even if it *were* true, you couldn't keep something like that a secret in this town. I'd have read it on a bathroom stall by now."

We exited the car. He put his nose in the air. "Mr. Ed is *very* discriminating." He waggled his eyebrows at me from across the roof of the car. "But look at you! I can still make 'em cry!" He ducked in, grabbed the duffel bag, and headed for the house. I stood still, dumb struck. He yelled, "Come on, slowpoke, toss me the keys!"

I threw them to him and gathered my notes. I closed the car door just as he got the front door open. I thought about warning him, but just smiled as he shoved the door open.

Wesley catapulted across the threshold and planted his enormous front feet on J.J.'s chest. They both flew off the porch and hit the ground. J.J.'s duffel bag bounced and rolled to my feet. I picked it up and walked past the roiling mass of big man and big dog.

I met Hill on her way out to greet J.J. She waited patiently until Wes and J.J. were both exhausted from rolling around on the ground. She walked forward and put her head in his hand. He rubbed her ears and asked, "How's my best girl today?" Hilary closed her eyes in ecstasy and delicately passed gas.

He jumped to his feet. "Whew! I guess that answered that question! Come on, guys." He strolled through the front door, the dogs happily trailing behind him.

I called from the kitchen, "I ordered the pizza and your duffel bag is on the couch." I set the coffee pot on automatic for the morning and walked back into the living room. It was empty. I walked down the hall. "J.J.? Wes? Hill? Where the heck is everybody?"

I heard water running and went into the master bedroom. Sure enough, my shower was running. "J.J.? What are you doing?"

"Playing Parcheesi, what does it sound like? Or would you rather come in and take a look for yourself?" He proceeded to neigh.

I laughed and shook my head. "No thanks, John Stud. You get that pony corralled all by yourself. When you're ready, come down and have pizza and beer." I walked out and laughed again when I heard neighing and pawing from behind the door. The dogs cocked their heads and stared at the door.

I was almost to the kitchen when I had a sudden thought. I was not expecting company today–especially of the male variety. I tried to remember how I'd left my bathroom. Did I leave any unmentionable or humiliating things lying around?

I chewed my fingernails and feared the worst. J.J. came whistling around the corner and stopped in the doorway. I took one look and my brain turned to mush. Fresh from the shower, he wore an old threadbare football jersey with the sleeves torn off. His sweat pants rode low on his hips and his feet were bare. He looked good enough to take a bite out of and smelled like a dream. That wonderful combination of soap and testosterone; *ggrrrrr*, come to Mama! I pulled up short, but sneaked in one more whiff. *Whoa, there! Get hold of yourself, girl.*

He smiled slowly and knowingly. I thought my goose was cooked. He put his hands on his hips. I held my breath and he let out with, "Where're all da women at?" That broke the spell. I exhaled and we laughed. I shoved a beer in his hand. He grabbed up the box of pizza and headed for the living room. He put the pizza down on the coffee table and flopped on the couch.

I picked up the remote, turned on cable T.V. An NBA game was on.

"You ok with sports?"

"Unless you got *Debbie Does Dallas* on tape."

"What is with you tonight?"

He looked thoughtful and then confused. "I don't know, but I'll stop it now."

I turned off the television and turned on the DVD player. "How about a movie instead?"

"Great idea," he said. "What do you want to watch?"

I thought about it. "That depends. Are you in a *Lethal Weapon* mood or a *Rush Hour* mood?"

He laughed and shouted, *"Do You Understand The Words That Are Coming Out Of My Mouth?"*

"All-righty then. *Rush Hour* it is."

"Buzz, you are the perfect woman!"

I batted my eyes. "Yeah, yeah, move over and quit hogging all the pizza."

We polished off the pizza and laughed all over again at the outrageous comedy of Jackie Chan and Chris Tucker. At the end, he went to grab the remote. I dove after it.

"Wait! The outtakes are the best part!"

He settled back and said, "Aww, man! I almost forgot." We laughed some more.

I wiped the tears from my eyes. "Wow. I needed that."

"I agree. I think I'm a whole new man. Thanks, Buzz."

"I couldn't have done it without you, J.J. It's not quite the same watching it with Wesley. Besides, he eats most of the pizza."

He yawned and popped the top of another beer. He settled back. I turned light classical on the stereo. I took the pizza box and the paper plates to the kitchen.

I dumped them in the trash and thought, "Now that's how I like to do the dishes." I wiped down the counters and turned off the lights.

"Wes, Hill, do you guys need to go out one more time?" There was no scuffling, and no vying for position to be first out the door. Odder than that, there was no noise at all coming from the other room. I walked quietly to the door and peeked around the corner. I smiled and sighed. This was a Kodak moment if I ever saw one. J.J. was sound asleep, slouched sideways on the couch. His untouched beer was perched precariously on the table. Wesley was on the other half of the couch, grinning proudly and waving his tail. Hill was in J.J.'s lap, daring me to chase her off.

I went to the fridge and grabbed a hot dog. I stood in the doorway and broke it in half. Wes was my slave in about two seconds. Hilary quietly got off J.J.'s lap and waddled over to get her half. I pulled a quilt from the linen closet, threw it over J.J., and turned out the lights.

The dogs both looked at me questioningly. "Come on, kids, go to bed." They trotted down the hall to my bedroom. Wes jumped up on the king-sized bed and I lifted Hilary. By the time I got out of the shower they were both snoring softly. Wes was sprawled across one side, with Hill curled up next to his big warm belly. I crawled in next to them and turned off the light. I lay listening to their familiar snorts and snores and drifted off to sleep.

* * *

I was dreaming about great smelling guys, and one in particular. I came slowly awake still dreaming of burying my face into a hairy chest smelling of Irish Spring and man. My subconscious mind told me I would probably wake up with a face full of dog butt.

My semi-conscious mind, however, registered a couple of indisputable facts. One, Wes was on the floor, licking my hand. Two, I was now fully awake and I still smelled Irish Spring and man, but I also felt very warm skin under my chin and nose. I opened my eyes and registered a third indisputable fact. I was face first in J.J.'s chest, and there was a pool of drool next to my mouth. I made an unladylike slurp and J.J. moved the hair out of my eyes. I looked into those startling blue eyes and melted.

"Good morning, beautiful." Hilary preened and I let her have the spotlight. I had to–she looked much better than I did this morning.

I lifted my head and said, "It is a good thing we're friends, or I might have had to kill you. Where did you come from anyway?"

He picked that moment to stretch and wipe the wet spot from his chest. "The dogs woke me up, so I took them for a walk. The coffee was already made so I poured a cup. I took a phone call from one of my deputies, and I came in here to wake you up." He pointed to the cup on the night stand. "I leaned over to wake you up and you rolled me over the top of you." He clutched his heart. "I was rendered helpless when you burrowed in and flopped face first on my chest. That was about, oh…" he consulted his watch, "Fifteen minutes ago."

"Oh geez, J.J. I'm sorry."

"Don't be. It was my pleasure. Believe me, it was all my pleasure."

I yawned. "What the heck time is it, anyway?" He started to answer me when my phone rang. I heard my mom's voice and let the machine pick it up.

24

Alejandro and Moe picked up the horse trailer from Mitchell Field Airport. They arrived back at the Miller Farm by 10:50 a.m. Bill waved them to a stop and gave them instructions for the placement of the trailer behind his barn. Alejandro thanked him and drove around the barn. Moe got out to direct and Alejandro started to back the trailer perpendicular to the northwest corner of the barn. Moe moved, so Alejandro could see him in the mirrors, and tripped and fell forward over something sticking out of the ground. Alejandro slammed on the brakes and jumped out to check on Moe. He found Moe staring at the ground, brushing at the dirt. Moe sat up and shoved some more dirt aside with his heels, and looked down again.

Lifting his ball cap and scratching his head, Moe looked at Alejandro with a bewildered expression on his face. "Well, I'll be dipped. Montoya, would you look at that?"

Alejandro moved closer and looked at where Moe pointed. A patch of brown hide and a piece of halter could be seen where Moe had scraped away the topsoil. Alejandro squatted and brushed more soil away. He inhaled sharply and made a small noise when he uncovered a horse's head. Moe just stood there looking baffled. Alejandro realized he was looking at the mare from which the bad guys had removed the bricks of cocaine two days ago.

"Oh my God!" He fell backward, scrambled to put distance between himself and the dead horse. He choked back bile and fought to control his breathing. He didn't realize he was praying aloud until Moe put a hand on his shoulder, startling him. Alejandro jerked his head around. Moe backed away from him, wary of the desolate look on his face.

"*¡Margarita, mi caballito!*" Alejandro looked down at the little mare, speaking softly, stroking the horse's face. Not turning from the horse, he said quietly to Moe, "Call Sheriff Green right away. This is my mare they murdered at Graff's."

Moe fumbled with his cell phone and finally hit speed dial. J.J. answered right away. Moe moved away from the truck. Alejandro listened as Moe spoke in low tones.

"J.J., it's Darryl. Uh no, Sheriff, I'm the other Darryl. Darryl Swanson." He enunciated into the phone. "I'm your deputy you sent to Milwaukee with Montoya." He sighed again. "Yeah, that's me. Moe or Tom or whatever you want to call me. Anyway, we're over at Bill Miller's place, parking the horse trailer. No, we didn't run into the barn. Listen...I uh, stumbled across a dead horse." He glanced at Alejandro and winced. "Yeah. Montoya says it looks like the one he claims died over at Graff's the other night... Okay, we won't touch it. Huh? Montoya? No, boss, he looks like he saw a ghost. Yeah–good idea, she'll know what to do... Okay. Will do, Sheriff. Yep, you too. Bye."

He flipped the phone shut and walked back to Alejandro. "Come on, Montoya. Gerry Miller will have coffee on. We can't touch the scene until J.J. gets here anyway."

Alejandro drew in a shaky breath and wiped his brow with a bandana. "Whew. Yeah. Okay. Where do you want me to go?" Alejandro took Moe's arm and he helped him up. He was still trembling as they slowly walked to the back door of Miller's house. Moe knocked twice. They heard a cheery, "Come on in; the coffee's on!"

Moe held open the screen door and Alejandro took a

tentative step inside the kitchen. Gerry was just turning from the stove when she caught sight of Alejandro. "Oh, young man, what is wrong? Are you hurt?"

Alejandro shook his head, giving her a small smile. "No, ma'am. I'm okay, but I think we have some disturbing news." He turned to Moe.

Moe took over. "Ger, we found what we think is a horse buried out back of your barn. Sheriff Green is on his way. Montoya here is a little shook up over the whole thing, so we thought we'd beg a cup of coffee off you and wait until the sheriff gets here."

Gerry clasped her hands in front of her. "I should think so! Sit, sit, I have just the thing!" She turned and bustled back to the stove, snatching up the pan she just took out of the oven. She muttered to herself, "Dead horse, oof dah! Wait until I tell the girls, wait until I tell Buzz!"

She grabbed a plate and pried whatever was in the pan onto the plate. "Here, young man, have some of my rhubarb crunch. It will make you feel better." She distractedly plopped the plate and a fork in front of him, picked up the coffee pot and filled two cups. "Darryl, Mr. Montoya, would you excuse me a moment?" Without waiting for an answer, she scurried into the next room.

Wiping her hands on the towel tucked at her waist, Gerry picked up the phone and hit the speed dial. "Buzz? Mom. I think you'd better come over as soon as you get this message. Something about a dead horse some guy named Montoya found buried behind our barn."

* * *

I lay in my bed listening to the answering machine as my mom prattled on. I opened my eyes a crack and saw J.J. smiling down at me. I could not yet put together a coherent thought, let alone decipher what Mom was talking about. I pushed the hair out of my eyes and looked blearily at J.J. He was still grinning at me. Mom said something about coming over for lunch.

I sat up suddenly, grabbed J.J. by the arm, and tried to focus on the dial on his watch. "Lunch? What time did you say it was, J.J.?"

"I didn't, but it's going on 11:25."

"Oh, crap!" I scrambled from the bed and sprinted for the bathroom.

As I closed the door, I heard, "Nice outfit, Miller."

I looked down and had to laugh. I was wearing an old comfortable tee shirt Fred gave me a million years ago. It had a piano and a piano bench on it. On the bench was a pile of poop. The caption below read, *Beethoven's Last Movement.* This was paired with my favorite Green Bay Packers satin boxers. I must admit, I was quite the fashion statement. "You should see me when I really dress up," I yelled through the door.

I wet my hair down, yanked on a bra, brushed my teeth, and grabbed a sweatshirt with a picture of a Holstein cow and the sign for pi below it.

J.J. gave me a quizzical look when I came out of the bathroom. I elbowed him and said, "Get it? *Cow pi?"*

He moaned and threw an arm around my neck. He whistled through his teeth. "Hey Hill, Wes, let's go to Grandma's house!" We had to jump out of the way or get stampeded on our way out the door.

We made it to Mom's house a couple of minutes before noon. I groaned and clasped a hand over my eyes when I saw the black Bonneville, and red Crown Victoria in the driveway. "Oh no! It's the geriatric *Mod Squad.* I'm going to kill my mother–but at least we don't have to deal with Dead Butts,"

J.J. flicked my earlobe. "You spoke too soon, my sweet."

"My sweet patootie, pal. What are you talking about– oh crap, I spoke too soon–"

Zoom! My car rocked as the township squad blew past us. Putz slid sideways, spraying gravel in all directions, pelleting my car. He bumped over the ridge along the driveway, fishtailed in and out of the first few rows of corn, tearing stalks out by the roots fighting to control the squad.

"Oh, boy, is your dad going to be pissed when he sees this," J.J. said.

I blew out a big breath. "Wow. You got that right, flatfoot." We pulled past the line of cars parked by the house.

We let the dogs out and they bounded straight for the back door. A hand was seen opening the screen door and the two dogs disappeared inside. I smiled and looked at J.J. He smiled down at me and said, "Ah, the joys of Grandma's house."

"You are right again, James J. Green–oh my God, look over there!" J.J. turned in time to see Ted's mother, Mary, whack him in the back of the head with a dripping Tupperware lid.

"Now look what you did, you self impotent little chest beater!"

J.J. and I exchanged glances. J.J. whispered out of the side of his mouth, "Impotent? This gets better and better!"

"Self *important*, Ma. I don't think you mean impotent. I'm arrogant, not limp." Ted hitched his pants, nervously looking around. He caught J.J. and me looking and turned a sick shade of grayish-pink. He opened his mouth and Mary whacked him again with the Tupperware lid.

"You made me spill my Chinese noodle salad and you wrecked my car! Look at my beautiful car!" She leaned over and examined the dings. "At least it's not as bad as Bill Miller's truck. He's going to sue, you know. What are you doing here anyway? This is for the real police, not for members of Donut Eaters Anonymous."

J.J. and I couldn't stand it any more. He barked out a laugh, and I almost wet myself howling. I clasped J.J.'s arm and hobbled to the house, laughing the entire way.

I hit the bathroom running. Looking out the bathroom window, I saw Ted, with his head down, stubbing his toe in the gravel. Mary was still giving him what-for and waving the Tupperware container, showering him with Chinese noodles.

I snagged Mom's digital camera and went back outside. Wesley came bounding up, wearing noodles on his head and nose. "You were eating noodle salad, weren't you, Wes? Did you get too close to Mary?"

Grin, pant, tail wave, and grin. I picked a noodle off his snout and dropped it in his mouth. He trotted off toward his driveway buffet.

I looked around and realized J.J. hadn't waited for me. I jogged through the barn and out the far end. J.J., Dad, Moe, and Alejandro were armed with shovels, brooms and a leaf blower. Bernie Smiley pulled up in his tow truck. The men discussed the strategy for removing the mare from the shallow pit.

I left them to it and fired up the camera. I noticed Mike Dudley, our local veterinarian was down in the pit, examining the mare. He leaned over and scribbled on a clipboard he had placed on solid ground on the rim of the pit. I walked over to where he was. He looked up, smiled and said, "Hey Buzz, how'r ya doing? Where's my favorite girl and her two-ton sidekick?"

"I'm good, Mike. Hilary is in the house and Wes is eating Chinese noodles in the driveway."

Mike laughed. "I won't even ask, but I can't say I'm surprised." He gestured with his head to the mare in the pit.

"What's up with the dead horse, anyway? J.J. says he wants a full autopsy–concentrating on a toxin report and the reproductive organs. Care to let me in on it?"

I hesitated. "Look, Mike, this is part of an investigation, of which you are an important part. Let me talk to J.J. I think he will fill you in later, but not in front of Bernie and the others."

Mike smiled. "You got it, Kiddo–I'm almost finished here anyway, so I'll join you in a minute." He looked back at the mare in the pit. "Sure was a pretty little mare though. Whoever killed her must have collected a good chunk of insurance money. Is that what we're looking at here, insurance fraud?" He held up a hand. "No, never mind. You go talk to J.J. and I'll finish up here."

"Okay, and thanks, Mike."

I went over by the 'meeting of the mindless' and pulled J.J. aside. "Mike wants to know what he's looking for, and I think we should let him in. He's a good man and he would keep any information in a confidential file. He thinks he's looking at insurance fraud. When he finds out this mare died of a cocaine overdose, he will go through the roof if we don't give him prior warning."

"I know. I've thought about that too. Let's go tell him now. Maybe he can help us brainstorm."

We had started back toward Mike when we heard the roar of Ted's voice, "I don't care about your stupid noodles you crazy old bat! I'm here for an official Mexica–I mean I have Mexican papers...that is, Texas papers for a murdered Mexican...I mean Mexican murderer–oh, just get out of my way and take your damn noodles with you!"

J.J. and I looked at each other and said simultaneously, "Oh no!"

25

I caught sight of Ted strutting through the barn with papers in his hand. It is always a bad sign when I see Dead Butts gather himself up to his full five-feet-two-inches and puff out his chest. When he adds that superior smirk, I know there's going to be trouble.

I was across the pit when Butts swaggered up to J.J. and hitched his pants. I kept one eye on him while I finished up with Mike the vet. I saw Butts jawing at J.J. When J.J. pushed his hat back and shook his head I became wary. Butts gestured wildly with one hand and shook the papers at J.J. with the other. J.J. crossed his arms over his chest in a defensive stance not even Ted was stupid enough to ignore. He took a step back.

I slid close enough to hear J.J. say, "Ted, I don't care if those papers say he's the goddamn *Frito Bandito*, I am not arresting Montoya on Grand Larceny and Murder. Where did you get those papers, anyway?"

Ted's eyes grew large and he stammered, "I-I just dropped by your office and Edie was at the fax machine. The phone rang, she went to answer it, and I p-picked them up."

J.J. was incensed. "What did you do, Butts, steal those warrants from Edie? You have no business touching anything in my office!"

He yanked his cell phone out of his pocket and punched in some numbers. "Edie? J.J. No, I didn't listen to my voice mails yet. He what?" J.J. glared at Ted. "Yeah, that's what I thought. Well, he's here now. Who was the guy again, Martinez? Okay. No thanks, I got the number. What?

No need to be sorry, Edie, it's not your fault. Ted's an ass. Yep. See you later, Bye."

J.J. held out his hand and said quietly, "Ted, hand over those warrants. Edie ttyed Texas, but has not received confirmation of the hits yet. Those warrants are no good until we do.

"Didn't it occur to you to verify the hit before running out here? And what would the Mexican Police be doing picking him up, and not a Texas Ranger? For God's sake, Ted, use your head."

Ted tried to peek around J.J. into the pit. "Come on, J.J. These warrants are signed and I am here to deliver them. Get out of my way now, you cannot ignore international law. We have to hold Montoya on these warrants until he is extradited to Texas, and then deported to Mexico."

"Out of your way? Out of your *mind*, you mean! Just slow down a minute. I am willing to have Montoya come back in for questioning, but I am not sending him back to Mexico when I think his boss might be the one who wants him dead. It may even be his boss who showed up to get him. Give me those papers and let me read them before we go off half-cocked."

J.J. reached for the papers. Ted snatched them out of his hand. "What do you actually know about this Montoya anyway, J.J.? I have personally spoken to Eduardo Martinez and assured him there will be no miscarriage of justice in White Bass Lake, Wisconsin. Are you willing to risk your job and your freedom for some little foreigner you don't even know? Well I'm not–"

J.J. grabbed Ted by the collar when he attempted to sneak past. "You sniveling, sawed-off cockroach! Who gave you the authority to assure anyone of anything? You might have just assured the death of Alejandro Montoya with your big man in charge impersonation!"

Oh, boy, I thought, J.J.'s really pissed now. He walked Ted backward, clenched his hands at his sides and glared at him.

J.J. said through clenched teeth, "Ted, for once get your head out of your ass and listen to me–this might be the most important decision of your career. *I* am the sheriff of this county and *you,"* he poked Ted in the chest, "are a piss ant."

He kept walking Ted backward, poking him every step of the way. "You either hand me those papers right now or I will charge you with obstruction, disorderly, and anything else I can think of. By the time I get finished with you, you won't have enough backers to get elected Dog Shit Inspector!"

Ted's eyes bored into J.J.'s. His face turned dark red and his chins quivered in rage. He glanced around to see if anyone was taking up his side.

He suddenly seemed to become aware that the rest of us were all there, waiting for his answer–except, of course Mike and Bernie, who were in the process of winching the dead horse out of the pit.

Ted opened up his mouth to speak. I figured he couldn't get any more of his foot in it, so I shifted left so I could play 'Good Cop' to J.J.'s 'Mad Cop'.

A shred of color in the pit caught my eye. I blinked to make sure I was seeing correctly. As the horse cleared the pit, I could see she was not the only occupant down there. I sidled up to J.J. and elbowed him in the ribs. I used my pinkie to point into the pit. J.J. stiffened and grabbed my arm.

I cleared my throat loudly and made sure attention centered on me. "Gentlemen, I believe this entire argument may be moot, because if I am not mistaken, Alejandro Montoya is currently lying dead, there in the pit."

The crowd gasped as one. They all leaned forward to get a better look. I took a step back, hoping to slide out and get to the house before anyone recovered.

"Oh, no! He can't be dead!" All eyes turned when Ted yelled. He seemed to deflate in front of the crowd like a whoopee cushion under a fat lady's ass.

Bernie jumped out of the tow truck and walked back to check the winch. He stood scratching his head, looking into the pit. "Hey, ain't that the little Mexican fella what came into town the other day?"

J.J. stepped forward and put a hand on his shoulder. He steered him back toward the front of the truck. "Looks like it, Bernie. How about we get this horse out of here and I'll call the Coroner." Bernie nodded and finished the job.

I was almost to the barn door when J.J. came up beside me. He put an arm around my shoulders. I about jumped out of my skin. My first reaction was to shove him away before anyone noticed. I looked around and saw everyone was watching with avid interest. I tried to wiggle out from under his arm and thought what a stupid time it was for J.J. to be messing around.

His fingers dug into my bicep and he dragged me close. He put his lips on my ear and whispered urgently, "Hold still a minute and let them imagine. Smile like you like me." I showed my teeth. "Get to the house and hide Montoya. Somehow explain to your mother the importance of secrecy. We might have to ship her to Madagascar to keep her quiet. If so, I'll explain it to Bill. He'll understand, I'm sure. Now, I am going to pat your butt, so don't shoot me."

I opened my mouth to tell him I was already heading for the house before his macho playacting made us the center of attention. I scowled at him and J.J. smiled condescendingly. He turned me toward the open door, and I stage-whispered, "You'd better not slap my ass, cowboy!"

He whispered back, "Just go with me here." He gave my butt a pat, so I 'went with him' and gave the requisite, "*Oooo!*"

The crowd loved it. The air was so rife with gossip one could watch the town grapevine grow. The crowd clicked and snicked as cell phones were flipped open and speed dials were initiated.

I didn't have to hold my breath to turn pink. I was humiliated enough by the knowing *ooos* and *ahhhs* over J.J.'s behavior. I was going to have to kill him.

Someone was probably calling Jane at the damn bakery right now and ordering a wedding cake! Now every word and action between the two of us would be headline news. How the hell was I supposed to sneak peeks at his gorgeous Wrangler butt with half the town looking on?

I loudly announced I would contact Malcolm at the house and left through the barn. I passed Ted on my way through and felt him eyeball me all the way to the house.

I threw open the back door yelling "Mom," my mother called cheerfully from the family room, *"¡Hola Senora Buzz!"* I sighed and locked the door behind me. Mom must be badgering the heck out of Alejandro about Mexican traditions.

I closed my eyes for a moment and had visions of Mom stuffing Dad with burritos while she did the Hat Dance in the dining room. At least she wasn't harping on that damn cowboy snake lamp any more.

I found her and Alejandro ensconced on the sofa in the family room watching *Geraldo Rivera*. I said, "Mom, why on earth are you watching Geraldo? You never watch him."

Mom slid her glance toward Alejandro and back to me. "I just thought I would make Alejandro feel more at home."

"Mom, Geraldo is not going to make anyone feel more

at home. Besides, Alejandro is an American. For that matter, so is Geraldo."

"What about his accent?" She turned to Alejandro. "Mexico, right?"

"No, ma'am. Phoenix."

"Oh." She clicked the remote and turned off the television.

I was glad the drapes were already drawn in case Constable Shit Head was doing recon on the house. I pulled a chair up to the sofa and took my mother's hands in mine.

"Mom, I know you share all the antics of our town with your friends, but I need your utmost discretion on a matter of great urgency. Are you with me?"

"Oh, Buzz, of course I'm with you. You act like this is a matter of life and death."

I squeezed her hands to make sure she understood the gravity of the situation. "Mother! It *is* life and death. Alejandro's life may be in danger. Now, do you get it that I am dead serious?"

Mom pulled her hands back, crossed her arms, and stuck her nose in the air. "Alice Christine Miller, don't you raise your voice to me. And how dare you speak to me as if I were a child! Of course I understand, and I will do anything I need to do to ensure nothing passes out of this room. Now talk."

I blinked, momentarily stunned. She hadn't called me Alice Christine since I was about eight. "I, uh, okay–sorry, Mom. To make a long story short, Alejandro's boss had someone issue official looking paperwork to make it appear that Alejandro is wanted for murder. Ted Puetz got his hands on the papers and came out here looking for Alejandro to throw him in jail." Alejandro surged to his feet. Mom grabbed his shirt and sat him back down.

"Don't worry, kiddo–Buzz won't let them arrest you."

At my startled look Mom said, "That *is* why you're here, is it not? To hide this young man so the bad guys can't find him until this is straightened out?"

At my stunned and silent nod, Mom began bustling around the family room. She picked up the empty popcorn bowl and one of the soda cans, talking as she headed for the kitchen. "Of course you'll stay here, Alejandro. We have three empty bedrooms upstairs, so take your pick. There's a bathroom up there, and a television.

"All four girls were avid readers, so you won't be shy on entertainment. Just remember, we need to make it look like there are only two people living here: me and Bill."

I jumped to grab the teetering popcorn bowl. "Whoa Mom, I don't expect you to house him indefinitely; only until tonight, or maybe tomorrow. J.J. and I haven't thought this through yet, so we're all just flying by the seats of our pants at this point. Ted is suspicious, so be very careful around him. He might even sic his mother on you for information, so also be aware of that."

I turned to Alejandro. "And just for your information, I think the bad guys murdered Huerta and threw him in the pit with the dead horse–we told everyone it was you."

"Then Mr. Martinez will think I am dead and not send any more bad men after me."

"I hope he will want to come himself to make sure you are dead. By that time, perhaps we will have enough on him to make an arrest." Hah! I thought, wishful thinking. "I have to make some calls now, so settle in for a while."

I called Malcolm and told him we needed him out at Mom's. I called Mag and left a message to call me. I did the same with Ian. I told him that should they be back tonight, we would all rendezvous at my house.

I went back into the kitchen to brief Mom. "I have to get back out to the barn before Butts wonders why I was in here for so long. I'm putting Alejandro's life in your hands now, Mom. I'll call you later after we clean up the mess out at the barn."

I bent to kiss her and headed back out to the barn. In the pit, shovels and brooms had been used to brush away most of the dirt that covered the face-down broken and crushed body.

"No horse did that kind of damage," I said under my breath.

J.J. looked up from inside the pit. "No shit. Look at this."

He pointed to a hand. I saw all the fingers were bent back and pointed up the arm instead of down.

"Wow. I'll bet that hurt. Hey, is Ted still here?"

J.J. replied in a low voice, "Dutts is gone, but I'd bet not for long. Is Malcolm on his way?" I nodded. "Good," he said. "I already took the pictures. I'm just finishing the initial audio." He held up the new mini recorder. He grinned and I winced. I never gave him back his old one. "Don't worry about it, Buzz. The fact that you still have mine gave me an excuse to buy a new one. Anyway, it's not like I don't know where you live."

He waggled his eyebrows at me. I hazarded a glance around me. I was astounded at how large the crowd had grown. I wondered if they were here to see the body, or to watch the J.J. and Buzzi show. I should have been embarrassed, but I could only thank God there wasn't a Jell-O mold in sight.

Malcolm took that moment to arrive and the interest of the crowd shifted toward him. Rosie the News Whore was barreling through the barn toward me, followed closely by Al. I could see Al was livid, and that gave me a tingle of satisfaction. So no one told poor Alexandra there was another chance to grab the limelight. Boo-hoo, Al. I pasted a giant smile on my face and went to face the dragons.

"Rosie! How good of you to come all the way out here." Rosie stopped dead. Al bumped into her from behind. She stood staring at me like I'd grown two more sets of eyes. I inwardly smiled. This was going to be sooo easy!

I met her at the barn door and grabbed her limp hand. Shaking it hard, I said amiably, "I cannot believe there is another incident out here. I can take you through it and give a statement for the press. J.J. is pretty busy with Malcolm Evans down there in the pit, but if you want to step over here, I'll be able to answer your questions. Go ahead and get your visual set up."

Both Rosie and Al were still staring at me with their mouths hanging open. I signaled the camera man to go about what he did best, and the flurry of activity seemed to snap Rosie and Al out of their stupors.

Al narrowed her eyes at me and said, "All right. Who are you and where is my obnoxious sister?"

I laughed out loud. "I am here to serve, my dear." I made an elaborate bow and I heard chuckles from the crowd.

Al tried for snide. "Don't give me that crap, Buzz. Even when you were still 'serving' you didn't serve. You hate talking to the press. What gives? Why now?"

Rosie stuck out an arm and shoved past Al, knocking her sideways and almost into the pit. "Oh, shut up, Alexandra. Who cares?" Rosie tucked my arm in her hands and led me off to the side.

My skin crawled as her two-inch lacquered nails bit into my arm. "Okay, Buzz, let's move away from the crowd noise where just us girls can talk."

I swallowed bile and said sweetly, "Good idea Rosie." I watched her flip on her recorder and I began to weave my tale…

26

The limo slid to a stop on Rush Street in Chicago. Eduardo Martinez stepped out of the car and walked through the front doors of the hotel, arrogance dripping from his expression. No one would know he arrived early, he thought. The incident with the horse made him angry all over again. The approximately 30 million dollars it had cost him in the last three days, between the two horses and what Huerta stole, did not concern him any longer. Huerta was one liability taken care of.

Martinez looked around the reception area of the Conrad Hilton Hotel. The opulence of the grand old lady suited his tastes perfectly, as did the little bunny Gutierrez picked up in the airport bar. She certainly was ready enough to jump into the limousine, he sneered silently. Probably expected a fat tip. He calmly brushed a piece of lint from his sleeve, pulled at his cuffs, and allowed himself a small smile. He gave her a tip all right–he told her she should not get into cars with strangers, right before he broke her neck. My God! The ultimate high was the absolute power over life and death.

He thought about the look in her eyes at the moment she knew she was about to die and he could feel himself get hard all over again. He fought for control as he envisioned her crumpled body dumped on Lower Wacker Drive.

He glanced at Gutierrez, the bodyguard he took with him on most business trips. He had sent Gutierrez ahead three days before. He had picked up Martinez at O'Hare before they drove to White Bass Lake. It was unfortunate about the horse. It was more unfortunate about Carole

Graff. She would need to be replaced. Damn the woman's nosiness!

Martinez rolled his shoulders to shake off the inconveniences he had suffered of late. He looked around for his bodyguard and saw Gutierrez was, at the moment, playing valet and lugging the suitcase and garment bag through the door. He stopped and gave Martinez a barely noticeable sneer. Martinez stiffened. *Very well, if that is how it was going to be...Lake Michigan is a very large body of water, and three bodies can disappear as easily as two.*

He ignored the big man and continued toward the reception desk, already planning the task of finding a replacement bodyguard.

Planning was everything, and he had this trip planned down to the wire. The reception in his honor was in the morning, with brunch beginning at 9:30. The presentation was to be at 10:00, and he could slip out by 11:00 or so. A short drive out to Midway Airport and a quick flight over the state border would take less than an hour. He would be in White Bass Lake by two o'clock. He could have driven, but he wanted the plane for transport, not transportation.

He checked in at the desk, automatically answering the tiresome clerk. Yes, Mr. Martinez would take his regular suite. No, Mr. Martinez would not be attending the cocktail party of the National Latino Businessman's Association this evening. Yes, he was attending their brunch tomorrow morning. No, he did not require a courtesy wake-up, and yes, Mr. Martinez would be dining in his suite this evening; could he have a rare steak and a Caesar salad sent up please? Thank you.

Up in his suite, he stashed his near-empty suitcase and looked on as his clothes were hung by the valet. When he was alone, he pulled the refrigerator away from the wall. He opened the back panel and removed the 9mm gun, taped to the inside. He opened the freezer and removed the three clips, which were stashed in the icemaker.

The stage was set; the players were ready to take their places. Come this time tomorrow, he would be heading back to Mexico–alone. He would pick up Montoya, take care of him, and then after take-off, take care of Gutierrez. They could 'sleep with the fishes' at the bottom of Lake Michigan, as they said in American movies.

Room Service brought his meal. He dined, with exquisite pleasure, on American beef. He always ordered steak when he was in Chicago. What did they do to their steers up here? Midwestern beef was like no other in the world, and though he had imported an American Angus bull to breed to his cows, the beef was still not quite the same.

His evening passed quietly. He prepared himself mentally for the coming day. Like a matador preparing for a fight, he focused on the entrance, the attack, and the kill as they floated through his mind in slow motion. Meditation brought clarity to the plan. He could look upon each individual event and plan his actions for any eventuality. He slept soundly and woke early.

The day was breaking to a misty dawn as Martinez donned a robe and ordered breakfast. He dined on steak and eggs while he read the local newspaper. He eventually got dressed, calmly packed his belongings, called Gutierrez to retrieve the bags, and gave himself one final going-over in the mirror.

Unless one looked very closely, one could not see the bulge of the shoulder holster under his suit coat.

The reception went as planned, other than the President of the National Latino Businessmen's Association being a little long-winded. At 11:10 he tossed his 'Man of the Year' plaque into the back seat of the limo and climbed in next to Gutierrez. He rehearsed Gutierrez's role with him on the way to the airport. They found the terminal with no problem. They were in the air within twenty minutes.

This afternoon the pilot of the rented plane knew Martinez as Hector Barrera Diaz. Martinez let out a self-satisfied sigh, settled back in the cockpit of the rented Cessna 172. He had chosen this plane and pilot carefully. The little passenger plane was big enough to accommodate three men.

Since the days of Al Capone, the area they were flying to was known for its mansion-style summer homes of the very wealthy. Private airstrips abounded, and a private plane was not an uncommon sight.

The plane was common enough that it could also be flown into one of the many local resorts in the surrounding area and become lost among the guest planes for a few days. Martinez had ordered a company car over a week ago and had it waiting at one such resort.

The pilot owned the plane and flew businessmen on short trips for a living. He would not be missed until 'Mr. Diaz from Los Angeles' was long gone. Best of all, Martinez had hundreds of logged hours flying this type of craft. He would pilot it on the last leg of his mission.

Flying in the co-pilot's seat gave him a feeling of euphoria, but piloting an aircraft like this gave him a rush of supremacy beyond mere mortal men. Life was about power, and he was a powerful man. People were pawns to be moved around the chessboard of life, and discarded when they were no longer of use.

Martinez had made very few mistakes in choosing his pawns on the way to his preeminence. Huerta was one mistake, the greedy bastard. He took what was not his and paid for it with his life.

Montoya; now that was a shame. Hard working, loyal and very good at his craft, he had a special way with horses, which was rare even among trainers. Unfortunately for Montoya, he also had a strong sense of right and wrong.

In the beginning he seemed so obedient. Martinez misread those signs and thought Montoya would be easily corruptible. Mistakes like that would prove fatal–for Montoya.

Thank God for stupido peasants like that American policeman–he checked his notes–Theodore Puetz of White Bass Lake, Wisconsin. Now there was a man with no morals. Martinez had the entire story, plus the location of Montoya, out of him in less than ten minutes. Puetz bought the warrant story with no questions. This Puetz was a man Montoya could manipulate and eliminate without batting an eye.

There were many in Mexico of his ilk, placed in positions of authority specifically to do the bidding of those who wield the swords of real power. Martinez chuckled.

In his lifetime he had dealt with and discarded so many insignificant clods like Puetz, he could feed their egos and slit their throats without them suspecting a thing. Their incompetence was exceeded only by their arrogance, and that self-importance usually proved to be the death of them.

By now Montoya would have been arrested for murder, and would be awaiting extradition to Texas. Martinez was too smart to play the games of Immigration–deportation could take months, and Martinez had hours. He looked toward the rear of the plane at the 300-pound bodyguard posing as a policeman from Mexico.

Gutierrez smiled at Martinez and patted the forged papers in his pocket. The dim-witted Americans would hand Montoya his death sentence when they turned custody over to Gutierrez.

It was easy to dispose of a weighted body over Lake Michigan, especially when one had a big man like Gutierrez to do the bull work. Montoya's demise would be a rare treat for Martinez.

He let his mind relax, and thought back to his beginnings. It had been 43 years since a ten-year-old, starving, half-clothed, illiterate Mexican boy shoved a knife between the ribs of a bag boy for the Mexican Mafia.

Instead of stealing the money (that would have meant certain death were he caught,) he delivered the bag. Thus began a career of running drugs and money for the Mexican Mafia.

Having street smarts and no conscience quickly elevated his status. By the time he was twenty he had his own fishing boat and was running a drug boat up-river. Drugs from Columbia were brought in through Mexico, and smuggled across the border into the United States. Martinez was in on the ground floor.

His wealth grew with his reputation for ruthlessness. He had killed off the competition and owned a fleet of boats. As his wealth quadrupled, he found his assets coming under scrutiny by the law. He was very careful, but had too much dirty money stockpiled and nowhere to spend it. His Columbian associates suggested ways to clean up his money and it was not long before Martinez was laundering millions through the black market Peso Exchange.

Over the next fifteen years, Martinez spent his drug money wisely and built an empire of legitimate businesses in the Chicago area, as well as Mexico and Columbia. He became the Mexican Connection for the Columbian drug trafficking trade in the Midwest.

He bought real estate in Mexico and the United States. He employed thousands of people and built housing for the poor. He was a man of vision, a man of power. He was an unconquerable warrior on his own turf, but he tread delicately in the United States.

Montoya was a small glitch. For some reason he was still alive. Martinez would soon take care of that minor detail.

He smiled to himself. It is a lucky thing to be able to stare into the eyes of a man at the precise moment the man knew his life was about to end. Martinez was nothing, if not lucky.

The flight was smooth and they landed on the private landing strip without incident. The pilot stepped behind his seat to prepare for deplaning.

He had time to notice the plastic drop cloths covering the seats and aisle of the plane, but Martinez doubted he had time to comprehend its meaning before he shot the man in the back of the head. He dropped like a stone. Gutierrez folded the drop cloths around the body while Martinez opened the plane.

Nothing moved outside the plane. The two men silently made their way to the car waiting for them. Looking at the map, Martinez calculated they would be airborne around 5:00 this afternoon. As long as all went smoothly in White Bass Lake, he would be a happy man by morning.

The trip was short and they soon pulled into the parking lot of the Colson County Sheriff's Department. They exited the car and strode through the glass doors. Edie greeted them with a benign smile. Gutierrez stepped up and handed her the phony papers and Edie looked them over.

Martinez nudged Gutierrez aside and honored Edie with his most winning smile. He handed her his passport. "I am Eduardo Martinez, ma'am. I am the employer of Dr. Huerta, the poor victim, and also of his murderer, Alejandro Montoya. If you will please direct me to your employer, Mr. Theodore Puetz, we are ready to take custody of Mr. Montoya and be on our way." He looked around and could not quite contain the disdain in his voice. "I'm sure you people are very busy, so if you would be so kind..."

Edie bit her lip. She fumbled with the papers. As she picked them up, she discretely pressed a hidden button.

"Well, sir, I understand you want to get going, but there has been a slight change in circumstances." She moved slightly to her left, making sure Martinez was in full view of the camera behind her.

"Sheriff Green asked me to tell you that Alejandro Montoya was found dead before they could serve the papers."

Montoya sputtered, "Th–that's impossible! I demand to speak to Theodore Puetz immediately!"

"I don't know what Ted is going to do for you sir, he is only a Constable. J.J. Green is the Sheriff of Colson County and if you need to speak to him, I'll have to call him for you."

Gutierrez and Martinez looked at each other. Martinez's eyes turned cold as they leveled on Edie. "Are you telling me that Theodore Puetz is not in charge of this investigation?"

"I'm telling you, sir that Theodore Puetz is not *in charge* of anything. Buzz Miller and Sheriff Green are investigating the matter. If you would like to speak with Sheriff Green, I would be happy to call him. He is in the field working, as we had no prior notice of your arrival. If you would like to speak with Miz Miller, I believe she is down at the morgue."

Martinez angrily threw his hands in the air. "Call him. Get him here."

Edie picked up the phone and dialed J.J. in his office.

He picked up the phone and said. "Edie, be careful. If this guy is who I think he is, he could be very dangerous."

Edie said, "Sheriff Green? Edie. Yes sir. I'm sorry to bother you but a..." She made it a point to read from the passport, "Mr. Eduardo Martinez is here to pick up that Montoya boy. Yes sir, I'll tell him."

Martinez leaned over and grabbed the phone out of her hand. "You are Sheriff Green? I am Martinez. How long will you be? Fifteen minutes? Yes, I can wait. No, this is not a problem. Thank you."

Martinez slammed the phone down and swore in Spanish. Gutierrez stood in stoney silence. Martinez whirled on Edie and pointed at her. "You! Where is the sheriff's office? We will wait there."

Edie looked over her right shoulder. "Sheriff Green does not like anyone in his off–wait!" She held up her hands and stepped in front of Martinez when he made to move past her.

Gutierrez moved like lightning and had Edie by the throat. He lifted her to her toes and held her there.

She let out a squeak. Martinez laid a hand on Gutierrez's arm. He slowly lowered Edie to the floor. She gasped, her eyes huge.

Martinez said in a smooth voice, "Why do you not direct us to the sheriff's office and we will wait there? You, of course, will wait at your desk."

Edie eyed Gutierrez and felt her throat. "Uh, yes, it's over here." She led them to J.J.'s office and opened the door. Stepping inside, she opened the vertical blinds covering the glass wall looking out on the lobby. Neither man noticed when she left, as both were in opposite corners of the office, talking on their respective cell phones. Martinez picked up the newspaper J.J. had left on a chair and stared at headlines, which read, 'Murder Suspect Found Dead'.

Edie stepped gingerly behind her desk and dialed up J.J.'s cell. He immediately started yelling. "Edie, what the hell did you say to that guy. I told you to be careful! Are you all right?"

"Hello, to you too." She casually sat in her chair and faced the office. Both men had their backs to her and neither was by the desk. "I thought I'd invite them to tea, but they had a prior engagement."

She drew in a breath. "Seriously, J.J., I tried to stall them from going into your office too soon because I didn't want them walking in on you, you butthead."

"I got out just before you went in. I'll call there in a few minutes. You're a champ, kiddo. Thanks." J.J. hung up the phone.

Edie touched her neck one more time and went back to typing a barking dog report. She discretely opened a drawer and watched on the monitor while the camera in J.J.'s office recorded Martinez planting two listening devices, one behind a light on the bookshelf, and the other under his desk calendar. The bodyguard kept watch on Edie, who looked for all the world like she was engrossed in her dog report.

Five minutes later the phone rang again. Edie picked it up. She heard the click of J.J.'s office phone and hoped he did too. "Edie? J.J. Something's come up and I can't make it back. Could you please give my apologies to Mr. Martinez? Get a number and I'll call his motel when I finish."

"Will do, Sheriff," Edie said and hung up the phone.

Martinez came storming out of J.J.'s office. Edie turned, smile on her face. "Mr. Martinez, that was Sheriff Green on the phone. He said—"

Martinez threw a piece of paper in Edie's direction. "I know what he said," and slammed through the front door.

Edie smiled for real and went back to her typing.

27

Mag and Ian arrived at Mom's while I was in the house. By the time I made it back out to the barn, Ian was talking to J.J. and Mag was storming through the barn in my direction. We both stopped and gaped as the familiar red Crown Vic came roaring up the driveway, fishtailing in the gravel. A fluff of blue hair was all we could see above the dash. We braced ourselves mentally, and dove for cover.

We watched as the heavy driver's door of the Crown Vic flew wide open and bounced on its hinges. Two scrawny legs popped out and pulled back in quickly, barely avoiding being pinched in the door. Muffled cursing that would have made a sailor blush could be heard from inside the car. The door popped open again. A purse the size of a diaper bag was thrust between the door and the frame. We came out of hiding. Mag grabbed the door and opened it. She jumped back when Mary Cromwell kicked at the door again. Instead of hitting the door, Mary's feet met air, and she catapulted out of the car and slammed into Mag. The Maggot fell backward and Mary ended up on Mag's chest, with her knees on either side of Mag's head, and her crotch on Mag's chin.

Mary looked down at Mag with reproach written all over her face. "You Miller girls just can't stay out of trouble, can you?"

Since Mary was sitting on Mag's throat, Mag was having a hard time answering, as she was being suffocated by the 78 pound geriatric. I grabbed Mary by the armpits and yanked her off of Mag. Mag sat up and sucked air into her lungs. I yanked Mary so hard, her legs flew over her head like a rag doll. I set her down, barely avoided being clobbered on the head by that monstrosity of a purse.

She mumbled and tottered off toward the house. I grabbed the purse and hauled her to a stop. With barely contained rage, I fought for control as it registered Mom must have spilled the beans already. I tried for nonchalance and ended up with Spanish Inquisition. I glared down at her and barked, "Did my mother call you?"

She yanked her purse out of my hand. She paused to smooth her short blue curls into place and stuck her nose in the air. "No, I guess I'm not good enough for Gerry Miller anymore, my *son* had to tell me there was another party–I mean body–out here at the farm. There's been so much murder and mayhem going on, I didn't have time to make anything."

She yanked her purse out of my hands and this time stomped off in the direction of the barn. I held out my hand to Mag. I don't often say it, but poor Mag, she tried to be a Good Samaritan and ended up crotched by an old lady. Mag grabbed my wrist and I hoisted her off the ground. Brushing the dirt off her butt she said, "Man, why did you yell at Mary? I thought you were going to mash her bony little body to a pulp. It was pretty cool the way she stood up to you though. She must be really ballsy, or really, really stupid!"

We thought about it for a second and looked at each other.

"Stupid," we said together, and laughed.

"Mag, a lot has been happening, and I can't tell you all of it until we get out of here. Let's meet at my house, I have to get the dogs home anyway. Why don't you order pizza and drag Ian out of here. I'll get J.J. and meet you guys at my house around," I consulted my watch, "seven."

"Sounds good. It was all but over with back there,

anyway. The ambulance is bagging up the body and Mike called the rendering service to move the horse to his large animal surgery. Bernie posed for a newspaper photo with the horse on the winch like he was posing with a record breaking marlin. Ted was on his cell phone, probably calling Mommy."

When we parted, Mag held out a fist and I touched her knuckles with mine. We didn't know what it meant, but we saw it on television once and thought it was cool. The ambulance drove around the barn. Malcolm followed in his car. People came streaming out of the barn and climbed into their cars. Ted and Mary drew up the rear, arguing over something. Mag and I ducked behind some old hay to avoid them.

Only J.J., Mike, Bernie, Moe, and Ian remained out behind the barn. Bernie was just climbing into his truck when I walked up to thank him for coming out. "Aww, shucks, Miz Buzz, you know I'd do anything for your folks."

"Thanks just the same, Bernie. Not too many people would blow an afternoon dragging a dead horse out of the ground for a neighbor."

He blushed and pulled on the bill of his John Deere ball cap. With a nod, he backed his truck up and pulled around the barn. J.J. was bringing Mike up to date. He explained why he wanted the mare autopsied and a drug screen run.

Mike shook his head and looked at the ground. "I've heard everything now, J.J. I honestly thought I could not be surprised at what people were capable of, but I was wrong. If there is anything else I can do, you let me know."

J.J. put a hand on Mike's shoulder. "Just be careful, my friend. We think whoever did this probably destroyed a veterinarian's office in Texas. They also stole the carcass of a mare that sounds as if she died in the same way."

Mike slapped J.J. in the ribs and jumped back, chuckled and said, "No worries, mate. My office is separate from my home, and I'm going to cut her open right away. Where are you going to be?"

I piped up, "My house."

Mike, with a speculative gleam in his eye, said, "So I heard."

I narrowed my eyes and went chest to chest. "Knock it off, Doc, or I'll start the rumor that when you pass Jake Gustafson's sheep farm, the lambs look up and say, 'There goes my daaad!'"

He barked out a laugh. "You are one sick bitch. Okay, you win, Buzz. Your house and no teasing." He ruffled my hair and headed for his truck.

I ran a hand through my wild mop. "Why does everyone *do* that?" I grumbled.

J.J. ruffled my hair. "We've been doing it since we were all kids, and it pisses you off." He danced out of my swinging range.

"Come on you guys," he called to Ian and Mag. "I guess we're all going over to Buzz's."

28

The meeting at my house went off as planned, with everyone arriving within a half-hour of each other. We congregated in the kitchen, gathering around the table. Food was top priority, and Sal had really outdone himself. With the bribery of good information for his morning crowd, he put on an unbelievable spread. We were expecting burgers and chips, but Sal rolled in with salads with three dressings, roast beef, gravy, real potatoes, corn, and double chocolate turtle cheesecake.

In return, Sal went home happy with the facts of the case tucked safely in the back of his mind. The only information withheld was the part about Alejandro being alive. We had Alejandro stashed in the guest room happily eating, until Wesley gave him away (must have been the gravy smell). Sal left with the secret screaming for a chance to greet the gossip mill in the morning, but I felt what the heck? Everyone in town would know by morning anyway, when the body I.D. and autopsy came back. Hopefully, if all went according to plan, by morning was all we needed. Sal might as well be the one with his facts straight. Better Sal's almost first hand account than the crap I handed Rosie-the-News-Whore out at the farm!

Stuffed to the gills, we gravitated to the family room. I gave a dirty look to the partially blank whiteboard, which laughed at me whenever I passed it. The dogs joined us for coffee. Wesley sat on my feet and Hill crawled into J.J.'s lap.

We went over the facts as we knew them. Ian added what he had learned from the molecular boys. "The seeds from Carole's pocket were definitely Mammilaria lutheyi, and they did not match with the samples we took from the cultivars from the green house.

"In all probability this means it was a new strain from Mexico, which would coincide with the propagation-from-seed theory. The problem is that it still doesn't connect Carole to the drugs or murder. The laws in Mexico forbid the exportation of the plants, but are unclear on the subject of seeds. So as far as we know, there was no crime committed which would have gotten her murdered."

Ian twitched with excitement. "Where the plot becomes interesting, however, is when we learn that leuthyi is only found in the Mexican State of Coahuila–where Martinez calls home. While this will not convict, it is another circumstantial tie to the drug trail."

He shuffled more papers. "Jeff's boys also found the paper towel the seeds were wrapped in carried traces of pollen from the opium poppies, and that matches up to drugs confiscated off the southern wave of trafficking we already have a handle on."

I shook my head in awe. "Then the autopsy from the dead horse at Mom and Dad's will explain why the drugs show up in the south and up here, with none in the Heartland, because they were using horses to transport it straight here, and then on to Chicago, Rockford, Minneapolis and points beyond."

Ian referred to his notes. "You win the kewpie doll, Buzz. As far as Jeff Fuller could find, they are trying to use this Mexican Poppy to cut cocaine and heroin. The Mexican Poppy is considered a weed in southern Texas and in Mexico, so it can be grown and harvested for next to nothing."

He patted Mag's knee and rubbed a hand up and down her thigh. "What our Maggie grabbed in the lab seems to be a new designer drug the lab boys are calling *Totaled*.

"In small amounts, the toxin found in the Mexican Poppy, when combined with cocaine, reacts in the human body like a hot rush that will blow the top of your head off, thus, you're totaled. This feeling is followed by it doing just that. Blood vessels burst in the brain and the results are stroke, coma, and death."

He taped the lab results to the whiteboard and went on. "Our friendly neighborhood drug manufacturers are mixing small quantities of the poison into a cocaine cocktail, which we assume is supposed to stop the chain reaction short of the stroke part. However, Totaled is highly volatile, and not much is known about the chemical reaction when mixed with alcohol or other drugs. Flying on supposition tells us that the results would be devastating if this drug hits the rave crowd. Some recent unexplained deaths are being tested at this moment to see if they can detect the toxin."

Ian blew out a breath. "That about wraps it up, boys and girls." He handed the rest of his report to Mag, who hung it with the rest of the lab results. He folded his arms, stood staring at the whiteboard, and said, almost to himself, "There is still something missing."

I piped up. "I still think that Carole must have seen something she shouldn't have, or she unknowingly became involved in something and tried to get out."

Mag inhaled, opened her mouth, and slapped a hand over her lips.

"What?"

Mag looked at each of us. "I'm not a cop like the rest of you, but I agree with Buzz. What if Carole accidentally saw something she shouldn't have? Like the horse behind Dad's barn die, or witnessed that guy under the horse being murdered? It could have happened a day or so before we broke into Graff's, and the timing would have worked out perfectly."

I grabbed her theory and ran with it. "What if Alejandro's boss never went to Fort Worth and was up here the whole time?"

The idea clicked with Mag. "Yeah, if Carole happened across either incident and ran, she might have headed toward Mom and Dad's. Martinez could have ordered the murders, which would make more sense than the bad guys just offing each other."

"Oh, my God!" All eyes turned to Alejandro, who was holding his head in both hands. "I must have blanked it out. Of course Martinez was there! I couldn't believe my eyes at first, but he was there, in the shadows! He was there. I know it!"

He turned teary eyes toward me. "How could I forget that, Buzz? How could I forget my boss was there in the shadows? That means he knew. He knew the whole time." His eyes grew bigger. "Then it *was* him who almost had me killed! Jose…poor Jose knew nothing." He rocked in his chair and moaned.

J.J. added, "And what about Doctor Little? Martinez probably had his clinic destroyed in case there was evidence there. He must have stolen the mare so the drugs couldn't be found."

Alejandro began to sob. "Poor Princesa, so beautiful, so full of life!"

He looked up again, with tear-drenched eyes. We all sat and watched as his expression changed from grief to rage. He moved to stand. J.J. and Ian each put a hand on his shoulders.

J.J. spoke first. "Anger is good, my friend, but we do not run off blindly to seek vengeance. We plan, we organize, and we plan some more. I will let you be in, but you must follow orders exactly to the letter, is that clear?"

Alejandro nodded. "Yes, sir. I will follow orders, but I want justice for those two mares. And for Missus Graff."

"We all do, my friend, and we will get it. Come on. We'll go over what we have so far. I have a couple of calls to make to get the ball rolling. Please excuse me, everyone."

J.J. left the room.

My house phone rang and I jumped up to get it. It was Moe. "Buzz? Darryl...uh, I mean Moe. I'm sorry to bother you...uh, I mean, is...uh, J.J. there? I don't mean, uh, shit. Buzz, I need to find J.J. I found something important and he needs to know about it. I can leave a message with you if he's busy or not there, but I gotta find him."

"Whoa ,Moe! Slow down a minute! Where are you? J.J. is here–why don't you come on over?"

"I uh, I'm actually in the neighborhood. But I don't want to interrupt ,uh, anything..."

"Don't be an idiot, Darryl. Mag, Ian, and a whole group of us just finished supper. Get over here and get something into your stomach, and you can tell J.J. in person, okay?"

"You're on, Buzz, and thanks!" About three minutes went by before Moe arrived. Wes looked at the door a split second before we heard Moe knock. He was ready to spring when Ian grabbed the doorknob.

Mag and I tackled Wes at the same time the door opened. We all went down in a heap. The rest of the guests laughed and applauded. When Moe entered to the roar of the crowd, he not only got a double whammy beam shot of two Miller sister butts, he was witness to howling laughter, and general chaos.

The poor man probably thought he'd entered into a major orgy.

Moe stopped, frozen on the threshold when Mag, Wes and I rolled to a stop at his feet, all breathing hard. J.J. came in from the kitchen in time to see Moe throw him a helpless look. J.J. laughed, as he took in the scene of me flat on my back with a hand on Wes' collar, Mag sprawled on her belly across Wes' belly, and Wes panting, waving his black flag and grinning widely in doggy joy.

"I see you've met King Wesley, Moe. Welcome to the family. Come on in and join our nut house."

"Phil." Moe cautiously tiptoed around us and kept glancing over his shoulder as he followed J.J. into the kitchen. We collected ourselves and tried to put a semblance of order back into the room.

We picked up the fallen chair, righted the lamp, moved the footstool back across the room and picked up the pillows.

Hilary stood in the middle of all the activity, excited to be a part of it. She must have been really excited, because when Mag playfully poked her in the butt, Hill jumped and cracked off a doggy fart to end all doggy farts.

It fizzed long and hard. All movement stopped as everyone stared at Hilary. She was so proud of herself, she trotted toward me for a reward.

The stench, unfortunately followed her as well, and I found myself backing away from her. "Hill, go to Mag. Go on! Go to Maggie!"

Covering my nose, I passed Alejandro. When he got a whiff, he jumped up and followed me. We backed past Ian, who joined us as we passed Mag. When J.J. and Moe came out of the kitchen, they saw the whole bunch of us headed for the front door, followed by a smelly Bulldog and a smiling Newfie.

Poor Hilary stopped and looked dolefully at J.J. He bent to rub her ears and said, "Yes, Hill, it's your fault this time, but we love you anyway." He poked his head out the front door. "Hey, you pansies get in here and quit messing around!"

We all filed back in and jockeyed for the best seats while Moe and J.J. spoke. J.J. hefted a large brown briefcase and directed his question to Alejandro.

"Montoya, does this belong to you?"

"No, J.J. It is a briefcase I found under the truck seat when I was in Mundelein. I never opened it. I told you, I saw Dr. Huerta in the show barn in Fort Worth carrying a brown briefcase, but it must have been a different one."

He furrowed his brow. "At the time I thought it was strange, because all the important papers for the horses were in there, but then I thought maybe he grabbed the wrong case. I forgot about it when I spoke to you, but it should have been in the truck under the passenger seat where I left it."

Moe nodded. "That's where I found it."

J.J. looked at the ceiling and closed his eyes. He rocked on his heels. "Alejandro, do you know what is inside this case?"

"No, Sheriff Green. I never opened it."

J.J. blew out a breath. "I hope for your sake you're telling me the truth, Montoya. With Huerta dead and this case hidden in your truck, the evidence would be pretty incriminating if this case contained something worth murdering for, don't you think?"

Alejandro looked thoughtful. "Yes sir, I suppose you are right."

I jumped up. "Now, wait a damn minute J.J. Before you start jumping on the Dead Butts bandwagon–"

"Whoa, Buzz, I'm not jumping anywhere...yet. In fact, because the case's lock has *not* been tampered with, I figure Montoya is either telling the truth or he already knows the combination." He turned to Alejandro. "So which is it, amigo?"

Alejandro drew himself up and tugged on his shirt,

taking offense at the accusation. "I do not tell lies, Sheriff Green. I understand this does not look good for me, but I tell the truth. I do not know what is in that case. I found it under Dr. Huerta's seat."

J.J. straightened and let out the breath he had been holding. "That's good enough for me." He took off for the kitchen, and spoke over his shoulder. "Buzz? Find me a toolbox, would you, dear?"

I stood stunned for a moment while everyone in the room stared at me. I figured the offense was a good defense and I yelled, "How come you're always nice to me when you want my toolbox, Green? I'll 'dear' your ass, buster!"

I heard a collective chuckle when I left the room. I found my tools in the basement. By that time, everyone had followed me downstairs and we were crammed in my small work area. J.J. hoisted the heavy case onto the workbench. The men squeezed in beside him. Mag and I were left staring at three sets of Levis and one Wrangler butt.

Leaving the men to their manly pursuits, Mag and I walked over to my reading area, which consisted of a fireplace, two big overstuffed leather recliners, three fish tanks, and bookshelves to the ceiling. We flopped in the chairs and stared at the fish. In one tank, Golden Angels floated on gossamer fins past the Green Leopard super veils.

Green Laser Cory catfish swished the gravel, and a swarm of Cardinal Tetras played in the water column. Three brown, long fin bristle-nose plecostomus chewed rhythmically on the driftwood in the center of the tank. In the second tank, three Marlboro and three Blue Cobalt Discus gently nosed the glass. They were all about five inches in diameter, and stunning in their almost fluorescent colors. They recognized me and were performing for a snack. The *Brocus splendens* eyed me from behind the wood in the tank, waiting for bits of food to float down to their level.

The third tank contained all the rare specie of Corys, which were my sister Fred's South American passion.

Included in the tank were endangered Endler Live Bearers and other South and Central American cichlids. Each time Fred acquired a newly discovered species, she shared her treasures with me. The three huge tanks gave me variety to fit my mood. Wes and Hill loved to watch the fish, too.

We were startled out of our reverie by excited exclamations coming from the work area. The boys had succeeded in opening the case and were in the process of dumping the contents onto the workbench. We strained to look over shoulders and under armpits.

Suddenly, three men surged backward and pinned us to the opposite wall. J.J. yelled, "Back! Everyone back!"

A mad scramble away from the bench had us stumbling over Ian, Moe and Alejandro. Hands grabbed my arm, and I saw Ian had hold of me. I shook loose and started back toward the workbench.

J.J. held up a hand and I stopped. "Ian, I need you here," he commanded. Ian responded with a leap over the dogs. He pushed past me. The hair on the back of my neck stood up.

I held my tongue, but strained to see what they were doing. I about crapped when I saw J.J. hold up an incendiary device. The anger drained out of me as quickly as Ian sucked in a breath.

I backed away and joined Moe, Mag, and Alejandro. I looked at my beloved dogs and said, "Mag, help me get the dogs out of here."

We grabbed their collars and led them upstairs and out the back door. The kennel sat well away from the house. I figured they'd be safer out there.

I flopped on the swing and Mag joined me. "What the heck was that, Buzz?"

"*That* is a device meant to blow someone up and start a major fire," I replied. "It didn't look home made, either. If Alejandro knew what was in that case, no way would he sit by and watch us open it. He would have slid out the door and been to Hell and gone by now."

"Yeah," she said. "If he's in on this, I'd suck a pig's ass."

"Yo bitch, you are way too disgusting! Let's go back in and see what's going on."

Mag and I hopped off the swing and went back to the house. We jogged down the basement stairs.

Mag said, "Jeez, talk about pennies from Heaven!"

Alejandro and Moe were seated at the coffee table, with stacks of banded money in the middle. Ian and J.J. were at the workbench. J.J. held a piece of paper with my eyebrow tweezers and Ian held open a Ziploc sandwich bag.

Since Alejandro was not in cuffs, I figured J.J. had found something in the case to exonerate him.

I was about to make comment when J.J. looked up and said, "Over here, Buzz."

I figured it had to be something really important if it was better than a mountain of money on the table. "What's up, James?"

Ian held out the bag. "Look at this."

I took the bag and my blood froze in my veins. It was a hand-written note: 'Take care of Montoya–he is not to leave Fort Worth alive. Deliver the money to Escobar. I will meet you up north. M'.

I looked over where Alejandro was happily chatting with Moe and Mag, counting money and oblivious to how close death had come. I didn't realize I had swayed until I bumped into J.J. behind me.

I never failed to feel sick that someone would be so callous as to dispose of another human being like yesterday's garbage. Another reason I retired.

J.J. cleared his throat, and spoke quietly, "I'm not telling him at this point, and I hope you two will agree with this decision."

Ian and I nodded. "Ian called his office and they are on their way to pick up the device. Ian, I take it you have a gun safe, or something like it, in that black girlie car of yours?" Ian nodded again. "Then for now I'll put this in the trunk of your car."

J.J. took off up the stairs with the bagged firebomb and Ian's keys. I breathed a little easier when he came back in one piece. He had a determined look in his eye "We have to move on this before someone else is killed." J.J. slapped Ian on the shoulder. "Time to call in the Calvary."

Ian winked. "I'm way ahead of you. When I called the bomb squad, I also sent notice to my superiors that we required a response team. They are mobilizing and will wait at the Motel 8 by the expressway for our call. Bob O'Brien will be our contact. He's coming down now and will pose as your cousin, J.J. You'll understand why when you see him."

"Okay, if you say so. Right now I have to put a bug in the right ears to get this party started. Edie swept my office and found listening devices there and one at the front counter. I'm going to place a call and she'll put the phone on speaker."

I piped up, "If I could interrupt for just a moment, what am I doing now?"

J.J. jerked his head toward Mag, Alejandro, and Moe. "If you would go over tonight's itinerary with them one more time, I'd appreciate it."

He ruffled my hair and I poked him in the belly. "Knock it off or I'm going to tell your mother." He and Ian both laughed.

I turned to the trio across the room. "Hey, you Rockefellers, dump that into a box or something and let's go over tonight's plan."

We looked around for a container and Mag came up with the big cooler we used to put our fresh-caught fish in.

Alejandro laughed, "Now we know something is fishy here!"

We all joined in with fish jokes on the way back upstairs. J.J. was on the phone. "Hello, Edie? J.J. here. Do we still have that Luminal in the evidence storage area? Good. Pull it out for me, would you? Buzz and I are going to make another trip out to Graff's. I think that horse might have died out there in the barn. I'll stop by and pick it up. Yeah, about six o'clock."

He waited while Edie spoke. "My cousin Bob is coming for the weekend and I wanted to wait for him to get here so I could send him over to my mother's house until we finish out at Graff's. Yeah, about five or so. No, no, you go on home at 4:30 as usual. You can leave the stuff in my office. I'll pick it up on the way out. Thanks Edie–bye, now."

He flipped the phone closed and said, "Well, that's that. We're committed."

"Or we ought to be." I added under my breath.

Moe walked in from the other room, snapping her cell phone shut. "More bad news, guys."

J.J. turned. "What the hell is it now?"

"Rob disappeared from the hospital."

Mag piped up, "I thought he was in ICU?"

"He was. They upgraded his condition and moved him to a regular room. It seems when Joel–that's who you call Curly–was helping the nurses move his stuff, Rob must have disconnected his IV and wheeled himself down the hall. The wheelchair was found in a waiting room, and a man is missing a long coat. What he used for shoes is beyond me, but Curly is out looking for a guy who looks like a barefoot flasher, as we speak."

J.J. rubbed his brow. "Geeez, what next?" He picked up the cell once more and called Edie at the station. He put out an all-call on Rob Graff. He'd fix *his* disappearing ass.

J.J. had Edie notify everyone–including the Wisconsin and the Illinois State Police. "Robert Graff just jumped to the top of my most wanted list. Let's wait for Bob to get here. Moe, keep an ear close to the radio. I want that little bastard back in custody."

"Right, Boss."

The afternoon faded into evening while we tossed ideas back and forth about how to proceed. Bob O'Brien arrived about four. I opened the door, stood for a moment, staring at a man who could have passed for J.J.'s twin, or at least his younger brother.

He held out his hand. "You must be Buzz Miller. Ian described you perfectly."

I gave him a wary look and shook his hand. "I'm afraid to ask what he said. Come on in and meet everyone." Bob gave me an easy smile and walked past me into the house.

J.J. did a double take. "Hol-ee crap! Did my momma forget to tell me something? Are you a handsome devil or what?"

Bob laughed. "I must be. I look just like you, my friend."

29

Chest heaving, feet killing him, Rob Graff stepped around the side of a house and stood with his hands on his knees, willing his heart to slow. It seemed like he had run miles, but he could still see the tower on the top of the hospital about a half mile away. What the hell was he going to do? He had to get out of here. He had to pack and go…go somewhere. L.A. or Mexico maybe.

Jumping over a hedge Rob crouched near a shed. Good. No dog. He spotted clothes hanging on a line and couldn't believe his luck. Keeping an eye on the back door, Rob scuttled across the yard and snatched sweatpants and a tee shirt off the line. He heard a dog bark and his heart jumped to his throat. He ran like Jesse Owens toward the hedge and flew over the top. As he stumbled around the corner, he dumped the stolen coat on the ground, dragged the sweats over the hospital gown and pulled the too-small tee over his head.

The sound of a diesel engine kept him heading toward the street. *Wow. That's Bill Miller at the stop sign.* He ran to the intersection.

"Hi Mr. Miller," he called through the window.

"Well, hello there Rob, I thought you were in some sort of accident or something. Shouldn't you be resting at home?"

"Yes I should, but I got stuck here in town. If you're heading home, could I catch a ride with you?"

"Sure enough Rob. Hop in, I'm heading out now."

Rob was deep in thought during the ride, mentally making a to do list. He jumped out of the truck at the entrance to the garden center, yelled his thanks, and ran toward the house. First on the agenda: band aids, socks, and shoes for his feet. Then pack up and get the hell out.

* * *

FBI Bob, J.J., and I drove to J.J.'s Mom's house where we dropped off Bob. He hugged J.J.'s mom when she answered the door and went inside. I thought what a great sport she was, hugging a stranger she had never met. Just in case someone was watching, Bob waited five minutes, and then went out the back door. He hopped Mrs. Leskowitz's fence, ran three houses over, and crossed the street to where Mag waited with her car. He jumped into the car and they headed toward Mom's house.

Meanwhile, J.J. and I picked up the Luminol at the office. J.J. took his time and listened to his messages. Knowing Martinez would pick up anything he said with the listening device, J.J. proceeded to bait the hook so he could lure Martinez to the greenhouse. He checked in with Curly, who was on patrol. J.J. told Curly we were headed out to Graff's greenhouse, and if he needed him to use the cell phone. Acting as he would if no one was listening, J.J. made a couple of return calls. He called his mother, told her we were a little later than we had expected to be, and for her to tell Bob he'd be home by 8:30 or so. He rang off, and we headed out to the Graff's place.

* * *

Bob, Ian, Mag, Moe, and Alejandro drove up my parent's driveway and pulled up close to the barn. Ian silently pointed across the field to Graff's greenhouses. Bob nodded. Inside the barn six ATVs and eight black-clad FBI agents waited.

Bob and Ian grabbed vests from the agent by the barn door and mounted the closest ATV. Moe and Mag climbed onto the second ATV, donned vests. Everyone was ready to go.

Alejandro headed past Ian. Ian grabbed his arm. "Amigo, remember we talked about this. It is way too dangerous for you to come. Those people want you dead. Go to the house. Bill and Gerry are expecting you. I promise you, I will see justice done."

Alejandro bit his lip. He looked at the ground and sighed. "I understand."

He looked as if he wanted to say more, but walked off through the barn toward the house. Bob gave the signal and everyone else set off toward Graff's.

Mag was surprised the machines made almost no noise. Moe leaned back and whispered, "Electric–like a golf cart."

"Cool-lee-O," she whispered back.

They covered the distance to the Graff property in less than five minutes and pulled quietly into place along the back fence. Mag stayed back with one other agent. She plugged in her ear phone so she could listen in. Bob, Ian, Moe, and the agents crept slowly through the tall weeds toward the barn.

Mag watched them seemingly melt into the twilight. A tingle crawled slowly up her spine. *Wow. This is real.* The ball was rolling, and she was a part of it!

Rob Graff was in the driveway in front of the main building when J.J. and I arrived. He gave no greeting, but opened the side gate so we could drive through. He left the gate open and got into the back seat at J.J.'s wave. He sat with his arms folded across his chest and stared out the window.

We rolled slowly through the yard. J.J. struck up a conversation, giving no indication he had just put out an all-points bulletin on Rob. "So Rob, is your dad back in town yet?"

"Why do you want to know? What's it to you?" was the

snotty reply.

J.J. sighed. "Because I care about how you guys are doing, that's why. I haven't heard from your father and I admit I am a little anxious, that's all. I would expect you would be concerned too."

Rob sat back and said sullenly, "He'll turn up–he always lands on his feet."

J.J. slowed to a crawl and looked at Rob in the rear-view mirror. "Rob, is there something you want to tell us? Do you know something about your dad's whereabouts you're not telling us?"

Rob grabbed the door handle, like he was going to jump out of the moving vehicle, and thought better of it. He rubbed the heels of his hands in his eyes and said miserably, "I don't know, man. It wasn't supposed to be like this!"

J.J. would have said more, but we had arrived at the barn. Rob threw open the door and bolted for the stable door. The lock was back on the door. Rob had it open before we got there. He stood back, looking at the ground. We entered the empty building.

"Sherriff Green–"

We stopped. "Yes Rob, do you have something to tell us?"

He scuffed a toe in the dirt. "Uh, I guess not."

Rob stayed by the door while J.J. and I entered the barn. J.J. flipped on the aisle lights and we proceeded toward the drain, about half way down the building.

Edie had prepared four spray bottles of Luminol. J.J. and I each picked one up and turned to the onerous task of looking for evidence of bloodshed. Luminol was not evidence per se, but rather a last resort tactic when other investigative methods have failed to produce clues to what transpired at a crime scene. Blood spatter patterns can be analyzed to determine what type of instrument was used to kill. Footprints, fingerprints, and other forensic evidence have been uncovered by the use of Luminol, and have connected killers to crime scenes. The type of Luminol police agencies used does not destroy DNA, so there was also a chance of picking up clues and evidence of the horse dying, or if Huerta or Carole bled anywhere in the stable.

Rob stood off in a corner with his hands stuffed in his pockets. He shuffled his feet and looked like he would rather be anywhere else but here. I looked at him and said, "Rob, do you want to help? Grab a bottle and go along the bottom two boards near the cross ties."

Rob dragged his feet over to where the remaining Luminol sat, looked around, and picked up a bottle. J.J. told him, "Be careful and don't breathe the fumes." He tossed Rob a paper mask. "The ventilation is good in here, but we need to be careful anyway."

J.J. and I worked opposite sides of the drain, methodically spraying the rubber matting leading to the drain hole in the floor. Rob walked over to the boards near the cross ties and gave them a couple of half-hearted strokes with the spray bottle. He stopped and looked over where we were working. Bending, he sprayed the boards once more before stopping again.

Rob looked toward the ceiling, shuffled his feet, fidgeted, and glanced back at J.J. "Sheriff Green, I gotta go to the bathroom, I'll be right back."

He dropped the bottle and sprinted toward the door. We watched as he skidded to a halt—his arms flailing and his legs going in opposite directions. Blocking his way was the shadow of a huge man. He stood there like a stone statue.

Rob slid smack into the giant's legs, but the giant never wavered. Rob bounced off the giant and landed on his back at the giant's feet.

The giant picked him up by the tee shirt and tossed the wheezing Rob aside with one hand. He straightened, folded his hands in front, and stared straight ahead once more.

J.J. grabbed my wrist to stop me when I started toward Rob. He gestured toward the stone giant by the door. From behind the giant strolled an elegantly dressed man. He slowly stepped into the light, fiddling with his cuffs and taking in his surroundings with an air of disdainful nonchalance. His black hair gleamed in the light, and his dark eyes were fixed on us.

He moved gracefully across the rubber floor to where we stood. He looked down his nose at us as if we were fly specks on a window. I felt my hackles rise as his dead black gaze slithered up my body.

Hands on hips, I spoke. "Martinez, I presume?"

The man sniffed and turned his profile to me. "American women do not know their place." With lightning speed he whipped a hand out and blasted me across the face.

I went down hard, smacking my head on the floor. My bottle of Luminol went flying, broke apart, and splashed up the pant leg of Martinez's expensive suit. "Clod! Stupido!" He shook his leg to rid himself of the liquid. J.J. never moved a muscle; neither did the gargantuan statue by the door.

I picked myself up, my cheek burning and my eyes watering. I stumbled sideways and collapsed on a bale of hay. Through my tears I eyed the giant in the doorway. Did the man ever even blink? I rolled my head to make sure it was still attached to my neck and tried to focus on the conversation between J.J. and Martinez. When the ringing in my ears subsided, I rose and stepped close enough to hear what they were saying.

In a dead calm voice Martinez said, "I want Montoya, and I want him now."

J.J. played the big dumb cowboy, exactly what Martinez expected him to be. He pushed his cowboy hat up with one hand and rubbed the back of his neck with the other.

"I am afraid to tell you this, Mr. Martinez, but we found your boy buried out back of the neighbor's place, along with one of your horses."

Montoya looked down his nose. "Let us not toy with each other, Sheriff Green. You know as well as I that the dead man is not Montoya, but a traitorous thief. A man named Huerta who was stupid enough to steal from me."

J.J. twirled his hat in his hand. "Well, that's where you're wrong amigo. I mean, he is dead and all, but that Huerta fellow never stole from you. All that time you had your boys torture him? He was telling you the truth from the beginning. Huerta grabbed the wrong case from the truck. I have the case with your note, your money, your fingerprints, and your little bomb."

"You lie, policeman." Martinez pulled out a gun and trained it on J.J.'s chest. "That case held 15 million dollars of my Columbian money. The Columbians came looking for it in Fort Worth. Huerta ran with it and came here. I was afraid they would come after me if the mares and the drugs were not delivered. The Columbians blamed my operation for the bad bag that leaked and killed my horse though it was their defective bag.

"I had to clean up after their bumbling in Fort Worth, and I lost a champion mare in the process. Instead of terminating Montoya in Texas, I sent Montoya with the mares to Chicago. That imbecile followed my men here and went running to you. Too many loose ends, Sheriff Green, and now the two of you. I am tired of this mess. Sometimes I think I am the only one with a brain in this world."

Martinez stepped closer to J.J. and I began to sweat. I

wondered how long J.J. could keep him talking. I also wondered how the hell long Bob was going to wait before the Calvary came-a-runnin'. I inched my hand along my leg and under my sweatshirt. I touched the butt of my revolver and left my hand there. I could barely see the stone statue in my peripheral vision, but I knew he was still there.

J.J. kept his hat in his left hand and dangled it by his side. "What about Carole Graff, where does she fit in? She was neither running drugs nor was she a murderer."

"Ah, Carole. She was ready to bend the law when it came to her plants, but she witnessed an unfortunate event and had to be terminated. She was useful, but expendable. She was yet another unfortunate loose end which had to be, how would you say it? Snipped."

I was really pissed now and drew his attention toward me so J.J. could get into position. "Unfortunate event? Which one did she witness? The murder of Huerta or the murder of the horse buried behind the neighbor's barn? Maybe she saw both, and to you she was just a 'loose end' so you murdered her. You're just another arrogant asshole who thinks he's above the law."

Martinez swung his hand again and J.J. caught it in mid-air. "Can't let you do that, amigo, she's my woman. If anyone slaps her around, it's going to be me—you understand I'm sure."

"She needs to be taught her place."

J.J. let Martinez's hand down slowly. Martinez glared at me. I could feel the hatred pouring off of him. I saw the man blocking the door lower his hand from his chest and realized he had reached for a weapon.

Whew Buzz, close call that time. Where the hell was Bob? How long did they expect us to keep this psychopath talking?

Outwardly calm, Martinez turned to J.J. "Using the

mares to transport the drugs was a stroke of genius," he bragged. "And this," he stretched his arms to encompass the barn, "was another stroke of brilliance. I call this place, *The Martinez Research and Development Center*." He chuckled at his own cleverness. "The stupid Columbians will never suspect I use their own drugs to produce designers and then sell back to them at quadruple the price." His chest puffed out and he bounced on the balls of his feet, reveling in his own self importance.

J.J. held his cowboy hat in his left hand and discretely slid his handgun from inside the hat with his right. He never took his eyes off Martinez as he held his hat in front of his right hand. He was about to make his move when the statue blocking the door turned toward my right. J.J. froze.

Martinez was still basking in his own glory when the shadows to my right also shifted. I almost collapsed with relief that Bob was finally here. Instead a small, handsome Latino-looking man flanked by two other men with dark complexions materialized. I had a sinking feeling this might be the 'Columbian Connection', Martinez was bragging about duping, and J.J. and I were in the crossfire of what was about to become a Latino bloodbath.

Dressed in conservative Armani with an overcoat around his shoulders, the man bowed slightly to me and to J.J. "Emilio Escobar," he said in a cultured voice. "I am the 'Stupid Columbian' who cannot tell when a minor employee," he slid his eyes toward Martinez, "is stealing from me."

Martinez blanched and stepped back. He said nothing, but seemed to shrink in his shoes, breathing shallowly. Rob stirred on the floor but didn't get up. The statue didn't move a muscle.

Striding slowly forward in deadly determination Escobar backhanded Martinez. The diamond on his pinkie left a red slash across Martinez's jaw. Martinez stood motionless while blood dripped onto his suit.

"Eduardo," Escobar calmly said. "You leave a bloody trail across the United States. You get sloppy with the transport of merchandise. You murder women. You leave witnesses alive to spread tales to law enforcement officers in-in..." He waved a hand in a circular motion and looked around the room. "This place, what was it? Your research and development laboratory?" He spit on the floor. "You are a peasant."

Martinez began to shake.

"I should not have to come to the States to clean up after you, Eduardo." He smiled a slow, evil smile. "As of this moment, I am terminating our relationship."

The silence was so thick I could feel it settle around my shoulders. Recognition from a late night CNN broadcast struck me between the eyes. "Wait a minute. Escobar. Emilio Escobar, son of the late Pablo Escobar, the world's richest drug trafficker?" I looked at Martinez. "Is this who you are calling 'stupid'? You are dumber than you look, buddy."

I could see Martinez boiling with rage, but he kept silent. With guns pointed toward his head, I guess he didn't have much of a choice.

Escobar allowed himself a small smile. "You have heard of me." He bowed slightly. "Yes, I am Emilio Escobar."

Out of the dark a voice said, "Emilio Escobar, born January 1, 1969. Grew up in Medellin, Columbia, until November, 1993 when his mother fled to Germany." FBI Bob stepped into the barn from the opposite end of the statue.

Flanked by two FBI agents with automatic weapons held high, Bob stepped-and-dragged his feet up the aisle in beautiful S.W.A.T. formation. "MBA from MIT, picked up the scraps of his father's enterprise and once again turned it into a major player in the world drug trade."

Escobar did not move. With deadly calm he said to Martinez, "More loose ends, Eduardo? I am more than disappointed. You will die tonight."

Bob stepped up behind Escobar. "No more dying tonight, Mr. Escobar. FBI. By the power vested in me by the United States of America, you are under arrest."

Escobar sighed, shrugged, and gave me a half-smile. "I guess I was not so smart this time, eh?"

Ian stepped out of a stall to Martinez's left and drew his weapon. "FBI, Mr. Martinez. By the power vested in me by the United Sssss–" Ian slid to the ground as Rob Graff knocked him on the head above the ear with the butt of a semi-automatic.

Using the distraction to his advantage, Martinez lifted his weapon to fire at J.J. I barely acknowledged the fact before I flew through the air.

I stumbled forward and barreled into Martinez with a low tackle, hitting him head first in the scrotum.

I heard him squeak. My forward momentum sent us both flying into the front of a stall.

Rob followed us with his weapon trained on me. The statue suddenly came to life. With impossible speed for such a huge man, he kicked Rob's knee and drew a weapon on Martinez, who was now on the floor heaving in great gulps of air, crying and clutching his testicles. "DEA. Martinez, game's over." Over his shoulder he said, "You can come on out now, Greg."

A profoundly confused Martinez shook his head and shouted as he recognized his hit man, "Greg who? Gutierrez, what the hell are you doing?"

Gutierrez gave Martinez that same smirk he had given

him at the hotel in Chicago. "Waiting a hell of a lot longer than I wanted to, but I finally get to nail your drug-dealing ass, Martinez. I should have let Escobar have you."

Escobar calmly observed Martinez and shook his head. "There will be a time. Unfortunately it is not tonight." He hitched his coat on his arm and turned his back on all of us. Glenn Graff limped out from behind the statue called Gutierrez. J.J. and I looked on as he slowly made his way around Gutierrez. Arm in a sling and both eyes blackened, he looked at Rob sobbing on the ground, holding his ruined knee.

"Robert, I am ashamed to call you my son. You stand for the very thing I've spent my life fighting. You sold your own father out, and got Carole murdered for what? Drug money."

With tears in his eyes, a weary Glenn Graff held up an I.D. "Greg Henry, DEA. Carole was my sister, and also DEA. Sorry I lied to you J.J., but we've been undercover for more than four years now working this case."

J.J. sighed and looked at the FBI agents. "So much for cooperation between agencies."

Ian and Bob both said, "Shit."

Glenn (or Greg–did anyone go by their real name anymore?) limped past the hulking Gutierrez and leaned heavily on a stall door. "I've been in Mexico, tracking that research group Carole was mixed up in. Turns out the benefactor was Martinez, here. Under the guise of a man named Delgado, he funded the group that instigated the exportation of the Mexican poppy, as well as the cactus seeds." He looked at the floor and shook his head.

"They've been doing it for a few years now. I got hooked up with them when kids started dropping dead after using the new designer drug they call Totaled. Once the lab boys identified the toxin, the drug was broken down and traced to the Mexican research group."

I broke in. "But how did you connect Martinez to transport of the drugs?"

"Inadvertently, I happened upon the drop off point where the Columbian fishing boats drop the cocaine destined for the United States on the Rio Bravo del Norte at Nuevo Laredo.

"The drop off point just happens to be on a remote section of a huge ranch called Ranchero del Sol. The ranch is owned by none other than our own Eduardo Martinez. Martinez thought he lured Carole into the scam by dangling the Mammillaria luethyi project in front of her, when in fact, it was the perfect cover for us."

He turned again to Rob. "Until one of us sold out the other to Martinez. You didn't expect me to come back alive, did you, Rob?" He lowered his head in grief for the loss of his sister and his son. He sniffed and raised his head. "Well, have a nice life in prison, kid." Rob wisely stayed where he was, moaning and rocking back and forth, holding his knee.

Greg turned sad eyes toward us. "Buzz, when you pulled Carole out from under your mom's house, you opened up a can of worms the size of Cincinnati."

"Enough of this! Gutierrez, do your job," Martinez yelled, taking the moment of distraction to grab the front of my tee shirt and yank. He spun me around, grabbed my hair, and put a gun to my head.

A million thoughts spun through my head in those few seconds. *Oh shit, I don't want to die now. How did this thing suddenly go so FUBAR? I'm retired for God's sake! Where the hell is Bob? Who's going to feed my dogs? Damn I should have slept with J.J.!*

I choked back the hysteria and looked at J.J. I caught his intense stare. He closed his eyes and I suddenly got it. I abruptly went limp in Martinez's arms. He grunted and staggered. He had a hell of a time holding my happy ass up and maintaining a grip on my hair and his gun.

I was about at the end of my tolerance of pain when there was a loud commotion at the door. I heard loud metallic clacking and the unmistakable sound of pump-action shotguns all around. Though Martinez still had his gun on me, J.J. had his gun on Martinez. Gutierrez also had a gun on Martinez from behind.

Martinez looked up, looked around the area, and slowly moved his weapon away from my head. I cracked open an eye but didn't move because Martinez still had me by the hair. We stood like that when the barn door was nosily dragged open.

Gutierrez spun and had his gun on the door. The Columbians had their guns on Gutierrez. Rob reached for his gun and Greg stepped on his hand and held his gun on him. The FBI still had their weapons trained on Escobar, and six DEA agents slid down ropes out of the rafters. I vaguely heard Mag's voice say, "Holy shit, is Santa Claus coming down the chimney too? He's the only one not here!"

The DEA guys slid to a stop. Three had their weapons on Escobar and his cohorts; three on Martinez. No one moved. No one spoke.

Martinez suddenly went into action and his gun hand rose toward me again. A hollow thunk followed by the clear ringing of middle C echoed through the barn. Martinez stiffened and his grasp on my hair loosened.

I was yanked off my feet and out of the way as Martinez fell face first onto the barn floor.

The Columbians stared open mouthed first at Martinez, and then at an elated Alejandro. He stood behind Martinez, with a large manure shovel in his hands. He smiled as though he had just broken Barry Bond's home run record. Beside him stood his batting coach Mag, 'The Maggot'

Miller, arm around him and proud as a peacock. I turned toward the barn door where the commotion took place, and saw Ted Puetz standing there with his weapon at his side, his mouth hanging open, eyes the size of saucers, and a puddle forming around his shoes.

Ian was still knocked out in the stall. Moe was the only one who did what he was told to do. He strolled through the door with the agent from the command post.

The next few hours were a blur of activity. Federal agents argued over who took custody of whom and ambulances arrived to take Ian and Rob off to the hospital. I yelled at Mag and Alejandro for disobeying orders, and J.J. yelled at me for putting myself in the line of fire. Then he yelled at Moe for not stopping Mag, and Mag for not stopping Alejandro, then yelled at Mag again for giving Alejandro the shovel and the idea.

Feeling better now that he had vented his spleen, J.J. wandered off to referee the Who Has More Clout game between the FBI and the DEA.

The Luminol tests were completed, and the blood evidence was collected for the prosecution of Martinez. Escobar stood stoically, awaiting his fate. Martinez ranted and pleaded not to placed anywhere near the Columbians. It wouldn't matter because Martinez would be a dead man if they housed him in White Bass Lake or Timbuktu.

No one saw Ted leave, but it was a great story and I couldn't wait to tell Sal. And Dad. He'd probably use it as blackmail against Ted in order to get his truck fixed.

Mag said it best when she pointed out that tonight gave new meaning to scaring the piss out of Ted. "Why was he even here, I wonder? How did he know we were here?"

J.J. shrugged. "Maybe he listens to our frequency and heard me call Curly and tell him we'd be here. Maybe he was at his mom's, listening to her scanner."

There was a collective "*Ahhh*," as we all realized what must have happened.

The hour was late when we finally parted company. J.J. and I had Moe and Alejandro in my car. They dropped me at home and Moe at the police station. Alejandro stayed the night with J.J., with the promise that he would start looking for a place of his own in the morning. Mag went to the hospital to sit by Ian.

My dogs met me at the door with great enthusiasm, and we trooped out to the back yard for a pit stop. I sat on the swing, absently throwing the ball to Wes. The floodlights near the back door illuminated most of the yard, so I could watch Wes bring the ball back to Hill. I thought about the paths we took in life, and why we chose to take certain routes rather than others.

I thought about Rob and wondered what had led him to make the decisions he made. Wes trotted up and laid his massive head on my lap. I rubbed his ears, called for Hilary, and we all went back inside.

I mentally made notes on what I had to do the next day. By the time I had showered and wandered into the bedroom, both dogs were sprawled across the bed, snoring and twitching in doggy la-la-land. I wedged myself in between the two and they snuggled close. I drifted off to the soothing sounds of their snorts and snuffles.

Epilogue

A week later we were all kicked back at Mom's. J.J, Alejandro, Ian, Mag, FBI Bob, our families, friends, and neighbors all gathered in Mom's backyard for the first cookout in two weeks that did not star a dead body. We sat in camp chairs in a large circle, the smell of grilling brats and Jell-O salad rife in the crisp late-fall air.

Ian was once again looking hail and hearty after suffering a slight concussion from being hit by Rob Graff. He had a bounce in his step as he carried a couple of beers to where we sat. He dropped a kiss on Mag's head and held out her MGD with great ceremony. "For you, my Lady."

She wiped her hand across the label and flicked the cold water at him. She looked over at me and said, "How about that? Cute as a button, and he fetches beer too. The perfect man."

She saw Mom coming toward us and whispered, "Watch this."

"Hey, Mom!" Mom looked over and Mag patted Ian's knee. "He followed me home, can I keep him?"

Mom bustled about, smiling absently. She waved a hand in the air, and replied with the same words we'd heard all our lives. "Yes, dear, but make sure he has all his shots."

We all roared. Ian looked confused. Mag patted his leg. "Never mind dear, it's another Miller thing."

Ian looked from person to person with a dazed expression on his face. J.J. took a beer from him and said, "You'll get used to it, it only took me about 35 years."

Naturally, the conversation turned to the Graff murder and the subsequent events.

Bob said, "I heard Escobar bonded out to the tune of ten million dollars. His lawyers are trying to get him back to Colombia, but so far the U.S. has blocked legal passage. He'll slip out of the country one night, and the hunt will be on again."

Ian added, "Martinez disappeared from protective custody yesterday. All that was left of him were two knocked-out feds and a blood splat on the bathroom wall.

"One shot, bits of bone fragment and a little gray matter mixed in for good measure. Courtesy, I'm sure, of our local Colombian drug lord."

Alejandro sighed. "Justice done."

We all were quiet for a moment. I said to Alejandro, "Hey, I heard you found a job already."

"Yes, I did. I was caring for the mares that did not die, over at the vet's office and Dr. Mike told me of a job opening. On Dr. Mike's recommendation, I was offered the job of managing the Colson County Equine Rescue outside of town. The job comes with living quarters and insurance. Wow. County benefits. I am now set for life, and I get to stay here with all of you." He looked down at Wes who was grinning up adoringly at him. "I can even get a dog!" Wes sneezed on cue and Alejandro slipped him the rest of his hot dog.

J.J. laughed. "Now all we have to do is find you someone who will spend all that money you'll be making!" We all laughed and Alejandro blushed.

Just then my little sister, Fred, walked up with a dark haired beauty. "Everyone? This is my college roommate Sam Fernandini from Peru. She's visiting for about a month." Fred looked at me. "Sami is the one from whom I get all my rare specie tropical fish. She's an ichthyologist with the National Environmental Agency of Peru in Lima. She had vacation time coming and decided to become an honorary Cheesehead for a month."

We all saluted her with our beers and said hello. Alejandro just stared, with his mouth working like a fish out of water. I poked him in the ribs and he snapped his mouth closed. "Hi."

He stood and gently took Sami's hand. "I am Alejandro. Will you marry me, beautiful lady? I have a great job with County benefits. I like fish, too."

"Subtle, Montoya, *reeeal* subtle," I said.

Sami laughed and was saved from answering when Greg Henry drove up the driveway and got out of his car. The black eyes were gone and he had a barely discernible limp, but he wore his grief like a heavy load. His shoulders drooped and pain lurked behind his eyes.

He looked at Ian and Mag holding hands and the fake smile faltered. He straightened and took a deep breath.

The smile was back in place when he wandered over. "Hi everyone." We all called out a greeting. He kept looking at Mag. "I wanted to stop by and tell you all thank you very much for all you did for Carole."

He laid a hand on J.J.'s shoulder and looked at me. "Especially you two. Without you guys, I still might not know what happened to my sister."

J.J. and I stood. He shook Greg's hand and I hugged him tight. "She was a good woman, Greg. You should be very proud of her."

Greg nodded. "I am." He turned to Ian. "Ian? I'm going to get some food while there's still some left. Would you join me?"

Ian hopped out of his chair. "Sure. Excuse us, everyone."

They took off across the yard where the Geriatric Mod Squad was re-arranging food bowls and keeping a sharp ear out for tidbits of neighborhood news.

Bob said what we were all thinking. "Sure must be hard losing a sibling like that." I thought of my sisters and thanked the Lord they worked relatively safe jobs.

Mag said, "That sure explains why Glenn 'The Masher' Graff thought he could chase me around the potting shed with no remorse. He *wasn't* really married!"

I remembered the conversation Mag and I had about Greg and Rob. "No, but he's got a long row to hoe with that son of his. He told J.J. that he didn't even know he had a son until a few years ago. Seems the mother was some old girlfriend from way back. She was an addict, and they parted ways. He never even knew she was pregnant. One day Rob shows up at his door with a letter. *Hmmm*–I wonder if Gregg will quit the DEA. They might even force him to retire. Who knows?"

J.J. said, "I heard Rob was out of the hospital and was 'persuaded' to cooperate with the feds in return for a lighter sentence, counseling, and perhaps parole."

"Rob's going to prison, and Martinez is dead. What a bloody miserable end," I said.

Bob had another thought. "Hey Buzz speaking of blood; did I tell you? We also found a couple of drops of blood on Martinez's pants where you splashed him with the Luminol. We think the DNA will match up with a pilot Delavan P.D. found murdered out in the woods behind the school. Gutierrez gave us the lead on him."

A scratchy female voice interrupted. "Fat lot-o-good that'll do 'em with that Mexican drug lord getting croaked by the Colombians!" Mary Cromwell threw a couple of boxing moves. "You should have called us, Sheriff. Me and the girls would have kicked some major drug dealing booty down at that barn."

Mary gave an enthusiastic imitation of a football punter in action. She backed up, her tongue at the corner of her mouth.

"No, Mary, no," Mom hollered.

Mary swung back her scrawny leg and let it fly just as Greg came around the corner with a mounded plate of food.

Mary's toe caught the edge of the plate and sent it sailing through the air. Wes and Hill tore after the flying food and Wes clipped Mom as she walked toward the buffet table with an armload of desserts. Jan's apple pie popped out of her hands and landed on Dad's chest. Dad stood up suddenly and upset the chips and dip of which he was currently partaking. Jan caught the chips, but the dip bounced on the ground, giving everyone's legs in the near vicinity a tangy French onion flavor.

Jane laughed and picked up a cream cheese ball. She wound up and threw it at Mary yelling, "You crazy old bird! Act your age and not your son's I.Q., for God's sake!"

"Don't you call me a lazy old turd, Jane Broussard!" Mary wrestled a drumstick away from Wes and threw it back at Jan, bonking Reverend Hutchins on the head.

Bob, Ian, and Sam looked on the chaotic scene with stunned incredulity.

J.J. laughed and slapped Bob on the shoulder. "Get used to it, *Cousin*!"

Fred patted Sami on the back. "Before you ask, the one with the Boston Cream Pie on her chin and the cupcake attached to her knee is my mother."

Mag put her arms around Ian's middle and laid her head on his shoulder. "Welcome to the family, honey."

Ian whispered to her, "I'm glad you said that, because I just made a deal with Greg to buy the greenhouse property.

I can set up a lab and an office and work out of White Bass Lake. It's already clear with headquarters."

Mag squealed and threw her arms around his neck, giving him a smooch deluxe.

Wes sat there grinning upon the scene. He had noodles on his head and he was wagging his tail, while Hilary delicately passed gas. She cleared the area, everyone running for cover. I held my nose and yelled, "All right, who's the wise guy who fed the Bulldog *sauerkraut*?"

A UPS van drove up the driveway. Alejandro knocked his chair over running toward it. He bobbed his head up and down and danced to the back of the truck. Together he and the UPS man unloaded a long rectangular box. J.J. and Moe jogged over to help. They carried the box and set it down near the back door.

Alejandro cleared his throat and took my mother by the arm. He called Dad over and spoke to the crowd. "Ladies and gentlemen, you all have been very kind to me since I came to your town. The Miller family gave me shelter when I could have been murdered. For this I can never repay them. As a token of my gratitude, I offer you this gift. I ordered it special from Arizona."

The crowd gathered around as Mom cheerfully opened the box. Jan and Jane helped her with the lid. My dad moved in so he could see better and froze. The women *oooed* and *ahhhed* over the gift, and when the lid fell back, I about fainted.

There, staring my dad in the eye was a goddamn cowboy lamp with a rattle snake crawling up the pole. My mom clapped, Dad stood there stunned, and Alejandro grinned from ear to ear. I put my arm around Mag and Fred and said, "Here we go again, girls."

Gale Borger has been involved in law enforcement for over 20 years. This gives Gale an endless source of background material for her books. Growing up in a screwball household also gives her a sense for the zany and the bizarre. Gale writes what she knows, and she knows bad guys and funny stuff—but not necessarily in that order!

Gale lives in Southeastern Wisconsin with her husband and daughter, a Dogue de Bordeaux, two cats, about 1500 tropical fish, an African Horned Toad, a side-neck turtle, two dwarf hamsters, and a leopard gecko.

When Gale is not writing, she and her husband breed and swap tropical fish. Gale is also a Master Gardener and after work can usually be found in a flower bed up to her ears in weeds, or volunteering at a local gardening event.

Totally Buzzed is the first book in the Miller Sisters Mysteries.

See what's up with Gale at
www.galeborgerbooks.com

check out her blog at
www.galeborgerbooks.wordpress.com

or contact her at
galedborger@gmail.com

CPSIA information can be obtained at www.ICGtesting.com
227420LV00001B/3/P